BALIOS PUBLISHING

Austin, TX

Resurrecting

RANDI

a novel

David P. Shepherd

Susan,
Here's hoping you
find hope amid
life's challenges.

[signature]

BALIOS PUBLISHING

Balios Publishing and colophon are registered trademarks of Balios Publishing.

For information about special discounts for bulk purchases, please contact AtlasBooks at 800-247-6553 or orders@bookmasters.com

Printed in the United States of America

1 2 3 4 5 6 7 8 9 10

Cataloging-in-Publication Data
Shepherd, David.
Resurrecting Randi: a novel / David Shepherd
1. Adult—Fiction.   2. Psychological Thriller—Fiction.
3. Campus Life—Fiction.
LCCN: 2008922268

ISBN-13: 978-0-9705965-0-5
ISBN-10: 0-9705965-0-2

For those who
came before.

ONE

OVER THE past year, I've thought a lot about whether my life has been worthwhile. I think about it now as I loosely grip the handle of my revolver. I think about it as I hear the words of my young friend resonate in my brain as loudly as a gunshot: "Life is always optional."

My young friend. Is that what she was? Was that the compromise I had accepted? How pathetic. Those who know me, of course, would more likely say that she was the source of my destruction, and they would be correct. I understand that. But she was also something more, something so much more. She was something that none of them could ever understand, and I do neither of us justice by using a word as passive as *friend*.

A sliver of cold air slices through the worn window seal of my old Buick and further chills me. I doubt that most people know how numbingly cold it gets on the plains of West Texas in the winter. Whatever the temperature, the bleak landscape and relentless howling of the wind always make it seem colder. Or perhaps it's the vastness of the gray sky that offers no prospect of change. For mile after mile, there's little more to see than wiry shrubs rolling over hardened earth and around abandoned oil pumps. Parked on the side of this desolate highway, I'm only about seventy miles from where I was born; I had once thought this barren land to be the most beautiful on Earth.

I've decided to keep the engine of the old Buick running, not only for the heat, but also because it barely started back at the Chevron where I had filled my Thermos a couple of hours earlier. The car is a twenty-three-year-old tank that had belonged to Puddy, the old woman who lived next door to me on Preston Street. She hadn't driven it in a decade, and when she passed away six months ago, her nephew had insisted that I should take it if I could get it started. Having just sold my Wagoneer for much-needed cash, I accepted.

I've sold just about everything I owned. For much-needed cash.

I set my cup of coffee on the dash; a glob of condensation spreads across the windshield and obscures my view. I hear a car coming up behind me, sit up straight, and adjust the rearview mirror. My heart races as I lay the revolver on the passenger's seat, trading it for a pair of binoculars. Also on the seat is the cellular phone given to me by my good friend, Ben. He gave it to me along with the instructions to call "before doing anything rash."

Too late, Ben. Just being here is rash.

Ahead of me, about a quarter of a mile on the right, a lone brick building stands amid the bleakness. It looks like an old schoolhouse, absent the children. Three bare trees line a circle drive in front; four cars are parked to the side. A path has been plowed through fresh snow that is piled up two feet deep on either side. Barbed wire fencing surrounds the building but falls to the ground in places. Despite the binoculars, I detect no sign of life save a lone crow, its black feathers rippling as it tries to stay atop one of the bare trees by pressing into the wind.

I watch anxiously as the big Cadillac roars past me, its dual exhausts carving smoky vortexes out of the cold air. It does not turn into the circle drive, and I feel a mixture of disappointment and relief. I look at my watch and realize that I could have another hour to wait. Maybe more. The gas gauge falls below a quarter tank. When the coffee reaches my lips, it is cool. I try to recall how long it took me to get here from the Chevron.

Do I have enough gas for another hour? What if I make a run to the Chevron and miss her? These are the considerations that momentarily make life worthwhile on the side of the highway. Or do they? I pick up the revolver again.

As my finger tightens imperceptibly on the trigger, as I glance into the callous barrel, I am not afraid. My heart is not racing, and I'm not at all uncertain. I know I'll pull the trigger—should I choose that option—because I've done it once before. Same gun. Same reason. Only this time, it will fire.

A philosopher once said that we could consider our lives worth living only if we would live them over and over again without the slightest change. Wouldn't I want to change the fact that I had lost my professorship in disgrace? Wouldn't I rather be happily married to Kathryn and have my best-selling book back if I could? Wouldn't I prefer a life in which I had *not* been charged with murder?

And, wouldn't I change the fact that Layla Sommers, a nineteen-year-old human incendiary, had ever come into my fucking life? Yes, above all, wouldn't I change that?

I guess that's what I'm here to find out.

The ancient Buick sputters, the crow gives in to the wind, and I study the old brick building, waiting for my answer to emerge.

Two

I LOVE the fall semester, and last fall had promised to be the best of my career. The first day of classes is the favorite of any professor who truly loves to teach, and while the prestige of research and the inconvenience of students make that breed more and more rare, it certainly described me, Dr. Travis Harrison.

No matter how long I had been teaching—and it had been more than twenty years—the first day had always held a nervous anticipation that was as exciting as a first kiss. Nothing got my juices flowing as much as the thought of standing in front of a few hundred bright young minds that were waiting to be challenged and possibly even changed.

But last year the anticipation of the first day was only the beginning. There was so much more going on in my life, and for the first time in so long, it was all wonderful. There was no better evidence of that than the fact that the semester began for me not in a classroom but at a book signing at the Barnes & Noble on the edge of the University of Texas campus. My book signing! And it wasn't just some academic work where the twenty copies sold that day would roughly equal lifetime sales. No, it was a mainstream novel that was doing remarkably well less than a month after its release.

I arrived at Barnes & Noble thirty minutes before the store opened in hopes of finding an old friend. I walked toward a small Catholic church two blocks down where two homeless men slumped against a urine-stained wall; a third sat on the steps with his head in his hands. They were uniformly dressed in medieval layers of dark cloth, and feeling the hot morning sun on my back, I wondered how they would survive the day.

I recognized the one sitting and walked toward him, weaving my way past booths that had been set up to hawk subscriptions, telephone services, and credit cards to new students. I also walked past a girl with the most unusual copper shade of hair I had ever seen. Strands of it fell from beneath her wide-brimmed leather hat and seemed on fire in the sun.

Despite the heat, the homeless man with his head in his hands wore a knit cap; a scraggly black beard covered his face and fell to his chest. He noticed my approach, lifted his head, and quietly said, "Hello, Dr. T."

"Hello, Dale," I said, sorting through the various receipts in my wallet to find a five-dollar bill among the ones. "Where's Shawn?"

I often gave money to the homeless who seemed drawn to campus life, and one in particular had caught my attention over the years. His name was Shawn, and he was a gray-haired man who perpetually wore a blue and white seersucker suit with a white fedora and black bow tie. Like those of the others on the street, Shawn's clothes were soiled and reeked, but he had a dignity about him that was both unsettling and compelling. "You look like Mark Twain," I had said to him playfully one day, by way of introduction. He replied, "You mean Samuel Langhorne Clemens? He's not bad—despite *Tom Sawyer*—but he's nothing like my man Faulkner."

Turns out that Shawn had been born near Oxford, Mississippi, Faulkner's home, and had read just about everything he had ever written. He could quote full paragraphs from *As I Lay Dying* and told me how Faulkner had written it in the early morning hours when he had worked the night shift at a local power station. "Might write something like that myself someday," Shawn had said. Part of what drew me to him was that I suspected maybe he could.

"Haven't seen him, Dr. T," Dale said as he accepted the bill with dirty fingers and unblinking eyes.

"Haven't seen him?" I asked. "I thought you two were joined at the hip."

"Took off in the middle of summer. Said he was going to Mississippi if he could get there. Maybe he'll show. Either he will, or he won't, and that's all a man really needs to know about life."

I'd been giving money to Shawn for a decade, Dale for about half that time, and Shawn's absence disturbed me because I don't like people disappearing from my life. I've had far too much of that. For better or worse, Shawn had become a part of my routine, and I don't like changes to my routine, either. "I hope he shows," I said. "Take care, Dale."

I heard Dale mumbling to himself as I turned and left, "Either he will or he won't, and that's all a man needs to know about life."

* * *

I returned to Barnes & Noble, and as I stood in front of the still-locked storefront, the girl with the gleaming copper hair approached me. She wore torn, faded jeans and a threadbare ribbed undershirt, the sort I would imagine someone's grandfather wearing under a dress shirt. It failed to hide the darkness of her nipples. In the manner I had perfected, I glanced at my watch, attempting to ignore her, but she placed her hand gently on my coat sleeve.

"That was nice, what you did," she said.

I looked at her and was overcome with a feeling I could not fully explain. I felt both queasy and anxious. "What did I do?" I asked her.

"Gave money to that poor man."

"Oh, yes, well, thanks for saying so." I was taken aback by her eyes, which were intelligent and dark brown like those of a fine animal yet with little flecks of copper like her hair.

"Layla," the girl said, extending her hand. "Layla Sommers."

I shook her hand and was struck by its bony, delicate nature. "Dr. Harrison," I said. "Nice to meet you, Layla."

Not knowing what to say next and realizing that her hand remained in mine, I was relieved to hear the click of the door as it was unlocked.

"Well, I've got to go now," I said, nodding toward the door.

"Yeah, me too," she said. She looked down the block to where Dale sat at the base of the wall and then looked back at me. "That was really nice, what you did."

As she turned and left, a hollowness formed in my stomach as if I were suddenly hungry.

*   *   *

I entered Barnes & Noble and walked up the wide stairs to the second floor where I took a seat in the coffee shop. My table fronted a large picture window directly across from the Texas campus. The Drag, as those few blocks of Guadalupe Street are called, was coming to life. Along the sidewalk, vendors were selling egg rolls and breakfast tacos, police were patrolling on bikes, and aging hippies were setting up carts from which to sell their wares. Hundreds of arriving students humped out of buses and across the campus like Marines under the weight of their backpacks. I pressed close to the glass so that I could see as far down the block as possible. I looked in Dale's direction. I looked for a girl with copper hair and a leather hat, but did not see her. I then looked directly across the street for Kathryn Orr.

While Kathryn's name was nowhere to be found in my novel, the book was in many ways as much hers as mine. Kathryn and I had met four years earlier during a period when I was trying hard not to meet anyone. Ever since the death of my daughter, Randi,

I had avoided making friends. To me, people were little more than tragedies in waiting, and the closer I allowed them to get, the greater the inevitable pain would be. I met with my own students, of course, but only in my office and only in a formal manner. Beyond that, I walked across campus with my head down and brow furrowed—aspiring to be the curmudgeon whom no one dared approach. I was going through the motions of life.

My lone exception to this rule of avoidance was that I enjoyed eating lunch on one of several concrete benches outside my office in Garrison Hall, the history building on Austin's University of Texas campus. I loved the towering oak trees, the sunshine, and I loved feeding the squirrels that would audaciously take food from my hand.

The building immediately south of Garrison is the GSB, or Graduate School of Business. Its own metaphor, it stands as an island of steel and glass in the midst of a hundred Mediterranean villas. It was easy to spot the business-school students, and their professors, for while even I enjoy wearing a tie from time to time, I would not be caught dead wearing a suit.

"May I share your bench?"

I looked up to see who had uttered those unwelcome words and knew immediately that the woman wearing a suit was a business-school professor. Her hair and eyes were serious and dark, her face long but not unattractive. "Sure," I said unenthusiastically as I scraped my various papers and lunch items to my half of the bench.

The woman sat quietly enough that first day, but her presence there became fairly predictable. We said little as she looked over graphs and charts while I scribbled out pages of a manuscript I had in progress—or at least that's what I preferred to call it even though I knew it would eventually join the others in boxes under my bed.

I guess we shared that bench a dozen times over the course of a month though our conversation had scarcely extended beyond a sharing of names. Then one afternoon, Kathryn asked the question I knew was coming.

"What are you writing?"

"A book," I said. "A book about Thomas Jefferson and the changes in the election process from his time to now." She seemed genuinely interested, and somewhat out of character, I found myself elaborating. "I'm trying to contrast and compare how Jefferson would fare if he had to compete in a modern-day political campaign," I said, tossing a sliver of bread to a squirrel that had to fight off three low-flying grackles before it could race away with it. "My premise is that we could never elect a man of such thoughtfulness today."

Kathryn laid her papers aside and reached for the sheet I held in my hand. "Do you mind?" she asked. I did but handed her the pages anyway.

I shifted uncomfortably as she studied my sloppy script, which happened to contain an examination of what Jefferson would say to a contemporary—in this case, Ben Franklin—if he were trying to explain such a thing as a "sound bite" or the daily "news cycle."

"You should write a novel instead," Kathryn said, not looking up from the page. "Don't argue what he *might* have said—bring him back to life and let's find out. Put Jefferson in a modern election with the power to communicate with his contemporaries. Let us watch as he wrestles with his own integrity when he meets with PACs and lobbyists. Let's see how he handles it when he asks for six hours on CNN to explain an important issue and is given twelve seconds. I think you're on to something here!"

At the moment she mentioned it, the idea excited me. I had always wanted to write a book that would be sold in real bookstores, not just the academic ones. Because of that, my academic publishing record was sparse, and my bed hid boxes full of unfinished manuscripts. But all my manuscripts were nonfiction, and at the moment Kathryn mentioned a novel, Jefferson's voice began whispering in my head. From the forty minutes I usually spent writing at lunch, I suddenly felt an urge to go back to my office and write for hours.

"But I have no idea how to write a novel," I said, allowing that reality to surface.

"I'll help you, if you like," she said.

"Are you a novelist?"

"No, but modesty aside, I can organize anything. You give me the goal, and I'll give you the process to achieve it if you believe in it. If you believe in yourself."

I looked at her, and in that moment, it was impossible to doubt her.

*   *   *

I waited at Barnes & Noble for the book signing that Kathryn had orchestrated, having not seen her in two months. She spent summers in Germany where she earned $40,000 a month consulting for automotive companies. That was about half my annual salary as a tenured professor in the history department, but I wouldn't have traded jobs for the world. I had never told her in so many words, but business bores me.

My good friend, Ben Frizell, was also due soon, though I hoped Kathryn would arrive first. Ben is my most loyal friend in the world—perhaps my only friend in the world—but with so many things on my mind, I just wasn't sure that I could feign interest in his annual first-day stories one more time. There is a limit, even for me, as to how often one can pretend to enjoy Ben's theories about being able to smell freshmen or his five stages of peach maturation as they symbolize female aging. Something about buds and blooms . . . and rotting.

As I moved back to my table, I heard chairs being dragged across the tile at the opposite end of the floor. Looking up, I saw two bookstore employees and a young man with spiked blonde hair in a black suit. Together, they placed the chairs into position for the book signing. *My* book signing.

*   *   *

"You can smell them, you know—freshmen."

My trance broken, I turned to see the broad smile of Ben Frizell, obviously pleased that he had managed to get his wheelchair next to me without my noticing. Ben's eyes looked twice their normal size through thick yellowed glasses. His complexion was ruddy and his hair was an Einstein-like shock of white. He wore a skin-tight Banlon shirt that highlighted both his muscular arms and the rolling mounds of his ample gut. Khaki slacks were tucked under his legs, just above where his knees had once been.

As a young man, Ben had excelled on both the cross-country team and at the divinity school at Yale. His dream was to work in Africa, literally spreading the Christian message by running from village to village. On the night before his ordination, he was standing on his seventh-floor balcony in New Haven, overlooking Long Island Sound and ignoring the blustery wind. He was giving thanks to the Lord when he heard an eerie squeal, something that sounded like metal on metal. He felt a tiny shift in the wooden surface of the balcony and heard a woman scream from the floor below.

Ben has told me a hundred times that he'd felt precious little fear during his seven-story fall after his balcony had collapsed. "I remember being semiconscious, aware of how the Lord had saved my life," he said. "There was screaming all around, and I was trying to find the strength to give aid. Then, I heard a deep and ominous rumbling . . ."

Seven stories of brick, glass, and steel came down on him, pinning his skinny runner's body beneath tons of rubble and pinching his legs off at the knees. One of his legs was amputated at the scene in order to free him; the other came off in the hospital two days later.

The official who was to have conducted Ben's ordination came to see him at the hospital. Ben remembers him as a small man with sharp features and gleaming black hair. "What a miracle that you survived, my son," the priest had said. "Oh, yes, God has something special in mind for you in order to test you in this manner. God loves you, my son."

Ben fought through the painkillers and pulled himself up in his hospital bed. He threw the sheets aside, exposing the blood-stained bandages on his two stumps. "Yes, I know," Ben said. "God clearly loves me. But can you tell me, Father, why did He hate my fucking legs?"

The priest gave him a disdainful look and left abruptly. After two years of debilitating grief and painful physical therapy, Ben returned to school for another degree. He chose philosophy, the subject he teaches at Texas, and as he was fond of saying, "The more godless the philosophy, the better."

* * *

Ben shut his eyes and raised his hands dramatically. "You *do* smell them, don't you? Not the emanation of sophomores, not the redolence of seniors, and certainly not the malodorous transfer student. No, my friend, I am talking about the wafting of that most fragile and fragrant gland, the freshman gland. You can smell them, *can you not?*"

Ben didn't expect an answer, of course—hadn't gotten one from me in years, though that hardly discouraged him. "Kathryn should be here any minute," I said, looking at my watch and hoping to change the subject.

"Oh, then perhaps I should leave," he joked, pretending to wheel his chair away from the table.

Admittedly, Kathryn didn't see much in Ben. While he avoided labels such as fatalist or hedonist, he lived his life as if each day might be his last. And although, like me, he loved to teach, for Ben the ultimate escape from life's pain was plotting his particular form

12

of sexual conquests. Whenever he played his role as lecher, Kathryn turned to cold stone. I knew why, but her reasons would hardly have mattered to Ben.

In fact, it was widely known among the faculty that Ben Frizell was the most abusive professor on campus when it came to the time-honored seduction of students. Even Ben didn't deny it. In fact, he privately reveled in it, once telling me, "I dare those politically correct cowards to find even one of my angels of mercy who will stand before them and accuse this poor old man in his wheelchair." As usual, his uproarious laughter followed.

"Is the wedding still on?" Ben now asked me. "Or has fate intervened on your behalf?" He laughed even harder than usual.

I gave him an appropriate scowl. "I'm lucky to have her, Ben," I said. "And yes, as far as I know the wedding is still on. I guess we'll both find out in a few minutes."

*　*　*

I had received the first e-mail from Kathryn about four hours after that discussion on the bench. It had a spreadsheet attachment with columns in which I was to track my time and daily word count. Based on a quick survey she had done, she concluded that my novel should probably be around 125,000 words broken down into thirty chapters. The spreadsheet enabled me to write in the title and objective of each chapter, and as I entered my daily word count, pie charts were automatically updated showing me how much I had left to do. Though a little uncertain at first, I did as she asked and e-mailed a completed worksheet to her each day.

Kathryn concerned herself not only with the time I spent writing but with anything that competed for that time. When I complained once that cutbacks in the history department had cost me a teaching assistant, forcing me to spend more time grading tests, she loaned me one of her graduate assistants and told me to let her know if I needed more.

At one point, to make sure I wasn't going too far down a dead-end trail, she had me polish one chapter as if for submission, and then she sent it to three Austin novelists whom she had contacted. Based on their feedback, I did in fact make several important shifts in the point of view. Kathryn also insisted that I have the manuscript professionally edited before showing it to agents, and when that step was completed she had agents lined up to read it.

She was, and is, the most organized person I have ever met.

The book, titled *Reelect Tom Jefferson,* sold only seven weeks after Saul Westberg, the agent Kathryn and I had selected, had sent it out. After commissions and taxes, the $150,000 advance wasn't life-changing, but the stamp of authenticity on my life as a writer decidedly was. And the sequel—a modern-day politician runs against Jefferson in 1800—was already alive in my mind.

On the night the book sold to Knopf, Kathryn and I celebrated over dinner. We toasted our respective futures, as it was also shaping up to be a big year for her. She had been named chairperson of the university's marketing department, a long-time goal of hers. She told me that it had been almost five years since she had first envisioned an evening of being feted at the chancellor's mansion, and that evening was now being planned. We raised a toast to what a great team we made, and to my astonishment, she wondered aloud if my book might be nominated for a Pulitzer Prize.

We also made love that night for the first time. Kathryn was unlike any other woman I had dated. Even as we began seeing more of each other, she was confident enough in herself to grant me the privacy I required. Soon enough, it became obvious that she wanted me in her life. I was slower to realize that the feeling was mutual.

*   *   *

"Look at them," Ben said, turning his attention to the view through the picture window. "It's nothing but a numbers game, you know. Getting laid. Think about it: fifty thousand students, twenty thousand freshmen, ten thousand freshman *girls*. A hundred of them will be in old Ben's introduction to philosophy class. Half of those will feel sorry for the old man in the wheelchair trying so hard to be cheery. Half of those will schedule office hours with him, and a few of those will hear from him how much their papers on love touched him, touched him to the core!

"A precious few will see a tear drip from his wrinkled old eye, though he will bravely try to hide it. They will lay a hand on his shoulder and ask him what is wrong. He will apologize for his vulnerability and say it is just that their papers about love moved him so very much that, for the first time in twenty years, he wonders if he too might someday be able to love again. But, of course, he couldn't possibly impose upon *them* to help him . . . What? They would? Oh my, he never dreamed of this!

"And from there, my friend, it is a very short path to the moment when that angel of mercy falls to her knees, places Ben's old stumps on her shoulders, and attempts to raise the dead. Now that's what I call a fucking miracle!" He bellowed so hard that his laugh quickly devolved into a deep, phlegmy cough.

At the far side of the floor near where the signing table had been set up, I noticed a wide-brimmed leather hat above a row of shelves. The hat of Layla Sommers.

"You're lucky you're not in jail, Ben," I said quietly.

"They're over eighteen, Travis. You should consider the young ones. They're like peaches in the first stage of maturation—buds, really."

"Ben, please," I interrupted with less than my usual patience, "you're *not* going to detail the five stages of peach maturation, are you?"

He shut his eyes and ran his fingers through his white hair. A hurt rippled through his fleshy face, and I wished I had just let him tell his story, but I really didn't enjoy most of Ben's crass stories: he laughed too loud and cursed too often while telling them.

I, too, had once been in a terrible accident, the one that claimed my daughter, Randi. I discovered later that I had been in a coma for eleven days, and for eleven days, one man had sat by my side in that sterile hospital in Lubbock. One man had held my hand when it twitched involuntarily, and one man had talked to me endlessly, even though the doctors weren't sure whether I could hear him.

The man, whom I barely knew at the time, was Ben Frizell. Apparently, the entire faculty had been notified of my accident and the tragic death of my daughter, but only one had thrown himself—and his wheelchair—into a van and come to my side.

"On second thought," I said to Ben, "tell me about the peaches."

Ben smiled broadly. "The first stage, you see, is when they are just buds on trees—spectacularly beautiful, but not yet ripe—"

"Good morning, gentlemen."

Neither of us had noticed Kathryn's arrival.

THREE

"I HOPE I'm not interrupting something important," Kathryn said. "Sounds like Ben is giving one of his horticultural lectures. Thinking of changing fields again, Ben?"

I stood and accepted Kathryn's light embrace. She wore a navy pin-striped suit, dark hose, and a gold Mercedes brooch. Her black hair had been cut short and was rounded on the sides. As I hugged her, I noted that she had gained weight while in Germany. She kissed me quickly on the cheek.

She eyed me critically, remarking, "I see you wore the wool tie after all."

I fingered my favorite old tie. Before she'd left for the summer, Kathryn had given me an expensive silk tie with mallard ducks on it, just for this occasion. I'm sure it had cost over a hundred dollars, but I'd rather have hung myself with that tie than to have been seen wearing it.

"How was Germany?" I asked with false enthusiasm.

She picked a piece of lint from my brown tweed jacket. "Did you have this dry cleaned?" she asked.

Of course, I had not, even though she had placed it in the front seat of the Wagoneer and put a Post-it note on the dash: *Don't forget to dry clean!* She had even sent three e-mails from Germany pointing out to me that it would be impossible to drive or take the bus past the dry cleaners every day for *two months* without remembering to stop in.

But it had not been impossible, not difficult at all, really. The only problem I had encountered was a moment of panic that very morning when I couldn't find the jacket! It wasn't until I had downgraded to my tired blue blazer and climbed into the Wagoneer that I spotted the tweed jacket on the seat where Kathryn had placed it two months earlier. Fortunately, I had not needed to change ties, since in my opinion the wool one goes with just about everything.

"They're setting up the table over there," I said, pointing toward the wall filled with magazines. At that moment, Layla Sommers stepped out into an aisle and waved at me, smiling. I jerked my hand back as if I had touched a hot flame. Kathryn did not see her, but Ben did.

"They'd better do it right," Kathryn said. "Did you talk to the publisher about sending the extra books? Who's in charge of this event? Travis—are you listening to me?"

"What? Oh, I think that young man in the black suit is with Knopf," I said.

"That *boy?*" Kathryn said with indignation. Then she abruptly changed the subject. "By the way, Travis, congratulations on the sale of your house."

"You heard?" I asked. "I was hoping to surprise you."

"You know I don't like surprises," she said. "Flo called me in Germany to see what I thought of the offer. I told her to tell you to take *anything*. I was the one that suggested the early closing."

"You suggested it? Flo told me that the buyers had—"

"They sent a boy?" Kathryn said, apparently done with the real estate discussion. "And here he comes. Good. I want a word with him." She rolled her eyes and looked down at Ben. "I don't mean to ignore you, Ben. How are you?"

"Fine, Kathryn. You?"

"Couldn't be better, Ben."

"Dr. Harrison?" The publisher's representative appeared at our table. "I'm Trey Holcombe with Knopf. We're almost ready for you, sir." Below his spiked blond hair he wore a huge white smile.

"I hope you brought enough books," Kathryn admonished. "If not, somebody's going to hear about it." She produced a facial tissue from her large purse, wet it with her mouth, and wiped a lipstick stain from my cheek. "Are you ready, Travis?"

Suddenly I wasn't sure. As I stood and collected my leather satchel, I was surprised to see the modest line that had formed in front of the signing table. I had spent the past few years mastering the skill of avoiding people, and here I was deliberately heading into a mix of my own creation. Kathryn sensed my anxiety and took my hand in hers, which somehow only heightened my apprehension.

There was a curious mix of people in line. I shook a few hands as I neared the table. "Dr. T" was uttered by several former students whom I only vaguely recognized, and a few university dignitaries were notable by their suits and ties. Howard K. Schramm, dean of the College of Liberal Arts, was there. He was a penguin-shaped man who wore his perennial three-piece suits complete with a gold watch chain. Bald on top, his thin gray hair fell lank to his shoulders in back, leaving a trail of dandruff on his coat. I was surprised to see Dean Schramm, as it was well known that he'd considered my publishing record prior to that day to be abysmal.

Next to Dean Schramm was the university president, Rodney H. Nevitt. Nevitt was an athletic man who wore no coat and had his tie loose and his shirt sleeves rolled up. Cocky, and a relentless fundraiser, he was the first president of a major university without an academic background. Until three years ago, he had been a lobbyist for the oil and gas industry, and the dollars he had collected for Texas had been nothing short of prodigious.

Before that day, Dean Schramm would have avoided me if he could have, and I doubt that Nevitt could have picked me out of a crowd. However, as Kathryn had predicted, my value had grown directly in proportion to the success of my book and the resulting national PR. Like the others in line, both Schramm and Nevitt held in their hands a copy of my golden-red book—those 123,608 words that I worked into shape according to Kathryn's spreadsheets and pie charts. Kathryn ordered Trey to bring an extra chair for her.

Ben also stayed a while, rolling up next to any remotely attractive girl in line. I have to admit I have never seen anything like it. Girls were drawn to him—his big smile, deep laugh, and wheelchair. He would have them laughing out loud within seconds and then turn their faces inside out with sympathy. He could pump them up and then deflate them within the span of a single sentence. He was, for better or worse, a true master, and despite his frumpy appearance, it was not so hard to understand how that angel of mercy invariably appeared.

It had been helpful to me to at least have Ben to talk to during my erratic dating life. Though he laughed hysterically, offering me fictitious rewards to repeat stories, I couldn't deny that most of my stories were indeed laughable. What an ordeal it is for a grown man to get laid, which is to say, to hang in there with a given woman until the third date. Because it was always on the third date that these women would, as if on cue, suddenly shudder with a strained fit of passion that presumably justified their advances. When I was growing up, that was supposed to be the man's ploy.

The sex was fine, I suppose, but the requisite "intimacy" before and afterward was pure drudgery. By the time we made it to one of their bedrooms—and it was always *their* bedrooms—I already had one eye on the clock, working over in my mind excuses for my earliest possible departure.

Kathryn, to her credit, had been different. When we finally graduated from lunch on our bench to dinner in a restaurant, she announced that she would like to see more of me, but that she felt it best that I complete and sell my novel before we even discussed a sexual relationship. She also said that before such an encounter there were some things from her past she would have to share with me.

But as I prepared to sign my first book, I was aware of little more than the fact that Layla Sommers leaned against the far wall near the telephones and restrooms. She was staring at me.

I glanced at her and wanted to turn away but could not. She did not even blink as she studied me. Despite the thousands of females that Ben points out amble across the campus daily, Layla was strikingly different. First, there was the copper color of her hair and copper flecks in her brown eyes, which seemed to sparkle even from this distance. Then there was her purple lipstick, generously applied to full lips. And, of course, there was the hat, its brim stained with sweat. I would describe it as an Australian hat, by which I mean that the brim was bent up on one side and down on the other.

As our eyes remained engaged, the hollow feeling returned to my stomach.

FOUR

THE ACTUAL signing of books began without fanfare, and my mild adrenaline rush made the first few attempts at small talk with strangers easier than I had feared. But the sensation that Layla was still staring at me began to make me feel uneasy. I glanced up again, so subtly that I was sure Kathryn had not noticed. A blue backpack lay at Layla's feet, but she had nothing in her hands, least of all a copy of *Reelect Tom Jefferson*. She did not appear to be there for the book signing, yet continued to stare at me.

"A friend of yours?" Kathryn leaned over and whispered.

I grimaced, realizing my glance had not been all that subtle. "I just met her this morning," I whispered back. "Do you think she's staring at me?"

"I know she's staring at you," Kathryn said. "That's very inappropriate. Perhaps I'll have a word with her."

"No, no, that's okay," I said urgently, but from that moment forward, I could see out of the corner of my eye that Kathryn was staring right back at Layla and was poised to leave her chair at any moment. I introduced her to a few familiar faces as I signed their books, hoping to refocus her attention, but it was futile. In less than thirty minutes, Kathryn stood and began walking toward Layla.

The two of them began talking, Kathryn through a wide, pa-tronizing smile, and Layla through an open-mouthed look of in-dignation. Kathryn never relinquished her grin as they talked, and after a few minutes, Layla grabbed her backpack and stormed off. As Kathryn returned to her chair, Layla looked back at her and mouthed the word *bitch*.

"She said you were the nicest man she had ever met and that the two of you were friends," Kathryn whispered in my ear upon her return. "But if I wanted her to leave, she would. Is there some-thing I'm missing here?"

"I met her an hour ago," I protested.

Kathryn patted me on the back. "Yes, well, remember, Travis, one of our agreements is that you're no longer allowed to pick up strays." She barked a deep laugh, told me that she had to leave for a meeting, and headed toward the stairs.

I wished she hadn't mentioned strays because while I'd finally sold my house I was still dragging my feet on finding a home for my dogs. I had told Kathryn that I was working on it, but the truth was that I couldn't even bring myself to think about it.

*   *   *

Within minutes of Kathryn's descending the stairs, Layla was back by the phones, staring at me. Only now her look was markedly different; her eyes were narrow, her shoulders rigid, and her jaw set. It was as though she was angry with me. She must have thought I had dispatched Kathryn to scold her.

Nevitt and Schramm reached the table and both gushed about how proud the university was of my success. Nevitt slapped me on the back, saying that however much I made as an author, he would bring in ten times more by marketing my name. Schramm mentioned that he had been speaking to Trey Holcombe in the coffee shop and had learned that a national book-signing tour was being planned. He wasn't supposed to tell me, he confided, since Trey was planning to surprise me after the event with the news that sales across the country were climbing impressively and a review in the *New York Times Book Review* was imminent.

I couldn't have been more excited as the line before me finally shrank to only a handful. Almost instinctively, I looked again toward the restrooms, but Layla was gone. I wondered whether I would ever see her again. I wondered why I cared.

Then as I accepted a book from a young man who had appeared to be the last in line, I saw a copper shroud behind him. My pulse quickened, and for a million dollars I couldn't have recalled a word I said to the young man. I wonder if I even got the spelling of his name right. He thanked me and left, leaving only me, the table . . . and Layla.

"It's me again," she grinned sheepishly.

Her hair was luxuriant, precisely the light copper color of a newly minted penny. It fell from under her hat in uneven strands, some of which stopped around her shoulders, others falling far below. A braided leather band around her neck matched the one around her hat. Her purple lips were full—oversized for her symmetrical face. A constellation of pale freckles, the kind one often grows out of, was scattered across her nose and cheeks.

As I stared at her, temporarily unable to speak, I suddenly understood the feeling in my gut. Randi had had freckles just like that, and her hair was just that color. Layla Sommers looked exactly as I imagined my daughter would have looked at that age if not for the accident.

I noticed again that her nipples were visible through the threadbare cotton. If she had been my daughter, I would have made her put on more clothes. As it was, I consciously averted my eyes. But curiously—and I suppose I'll have to apologize to Ben someday—I was struck most of all by the fact that I could *smell her!* She had a deep, comforting smell that reminded me of . . . something I couldn't immediately define. Perhaps it was something from when I was a little boy, like the blankets my grandmother kept in her cedar chest. Whatever it was, I was drawn to it.

"Thank you for coming," I said. She now held a copy of *Reelect Tom Jefferson* in her hand; I reached out to accept it. But I didn't get her book. Instead, I got her hand. Her fine, bony fingers were long and delicate; her nails were the same dark purple color as her lips. Her fingers were noticeably cool. She tucked her chin into her chest and bit her thick bottom lip slightly, as if she couldn't possibly think of anything to say.

"May I have your *book?*" I asked, gently pulling free of her grip.

Her head jerked up and she blushed furiously as she realized that I had been reaching for her book, not her hand.

"I am *so* sorry," she said as she jerked her hand away. Her entire body stiffened.

I could feel the pain of her embarrassment and tried to change subjects quickly. "Layla, right?" I said. "That's a pretty name. Was your dad an Eric Clapton fan?"

"My dad was an asshole," she snapped. Quickly, her tone softened. "I shouldn't have said that—I'm sorry."

"Well, Layla, what would you like for me to write in your book?" I turned to the inscription page.

She hesitated and then smiled. "You really think my name is pretty?" Her body language changed miraculously as she spoke those words. In a blink, she was transformed from a state of humiliation to one of shy-girl innocence. "Just say, 'To Layla . . .'" I began to write, aware that she was staring at me, daring me: "To Layla with love."

I lowered my head and blinked hard, as if pondering where to start the inscription, when of course I was considering its appropriateness. I heard a shallow sigh from above, as if she were either mortified or relieved by the request she had made.

One thing I knew, even at that earliest juncture, was that a rejection of her request would have resulted in profound embarrassment— probably for us both. There was no one else in line and Kathryn was gone . . . so I signed the book as she had requested and handed it back to her. "Well, I don't know about you," I said, "but

I've got to get to class." I stood and gathered up my leather satchel. As I moved toward the staircase, Layla fell in step with me. I struggled for something to say.

"Is this your first semester?" I finally uttered as we descended the wide staircase.

She opened the cover of her book and read my inscription as we walked. Her face gleamed as if it were illuminated by some internal light source. "Yeah," she said. "I'm a freshman. It's sort of, like, scary."

"I'm sure you'll do fine," I reassured her. "Are you taking History 315K?" It just popped out as the statistically improbable thought occurred to me.

"I'm taking some history class," she said, "but I can't remember the number." She stopped abruptly. "Hey, that would be cool if I was in your class," she said. She looked again at the inscription. She ran her fingers over the words as if they had been engraved.

"Well, good luck," I said as we neared the front door. Trey Holcombe made a well-timed appearance, smiling at Layla as if he expected her knees to buckle. He handed me a sheet of paper that summarized the book sales from the signing and also a fax from my Knopf editor, a patrician woman named Cindy O'Connell. The fax confirmed what Schramm had already told me—there was going to be a book signing tour, ten cities to start, possibly more to follow. Cindy was also going to talk to Saul Westberg, my agent, about a contract for several more books.

"Looks like you and I will be traveling the country together," Trey beamed.

"What luck," I said. Then turning to Layla. "Enjoy your book," I looked at her and wondered if I would ever see her again. I thought of Randi.

*   *   *

As I exited Barnes & Noble, Layla remained inside. I hurried to the crosswalk where the light had just turned red. The Drag is six lanes wide, and crossing against the light is unthinkable. I looked at my watch and grimaced.

After what seemed like an eternity, the light turned green, but at that same instant, I heard a shrill siren and someone shouting behind me. All my instincts told me not to turn around, but I did. There, trying to tear free from a security guard—kicking, shouting, crying, and gripping her copy of *Reelect Tom Jefferson* as if her life depended on it—was Layla Sommers. Her face was on fire, her copper hair in flight. Her leather hat lay on the pavement beside her.

FIVE

"WHAT'S the problem?" I asked as I approached the security guard, quite aware that I would now be late for my class. Layla stopped kicking, and a look of wonderment crossed her face as the guard released her arm.

He was a tall, skinny boy with an enormous Adam's apple and a face like a relief map. I glanced at his equipment belt and was relieved to find no gun among the myriad gadgets. I bent over and retrieved Layla's hat from the pavement and handed it to her. The morning heat was building; I felt sweat droplets trickling down my rib cage.

"The problem, sir," the guard began, "is that this girl exited the premises with unpaid merchandise, triggering the magneto alarm and requiring, according to store policy, that I apprehend her and file a complete report. A ten-fifty-five-dash-one."

"I forgot, all right?" Layla said, much too loudly. "I was late for class. *All right?* It's not like it's some fucking federal offense, you pimple-faced—"

"Layla, *please*," I said. "Let me handle this." She retreated to my side and clutched my arm.

"You tell 'em, Dr. T," someone shouted from the small semi-circle of spectators that had formed around us.

"What's your name, son?" I asked.

"Nathan," he said. "Security Officer Nathan Duckworth."

"Well, *Officer Duckworth...*," I said, and paused for effect. "My name is Dr. Harrison. I'm a professor at the university." I nodded in the direction of the campus. "I'm also the author of this book, Miss Sommers' book." I tapped the book still in Layla's firm clutches. "The publisher allows me a certain number of complimentary copies—free copies. I gave this one to Miss Sommers, believing that it had already been accounted for and, uh, deactivated, or whatever one does to ensure that the alarm is not triggered."

"Demagnetized," Nathan said proudly.

"Yes, well, what I would ask, *Officer* Duckworth, since we are all late for these very important first classes, is that you allow me to take care of this. After my first class, I will call Mr. Proden, your manager. He happens to be a personal acquaintance of mine. First, of course, I'll tell him what a professional job you have done, and then I will make whatever arrangements are necessary to square the accounting. Fair enough?"

To my disappointment, Nathan did not look as relieved as I had expected. His mouth fell open slightly and his eyes narrowed in what, for him, must have been the deepest form of contemplation possible.

"But the manual says that if the alarm goes off—"

"Set her free, Nathan!" The voice of a nearby student rang out. "Set her free!" Several other voices joined in. Layla, her head turning rapidly from side to side to view her supporters, smiled broadly. Another shouted, "Mace her, Nathan! She's nothing but trouble." Layla flipped the finger to that speaker and mouthed the words *fuck you*.

As the crowd continued to swell and the chants grew louder, Nathan appeared to panic. He fumbled with his radio for a moment, but when he couldn't make that work, he turned and abandoned the scene, loping through the small crowd like a dinosaur in retreat.

As a modest cheer erupted, I felt the grip on my arm tighten, and even at that early moment, I noted the curiously pleasant sensation. Layla tucked her head under my chin and I felt the coolness of her copper hair pressing against me. She was smiling widely, her face alive and glowing. Her fingernails dug into my tweed jacket.

"You the man, Dr. T!" a former student yelled. The nickname, which I'd been given many years ago and which had stuck, was repeated by several who did not even know me. But very quickly, the crowd lost interest and dispersed. Like extras between takes on a movie set, they melted into the morass.

"You *are* the man," Layla said softly, kissing me quickly on my cheek.

Her kiss surprised me. I tried to think of what to say. "Yes, well, *the man* is now late for his first day of class—"

She jerked her hand free from my arm. Her face reddened and she seemed to sink within her own body like a punctured raft. I was stunned by the suddenness of her transformation; she looked as if she might throw up right there on the sidewalk. "Here," she said, thrusting the book at me. "I can't afford it." I refused to take it from her. She threw it to the ground near my feet and stalked away.

"Layla," I said, uncharacteristically reaching out and grabbing her shoulder firmly, turning her to face me. "I didn't mean to hurt your feelings." I had never seen a person's mood shift so fast. "It's just that being late on the first day is . . . it's unacceptable. That's all I was trying to say. Here, please . . ." I hustled back a few steps, gathered up the splayed book and offered it to her. "I want you to have this. Really, I do. Read it, enjoy it."

She breathed deeply and sighed, calming down as quickly as she had heated up. The redness in her face dissipated, though the fragile outline of her cheekbones was still crimson, and her scattered freckles were cherry red. She stretched a slender arm forward and accepted the book. "I just don't have a lot of extra money right now," she said meekly.

"I don't want you to pay for it. It's a gift from me." I looked at her closely and saw the hint of a grin forming. "Now, I'd love to stay and talk," I lied, "but because I have two hundred students waiting to see if there really is a Dr. Travis Harrison, I've got to go. Okay?" She stared at her feet. *"Okay?"* I repeated.

"Okay," she whispered at last.

"Good luck, Layla," I said as I turned away, barely aware that I had just asked for her permission to teach my class. The light was green for pedestrians and I hustled onto the campus and up the West Mall, moments from the greatest embarrassment of my life.

SIX

I WAS scheduled to teach only two classes that semester—History 315K, a large freshman class on the history of the United States before the Civil War, and History 437L, an upper division course on the formation of the Declaration of Independence. Both would be held in Garrison Hall, an eighty-year-old Spanish-style building that was also the site of my office.

My freshman class was held in the main auditorium, which is my favorite one on campus. While it is large enough to accommodate several hundred students, its worn wooden chairs and traditional blackboards give it the old-style feel I prefer. As far as I'm concerned, if a professor doesn't leave a lecture covered with chalk dust, nothing of value could possibly have been conveyed to the students.

The only problem with the Garrison auditorium is that three doors at the back lead directly from the top of steep aisles to the outside of the building. The doors are extremely heavy and unusually loud, making it impossible for tardy students to enter discreetly. Within minutes after the bell, the windowpanes at the back of the room fill with young faces as they assess the risks of entering.

But on that first day, it was I who banged through the doors four minutes late. Ling Chen, my teaching assistant, was busy calling the roll; he could not hide his irritation as I approached.

"Where've you been?" Ling snapped under his breath. His hair was straight and uneven, as if self cut. He wore a black and yellow T-shirt trumpeting a rock band of some sort. Ling was always curt, but he never meant to be impolite. Besides, I had to be somewhat tolerant if I was going to keep him; the chairman of the computer science department had accused me of ruining this mathematical genius by luring him to the graduate program in history. I had argued that someone who understood the Declaration of Independence would be more valuable to his native China than someone who understood computers.

"Sorry," I whispered to Ling. "Please continue while I get ready." Ignoring the students, yet feeling the heat of their curiosity, I took a sheath of notes from my satchel and began to write an outline on the blackboard. The chalk etched the letters with a comforting and familiar symphony of clicks and screeches.

When I had finished, I sat in an old wooden chair and waited patiently as Ling quickly read the names of those students officially registered—the only time we would do so. Next he covered a number of administrative issues, including the fact that the class was full and no one could be added.

Finally, Ling introduced me as the most popular history professor in America. Enthusiasm, as much as genius, was what I liked about Ling. As I stood and looked over the packed room, the morning's craziness was instantly washed away. I don't know if the proper analogy is to a rock star, athlete, or politician, but standing before the rapt young crowd packed into the seats and aisles, waiting patiently for the din and rustling of papers to die down, is a potent feeling. I would not go so far as to call it God-like, although many other professors had no difficulty in rising to that metaphor, but it is undeniably intoxicating. For seventy-five minutes at a time, twice a week, it drew from this introvert every ounce of the performer and evangelist that I possessed.

*   *   *

I stood and walked to the center of the floor, placing my papers on a simple wooden desk. Though I knew all eyes were on me, I said nothing. I looked at my notes and paced in a small circle as if no one else was there.

The objective of my sustained silence was to establish a form of control that, if successful, would enable me to teach all semester with minimal disruptions. If I failed to quiet the room, however, I would have to retreat to the lavaliere microphone, trying hard to look as if that was precisely what I had intended to do.

Fortunately, silence did sweep across the auditorium, from the front to the rear, row after row. Within two minutes (which can seem like an eternity when you're standing silently) the room was impressively quiet. The doors at the back were motionless, though I could still see faces pressed against the panes of glass.

"Good morning!" I said at last, expanding the circumference of the semicircle I paced.

"Morning." The replies from the class were pleasantly enthusiastic, a good sign.

"Welcome to America," I continued. "The history of America, that is, at least from 1492 to 1865. That would be from the time Columbus sailed the ocean blue to the time Lincoln freed the slaves. That, my friends, is a pretty broad sweep for three months' worth of work. And work there will be.

"I realize this is a required course, which means that some of you may not *want* to be here. But it has been said that if we fail to understand our history, we are doomed to repeat it. For example, how many of you would like to repeat the importation of African slaves into this country?" I raised my hand as a signal that this was not a rhetorical question, that I was prepared to take a count of hands. "How many?" I urged. No hands went up. Those whose eyes I could see in the first few rows looked at me as if I were crazy. *Good!*

"None of you?" I challenged. "Well, how many of you have friends or relatives living in the northeastern part of this country?" Slowly, dozens of hands went up. "How would you like to take up arms against them because of a difference of opinion, perhaps to kill some of your cousins?" No hands went up.

I had them. I could feel it . . . and what was likely the first class at the University of Texas for most of these students was going to ignite their concept of higher education.

As I continued to pace and lecture, however, I suddenly became aware of Ling. He was standing by the side door—the lone door that led from the auditorium to the interior of the building. He stared at me intently, conveying a mild sense of panic as if he was desperate for my attention. When I finally gave it to him, he pointed to his cheek. I decided to ignore him, knowing that if I lost my concentration, the students would lose theirs. But each time I paced in his direction, Ling would tilt his head and point to his cheek, each time more urgently.

Then, I heard a single chuckle—the ember of a professor's greatest nightmare—embarrassment before his class. It came from someone seated near Ling. Then, I heard another laugh from a more distant point. A low ripple of laughter swept through the section of the auditorium nearest Ling, as if they had somehow caught onto the joke—a joke that I didn't get.

And then it struck me. *My cheek!* Layla's quick kiss on my cheek. Her purple lips. Kathryn, who wore a fraction of the lipstick that Layla did, had made sure to wipe off the residue of her quick peck, but no such thought had occurred to Layla. Or to me. Had I been on time, of course, I would have caught it in the restroom mirror prior to class, but Layla had seen to my tardiness.

With the suddenness of a wildfire, two hundred pairs of eyes fell upon me like flames—flames that were burning the side of my face. I couldn't see it, of course, but I imagined Layla's lip print as large and purple as a plum, as perfectly etched as a tattoo.

Even as the snickering continued to spread like ripples in a pond, I could not think of an escape, not while struggling to continue my lecture and maintain my composure. I couldn't just stop and rub my face, even had I something, other than my wool tie, with which to rub it. I certainly couldn't make reference to it, and I couldn't simply stop the class and excuse myself to the men's room. I began to sweat lightly as I forged ahead, speaking more loudly in a crude effort to regain control.

"Well, isn't that strange," I said, "because in the past our nation has done these things. They are part and parcel of your heritage, if you are an American or if America is the country you have chosen to study in. You must remember that . . ."

A rear door crashed open and slammed shut. Every head turned to see the offender—a copper-haired girl in a leather hat who began fearlessly working her way down the crowded center aisle, stepping over, between, and on those who blocked her path.

"Excuse me, excuse me," Layla whispered loudly as she worked her way toward the front. I stood open mouthed. Purple cheeked.

"Sit down!" I heard one girl say as Layla high-stepped over her backpack.

"*Fuck you,*" Layla hissed as she kept moving.

She made her way to the front row where she sat cross-legged in the aisle. I looked at her directly, coldly, not amused. I *assumed* she would offer me a look of some contrition, but she simply waved meekly and mouthed the words *It's me again* through plum-purple lips. Oh, yes, it was definitely her again.

Looking at her lips, I was reminded of the purple stain on my face and horrified by the thought that someone might make the connection. *My God!*

The remainder of my lecture was dry and tortured. Minutes seemed like hours. Oh, I said all the words I had planned to say, but my mind had long since wandered away, which meant that my heart was not in it. Layla Sommers had broken my momentum and I had lost the class.

I sighed with relief when the bell rang, and with two hundred students rising to leave as one, I was able to hurry through the interior door before Layla could reach me. While I felt guilty about avoiding the other students on the first day of class, my dour mannerism must have sent the proper signal because they cleared a path for my exit as though I was armed and dangerous. The stairs right outside the auditorium lead up to my office, which is in the same corner of the building, two floors above. I took them two at a time.

I could hear Ling's voice chasing me up the stairwell, but before he could catch up, I had made it to my corner office and closed the door. My office, my sanctuary. I loved the view of the Main Mall and the intimacy of that office so much that I had declined a larger office when I'd gained tenure. An old wooden desk occupied half the room, and books and papers lined every inch of the walls and much of the remaining floor space.

But as much as I loved my office, I loved the door even more. At least sixty years old, it must have weighed three hundred pounds—even though the top half was thick, opaque glass. When it shut, it did so with an intimidating brass register that was music to my reclusive ears.

I slumped into my high-backed leather chair, which creaked loudly. I swiveled toward the window and looked through the complex network of thick oak limbs at the Main Mall. Students poured across it. Several boys had shed their shirts and were chasing a Frisbee across low hedges. Noticing my reflection in the glass, I hoped that my fears about the purple lipstick would go unrealized. The grim reality was that my cheek bore a perfect purple oval etched with tiny hash marks. I put my wool tie to good use and began to rub vigorously.

When I swiveled away from the window, I noticed flowers on a table in the opposite corner. Tall, white gladiolas. I knew immediately they were from Kathryn, and a twinge of guilt struck me for not having done the same for her. I opened the small envelope attached to the elegant vase and returned to my squeaky leather chair to read her note.

Dear Travis,

Congratulations on your book! I knew you could do it, and I'm glad I was able to be a part of the process. May many more follow. I'm looking forward to this semester—you have your book tour, and I, my long-awaited departmental chair. Of course, I also look forward to our marriage. You are a good and decent man, and we are lucky to have found each other.

By the way, don't forget to mark October 25th on your calendar. That is the evening at the chancellor's house reserved for my formal reception.

With love,
K.O.

I logged onto UT's computer network and sent Kathryn a thank-you note via e-mail. I had been one of the last to give in, but even I could no longer deny that e-mail was a permanent part of university life. I would probably receive thirty such messages before the day was out, but it was early yet, and the only one I had waiting for me was from Ben:

A bumper crop of peaches! Prospective Angels of Mercy in every row! I'm lunching at the Cactus around noon. Care to join me?

Ben's e-mail was hardly necessary—the day that Ben did *not* lunch at the Cactus around noon would be the only fact worthy of note. I cared deeply for Ben, but that didn't mean I wanted to hear more of his stories and watch him drink martinis during the middle of the day. I told him I'd have to pass.

As I was about to log off the system, I heard the electronic ding that indicated I had received a new e-mail. I clicked open the window and stared at it in disbelief: It was from lsommers@utexas.edu. The subject line read *Aroused.*

> *Travis . . . tried to catch up with you after class . . . thought you'd wait FOR ME!!! your office door was shut though i'm sure you were there . . . whatever . . . need to talk to you . . . need to add your class . . . i know it's full and all, but I'm sure that will not be a problem FOR ME!* ☺ *you were brilliant this morning— even with purple lipstick all over your face (LOL!) wonder where that came from? watching you teach turned me on . . . do you always have that effect on girls? I'm totally serious . . . couldn't believe just sitting there watching you . . . I got aroused!*

There was more to her e-mail, but I quickly stood behind my desk and turned away from the screen. *My God!* I ran my fingers through my hair. How could she possibly write those words to me? What in the hell was I supposed to do with *that?* Had it never crossed her mind to simply write, "nice lecture?" I paced the tiny section of my office floor that was uncluttered and then stared out the window and watched students crossing the Main Mall. In a large grassy area near my building, more students had shed more clothes and now lay on their backs, letting the growing heat of the sun wash over them. I saw a large black student in a football jersey walk by and tried to think ahead to this weekend's game in an attempt to regain control of my own thoughts. Everyone on campus was wondering whether the new coach ($3.4 million a year, thanks to president Nevitt's fund-raising skills) would play the highly touted freshman quarterback. Kathryn had season tickets, and we planned to attend all the home games.

I looked again at the flowers she had sent, thought of summoning Ling (perhaps asking *him* to respond to Layla's e-mail as if I had not seen it), and then tried to focus my thoughts on the prospects of a book-signing tour. In other words, I tried to think of anything other than Layla's e-mail, other than Layla's . . . arousal.

But I lost that battle with my mind and slumped back into my chair to read the remainder of her message:

> *I'm using a pc at the academic center . . . probably won't be back here until tomorrow or the next day, so could you call me tonight . . . 473-2198 . . . call me after six but if a boy answers, hang up!!! i've been trying to get rid of enos because he's really hurting me . . . if he thinks another boy is calling me, he would really mess me up . . . i think he wants to kill me . . . it's getting so much rougher and more violent each time . . . i really, really need to talk to you . . . i'm so happy I met you, Travis . . . I think it was fate or whatever . . . thanks for the book . . . that was so sweet . . . YOU ARE SO SWEET! thanks for saving me from that fucking giraffe . . . for just being there for me . . . no one's ever done that before . . . can't wait to see you again. call me! ☺*

Before I logged off the system, I sent one more e-mail:

> *Ben, on second thought, I think I will join you for lunch.*

SEVEN

"SHE GOT *aroused?*"

"Ben! Please! Keep your voice down," I said, though his roaring laugh had already drawn the attention of every patron in the Cactus Café.

"Oh, that's rich!" Ben's shoulders rocked with uncontrollable laughter as he held the e-mail I had printed out for him. "That's good stuff. You're making my day, Dr. Harrison. How much do I owe you for this?"

"Ben!" I pleaded. "Be serious. I think I've got a problem here."

"Wouldn't I love such a problem!" he said. "I saw her at the book signing this morning, standing there with that dirty T-shirt and sweat-stained hat. I saw her wave at you. She didn't happen to say whether she was taking philosophy, did she?"

"Ben . . ."

"You sure you don't want one of these?" he asked, pointing to the martini in front of him. The fact that the Cactus Café had a full bar was the reason Ben lunched there every day.

"You know I don't drink at lunch," I said.

"Yeah, well, this might be a good day to start," he said, shaking the printout and taking a generous sip.

"So what do I do?" I asked. "This does seem like your area of expertise."

"Depends on the result you want," he said. "Want to see this girl again, or nip it in the bud?"

For a moment, I did consider ordering a drink, but I settled for iced tea. "That's the odd thing, Ben. I'm not sure. When I first saw her, I was overcome with a weird feeling. I felt like I was looking into the eyes of Randi."

Ben's eyes grew wide behind his thick, yellowed lenses. "Randi?"

"Yes. She'd be a freshman this year, and—it's uncanny—she would have looked a lot like Layla." I paused. "Though I hope she would have *acted* a little more appropriately."

"So this girl, the one who reminds you of your daughter, says that you arouse her. And you think *I'm* a pervert?" Ben's laugh filled the Cactus so raucously that half a dozen tables began laughing with him.

"Ben, please—"

"Is the problem that you don't know whether to screw her or adopt her?"

"I have no plans to do either—"

"Hell, if I were you, I'd do *both*. Nothing like a captive audience. Good stuff!"

My scowl of disapproval finally registered with Ben. He paused and then said, "Okay, my friend, let me give you the bare facts. This girl is bad news and you need to get rid of her. Of course, maybe Enos—Enos the Penos—will take care of that for you." He laughed again so hard that his bulky glasses fell into his lap. He picked them up, peered through the lenses to see if they were clean, and repositioned them on his face.

"Could we just call him Enos?" I asked in frustration.

"Look, *Enos*...may or may not even exist. This girl is probably full of shit. Most of them are at that age. But you see, Dr. Harrison has a little problem with guilt, and if he should wake up tomorrow and read that something *did* happen to this little girl who reminds him of his daughter, he would never forgive himself. True?" He plucked the olive from his martini and rolled it between his fingers.

"True," I admitted. "So what should I do?"

"Why don't you ask Kathryn to handle it for you?"

I stared at him blankly. "You're joking."

"I'm not."

"You mean, just call Kathryn and casually mention that the girl she pissed off earlier today has now discovered that I . . . I . . ."

"Arouse her! *That's good stuff!*" Ben howled with laughter, accidentally tossing the olive in his fingers onto the floor. "Somebody grab that thing," he shouted.

A young girl with striped pants and brown hair to her waist scooped the olive up from where she was sitting and brought it to him.

"Oh, thank you, my angel," Ben said with an excess of graciousness.

"I'm in your philosophy class," the girl said shyly. "Marie Patton."

"Yes, of course," Ben said. "Marie Patton. Now I recognize you. Now listen, Marie. When I assign the first paper, the one on Love, I want you to schedule time during my office hours to come discuss yours with me. You look like a girl who would think deeply on such matters."

"I do?" Marie said, placing her hand over her heart. "Thank you, Dr. Frizell. I'll do that. I look forward to it!" She returned to her table.

"Trust me, my darling," Ben said under his breath, "not half as much as I do."

Ben stared at me with an omnipotent look. I said nothing, but I'm sure my face registered the proper degree of wonder.

"Look, Travis," Ben said at last as he placed the olive on his plate. "Isn't Kathryn's job description to get rid of distractions in your life? Well, my friend, as of this e-mail, you've got 120 pounds worth of nuclear-strength distraction." Ben leaned in towards me; he was no longer smiling. "If you think about it, her message is really quite brilliant. First, she says that you turn her on, and most girls older than twelve know better than to say that to a man unless they want the consequences. But, at the same time, she's introduced another man who is hurting her—*sexually.* She doesn't use that word, but the implication is obvious. She even gives you his name, Enos the Penos. Sorry . . .

"In this way, you can start imagining this little lamb, whom you have already saved once, as the innocent victim again— doomed without your help."

"So, what do I do?"

"Well, she lays that out for you, doesn't she? A very simple request. Just a phone call. And for good measure, she lays the guilt of a parent on you should you refuse, reminding you that no one has ever helped her before. Conscious or not, the girl is brilliant."

Ben took the last sip of his martini and signaled to the waitress that he was ready for another. "Act shocked if you want when I mention Kathryn, but we both know that she *would* get rid of the problem, and if it is gotten rid of now—today—then a month from now it will be nothing more than a good story. Which, by the way, I will repeat on the first day of fall semester for the rest of my life!"

I sighed heavily. "If there's one thing I've never shared with you Ben, it's Kathryn's history with the men in her life and their younger women. I don't think it's wise to get her involved, but I know that I have to do something."

"Indeed you do. A student has confided in you that she believes her life is in danger. Bullshit or not, you can't just sit on that information. If you're not going to sic Kathryn on her, you should contact either the University Police or University Counseling. Yeah, you've got to do something. What's so damn fascinating is that Ms. Sommers clearly knows that as well.

"To my friend, Travis, his friend, Layla, and her friend, Enos the Penos," Ben said as he raised his second martini into the air. At a nearby table, Marie Patton thought Ben was signaling to her and an electric smile lit up her face.

"Good stuff," Ben said. "Damn good stuff! Is this a great university, or what?"

Then an odd thing happened. I watched as Ben grew quiet and tears welled in his eyes. He drained his second martini in a single long gulp. He took off his glasses and dabbed at his eyes. "I know you miss Randi," he said. "I wish I had known her."

EIGHT

"I DON'T like my freckles, Daddy." Randi stood on a footstool in the small bathroom in our house on Preston Street and studied her face in the mirror. I walked in behind her and studied her as well. She was perfection. Her long copper-colored hair fell almost to her waist and, although only nine, her body showed the unnerving hint of what someday was to come—womanhood.

It was ten years ago that I had finally given up on getting tenure at Texas, and with Randi turning nine, I had decided it was time for a little more space and a little more security. The best opportunity I had for a tenured position was from Texas Tech, and the interview I faced that day in Lubbock would be the deciding one.

"TJ likes your freckles," I said, referring to the twelve-week-old Labrador retriever I had gotten her for her ninth birthday. "I saw him kissing them earlier this morning."

"TJ likes everything," she said, "and besides, he wasn't kissing, he was licking; I had oatmeal on my face. When will my freckles go away?"

"Never, I hope. Your freckles are spectacularly beautiful. Brush your teeth, now. Daddy can't be late for his meeting, and Lubbock is a long ways away."

"Tell me again why I'll like Lubbock."

"For one, there's an indoor swimming pool at our hotel. That sounds fun, doesn't it?"

"Sort of."

"And two, if Daddy gets this job, it will mean a bigger house for us. It will mean you can have a bigger room and your own bathroom. TJ can have a bigger yard."

"Does it mean we'll have room for a mommy?"

No matter how many times she asked it, I never got used to the question. Sometimes I wondered if the curiosity of a child made her ask it just to see the ashen color wash over my face and my eyes lose their focus. Thankfully, TJ came sliding around the corner and into the bathroom, tossing a small stuffed armadillo in front of him, which he then pounced on like a lion. Randi and I both laughed; I picked the dog up and held him in front of her face. "We'll like Lubbock," I said, doing my best ventriloquist act.

"I didn't know you could talk, TJ," Randi said to the dog. "Are you going to Lubbock with us?"

"Not this time," I said on TJ's behalf. "I'm staying with Puddy, but if you move there, I'm moving with you."

"Oh, goodie," Randi said, rubbing TJ's ears gently. "Tell me, TJ, do *you* have a mommy?"

*   *   *

It wasn't as if I hadn't tried to find a new mother for Randi. In fact, it was mostly the sense that Randi should have a mother that forced me out into the dating life. The problem was that Randi so longed for a mom that she instinctively and passionately clung to any woman to whom I introduced her, which made separating true emotions from the base needs of a child all but impossible.

But soon enough, Randi became curious about girly things like clothes, makeup, and boys—things that I knew I could never help her with—and her teen years lurked on the horizon like a rising sun that would soon be too bright for me.

So it's not that I didn't try. I reached that third-date point with four perfectly adequate women and subsequently introduced each of them to Randi, who clung to them just as she clung at night to her stuffed lop-eared bunny. But every time I started imagining one of them living with us, all I could think about was what a pale substitute she would be for Randi's real mother, Helen.

Helen and I had gone to high school together in Colorado City, Texas, home of the Fighting Wolves. Our families knew one another, and everyone in the small West Texas town always thought we would end up together. We did. We went steady in high school and both went to the University of Texas at Austin for college; I studied history and she studied to be a high-school math teacher. I suppose we were the ideal combination of best friends and lovers. And from that first time that she'd unexpectedly hiked up her skirt and eased onto my lap in the back seat of my dad's car, we went for years unable to get enough of each other.

Helen was beautiful in her plainness. Her hair was dark red, and she paid little attention to it, letting it grow in long, natural waves. She dressed simply, wore almost no makeup, and wore thin black glasses that made her look like a stereotypically conservative librarian. I teased her about that fact anytime I wanted to unleash the ire of the most sexually creative woman I have ever known.

"Do I still remind you of a librarian?" she would ask as we both lay breathless on the small dining room table in our one-room apartment or on a hidden boulder under the stars at Mt. Bonnell or in a tiny bathroom stall in some obscure campus library.

I had to be careful with my answer because the slightest hint of a "yes" would lead to an immediate additional test of my endurance. It was a contest I could not win, but enjoyed the hell out of losing.

Our first years together in Austin were the happiest of my life. After graduation, Helen got a job teaching algebra at Austin High, and I was accepted into the Ph.D. program in history at Texas. We had enough money, enough time; we loved what we were doing, and we loved each other.

The first sign of trouble came the day I arrived home after classes and found Helen sitting in our apartment, crying. She was not due home from school for hours.

"Baby," I said as I sat down next to her, "what's wrong?" Her grief was palpable, and I could only imagine one of her parents had died. Or one of mine. She couldn't compose herself to answer. She just cried and hugged me weakly.

Then, at last, "I got my period today," she said at last through choked tears.

"I'm sorry," I said, not entirely clear as to why this news had so affected her.

She pulled away from me. "No, Travis, you don't understand. I was late. Very late. Travis, I was going to tell you tonight that I was sure I was pregnant. Now, I'm sure I'm not."

Even though we had talked about it often, it was only in that moment, watching her hunched over in emotional agony, that I realized how desperately Helen wanted a child.

"It will happen, Helen," I said.

"When, Travis? Do you realize that we haven't used birth control for almost three years now? There's something wrong with me, Travis. I'm sure of it."

*   *   *

Helen was never quite the same after that day. She seemed to lose a measure of her spontaneity as well as some of her sexual aggressiveness. Sex no longer served as the prospect of something potentially wonderful but as a reminder of something disturbingly wrong. She went to four different doctors, and we tried all sorts of things, but back then fertility enhancements involved little more than my rushing home from campus in the middle of the day if her temperature reached a certain level. We kept trying, but by the time I received my Ph.D. two years later, Helen had begun to talk wearily about a childless life.

*   *   *

Like most major universities, Texas is not fond of hiring its own doctoral students, so I sent out two dozen *curriculum vitae,* and Helen and I prepared to move to a place unknown. It was a trying time as we slowly, almost imperceptibly, gave up piece-by-piece on the vision we had so often shared after making love in the backseat of my father's car.

And then, like contestants on a game show who win a prize that is followed by a bigger prize and then by an even bigger prize, our lives suddenly changed.

On a Tuesday morning after Helen had left for work, the chairman of the History Department at Texas, a wiry old man named Alfred Stokes, called me at our apartment.

"Dr. Harrison," he said, in his high-pitched Southern drawl. "We've had a slight problem in the department. Dr. Franks is taking a medical leave, and Dr. Goldberg accepted a position at Harvard. What I'm saying, Dr. Harrison, is that while we don't normally hire from within, nor do we typically hire so young . . . we've got a spot on the faculty for you if you'd like it. It's tenure track, though I have to warn you that it could be a very long track."

Our apartment was in the path of the local airport, and as a plane was passing low overhead at the time, I think I shouted, *"Yes!"* to Dr. Stokes at least twenty times to ensure that he had heard me.

To prepare for the move we'd thought imminent, I had saved up about $1,500. I grabbed my checkbook and drove to a house for sale close to campus—one that Helen and I had driven by and fantasized about a hundred times. It was a tiny two-bedroom, one-bath cottage on Preston Street that, to us, had all the elegance of Tara. I wrote down the number of the real estate agent, called him from a nearby service station, and within four hours had submitted a contract and put earnest money down on the house. I told him it was an essential part of the deal that a CONTRACT PENDING sign be placed in the yard immediately.

I then drove to Helen's school, unannounced, and picked her up. I blindfolded her before driving her to Preston Street, helped her out of the car, and carried her to the front yard of the house, placing her down near the CONTRACT PENDING sign. Finally, I removed the blindfold and said, "Welcome home."

An old lady in the yard next door, who was tending to her roses, stopped her gardening to come over and introduce herself. Her name was Puddy, and she told us we would love it there.

I told Helen about my job and the increase in pay and she responded with a look of mixed happiness and pain that was all too easy to interpret. *If only.*

We closed on the house about six weeks later. Tired from the move and with most of our belongings still in boxes, we sat on the hardwood floor and enjoyed a pizza for dinner.

"I'm going to get tenure," I mused. "I'm going to be a Texas professor for life and write the best history books ever written. And you're going to be the best math teacher in America . . . and we're going to look into adoption."

"I don't want to adopt, Travis," Helen said.

"But I thought you wanted children in your life."

She gave me a strange smile, pushed the pizza aside, and got that librarian look in her eye that I hadn't seen in years.

"I do," she said, pulling me gently onto the floor with her. "Tell me, Dr. Harrison, have you ever made love to a pregnant woman? 'Cause now's your chance."

It was the happiest night of our lives, including the one on which Randi was born, for by then we knew that Helen was dying.

NINE

THE TWO weeks after my book signing—and the unsettling e-mail from Layla Sommers—brought little change to Austin's heat but great improvement to my outlook on life. Having opted to report Layla Sommers to University Counseling, I had neither seen nor heard from her since. And with the ceremonial lifting of Ben's martini, I had been officially declared "free of the copperhead."

I had not mentioned Layla's e-mail or my course of action to Kathryn, and as both the sale of the Preston house and our marriage grew closer, she seemed perpetually upbeat. *Reelect Tom Jefferson* was selling better by the day, and thankfully, I had managed to regain control of the undergrads in my class. Even after my embarrassing first day, it was turning out to be precisely the semester I had hoped for.

Oh, I won't deny that I thought about Layla. Occasionally I scanned the aisles of the Garrison auditorium in search of her, but she had not returned or attempted to add the class. I had even scoured the local paper a few times for news of a tragedy involving a young female student, but predictably, there had been none. As each day passed, the memory of Layla Sommers faded from all but the lascivious mind of Ben Frizell.

I was not the only one on campus whose attitude was growing upbeat. With a new coach and a 2–0 start by the team, the religion called football in Texas was finding converts everywhere. True, the team had not played a strong opponent yet, but Saturday's game against Notre Dame would change that. Press coverage and fan interest were heightened by the question of whether the new coach, Dabs Knowlton, would elect to start the sensational freshman quarterback who had looked so promising in the previous game. His name was Hy Bombgartner, or H-bomb, as he had been inescapably tagged by the press.

*   *   *

I slept until almost 8:00 a.m. on the morning of that game, a luxury that was brought to my attention by the pouting brown eyes of TJ as he rested his graying chin patiently on the side of my bed, imploring me to let him out. He was the only one of my dogs that I'd actually paid money for and the only one who got to sleep indoors. TJ had been Randi's dog.

I should say a word about my dogs, for as surely as I had learned to avoid people over the past decade, I had collected canines. Besides TJ, who was a purebred Labrador, the rest were mixed breeds, but each showed the dominant traits of at least one of its parents.

Abigail was a Dachshund mix that had emigrated from my elderly neighbor, Puddy. It was about three years ago when I first noticed Abigail ferociously digging under my fence as I fed my dogs. I investigated and discovered that Puddy, her memory failing her on many fronts, had been forgetting to feed Abigail, except on the one occasion when she had fed her rose fertilizer. I never really said anything to Puddy, but I took a shovel and widened Abigail's subterranean path; she soon began spending almost all of her days with my pack.

George was a mostly Weimaraner who I am certain loved me because I promised never to dress him in human clothes, despite that being the apparent plight of his breed. I'd found George on a highway during a rainstorm. Martha was mostly standard poodle and had been given to me by a woman I passed on the jogging trail some years ago. Martha was jogging at her side, but the woman wore a T-shirt that read, "My dog needs a home." I stopped and talked to her and discovered that when she bought the dog as a puppy she thought all poodles were small dogs until Martha quickly grew too big for her apartment and her irritable landlord. I let Martha's fur grow shaggy hoping to avoid the airs that well-shorn poodles often put on.

Sally was part black Lab; I had gotten her when my veterinarian showed her to me and said that her owners had abandoned her. Madison was a shepherd mix who just showed up in my backyard one day and refused to leave. He perpetually carried a slobbery tennis ball in his mouth, although he wasn't as adept at fetching as the Labs, TJ and Sally. In fact, I don't even think Madison enjoyed it. My theory is that he relentlessly brought me the ball because he thought I enjoyed it.

That made for six dogs in all; Kathryn felt strongly that one was too many. The irony was that her spacious house had an equally spacious yard that the dogs would have loved. But the compromise was that I would keep TJ and find homes for the others— something I had always vowed to do even before I had met Kathryn. I'd always imagined myself as a canine crisis center, not a long-term care facility, but I could never bring myself to run the ads or make the calls on their behalf. With less than a month remaining before moving out of Preston and in with Kathryn, I still had six dogs. Something would have to change. Soon.

*   *   *

I shuffled across the creaky hardwood floor and let TJ out. The other dogs rose to a welcoming attack, as if they couldn't wait to discover what had happened inside overnight. Madison's eyes pleaded with me as he rolled the slimy ball around in his mouth.

I managed to pull it free and threw it to the fence, where Sally retrieved it before Madison even got traction.

The large, circular thermometer on my patio indicated that it was already 81 degrees. I shuffled out front, gathered up the morning papers, and waved to Puddy, who seemed never to forget to tend her roses. I don't think one can truly appreciate the love that goes into a garden until one has witnessed a blue-haired geriatric lumbering down steps on a metal walker four times a day.

As I turned back toward the house, I stared for a moment at the real estate sign in the yard with the CONTRACT PENDING banner. How easily I was transported back to the day I had picked Helen up at the school where she taught, blindfolded her, and carried her to that very yard . . .

On the outside, the house hadn't changed much since that day. On the inside, sometimes consciously and sometimes not, I had expunged every indication that Helen and Randi had once lived there. Sometimes slowly, and sometimes in sudden weekend-long fits, Helen's wildlife prints and beaded pillows had found their way into boxes, as had Randi's Barbie dolls and colorful bedding. There were no pictures of either of them on display in the house. It was, I suppose, my way of coping.

I thought briefly about getting out an old photo album. Instead, I made coffee and toast and settled into my leather chair to read the *New York Times,* mildly disappointed, as always, with the paucity of Saturday's edition.

* * *

The day passed quickly. As was my custom, I visited a few garage sales in the neighborhood and picked up some books to add to my collection. Books covered virtually every wall inside my house and spilled out into the tiny garage at the end of a gravel drive, a garage that was actually more of a carport. It was much too small for the Wagoneer, which, like most of the cars on the neighborhood, usually wound up on the street. I had purchased the Wagoneer from a man named Craig Newby, and for more than five years, he'd been calling me once or twice a month, begging to buy it back, offering more than I'd paid him. I'd never been interested in selling, but I tolerated his long-winded family updates. He seemed a decent man.

Kathryn called once during the day to remind me of the timeline of our evening, and to make sure I would be wearing the *silk* tie, not the wool one. We were going to the Faculty Club just west of campus for an important networking event for Kathryn's fund-raising efforts—a vital measure of her early success as department chair.

"The Ganzes are going to be there," she raved. "The regents have authorized me to offer them the Ganz Marketing Research Center if they'll cough up $40 million."

"That should build a nice center," I said, admiringly.

"Oh, the center's already built," Kathryn said. "You know, the Texas Marketing Center. We'll just rename it."

"So the $40 million is essentially for a bronze plaque?"

"Precisely," Kathryn laughed. "And by the way, Norman's assistant told me that he's read your book and is looking forward to meeting you. I have to go early to meet with some other donors; you can come with me or meet me there at five."

"I'll meet you there," I said.

"Don't be late, Travis. This is very, *very* important to me."

"I won't," I assured her.

"Be charming and witty and help me pry $40 million out of the Ganzes, and I'll have a special reward for you later tonight."

I'd almost forgotten it was Saturday, the night of the week that I spent in Kathryn's bed.

*   *   *

I walked the dogs (an often comical undertaking that sometimes brought neighbors out of their houses), visited with Puddy for ten minutes, and then went inside to shower. As I passed the phone, I glanced at the caller ID to see if Kathryn might have called again: I found myself staring at the small device with a surreal sense of detachment as I studied the name of the lone caller: Layla Sommers.

I retrieved the message.

* * *

Travis.

Her voice was weak, raspy, and tear-stained. I wondered if I should even listen to the rest, yet I also knew that I would.

He found the book. Enos found the book.

What book, I wondered. What in the hell was she talking about?

He read your inscription . . . the part about your loving me.

Oh, *that* book.

He said he's coming back tonight to teach me a lesson and then stormed out. I can't keep him out . . . he just climbs up the fire escape in back . . . my kitchen window won't lock. I don't know where to go, Travis.

Her voice was pitiable.

I don't know who to call, what to do. It's been bad before, but I'm really scared now. The police won't do anything until after he's already hurt me. Been down that trail before.

I know you hate me, Travis, and you should . . . that inexcusable e-mail. I'm so sorry. I'm such a loser . . . I don't know where that one came from, but I do know it was totally inappropriate. I don't blame you for not calling me, for having that stupid bitch . . . that woman from counseling call for you. I deserved that. I really did. That's why I haven't tried to contact you. But now I really need your help. I'm still at 473-2198, still at 2368 San Antonio, number 303.

I jotted down the information.

You're right to hate me, Travis. I'm nothing but trouble. Everyone ends up hating me. But I know something about you. I know you wouldn't stand by and let Enos hurt me. I also know I have no right to put you in this position, but I'm scared and I don't know what else to do. I'm fighting for my life. I know you'll think of something. And then, I promise, I'll be out of your life forever. I just need to get away from him, from Enos. Then I'll be fine. I know it. Thank you, Travis. I . . . I...

Her voice faded to an undetectable whisper.

*   *   *

I sighed loudly as I queued the message again, wishing that, as with e-mail, there was a way I could forward it to Ben for his analysis even though I knew what he would say. He would say that Layla Sommers was again brilliantly manipulating me. Since I had felt compelled to contact the counselors initially, she knew I would feel compelled to act again. By citing my inscription in her book as the source of Enos's rage, she had in effect made the threat to her life *my fault*. She had even offered an apology for her e-mail and conveniently provided her phone number and address—an address that I recognized as very near the Faculty Club where I was to meet Kathryn in a matter of minutes.

I listened to the message three more times and finally did call Ben, but he wasn't home and I didn't leave a message.

Remembering that I hadn't yet showered, I looked at my watch. *Damn!* I was already twenty minutes late. I would have to tell Kathryn about Layla's call, but then again I couldn't possibly.

Not considering the great wound of Kathryn's past.

TEN

THE CONCERN I had over mentioning Layla's reappearance in my life to Kathryn stemmed from what I knew about her first marriage.

It was on our second night in bed together, the night after we had celebrated the sale of my book, that Kathryn and I had begun the confessions required of new lovers. True, we were mature beyond the point of needing a complete census of the other's sexual history, but former spouses would need to be addressed.

"I guess I've always been drawn to projects," Kathryn began, her head resting gently on my chest.

"So I'm a project?" I said playfully.

"I didn't mean that—"

I ran my hand over her body with a mixture of curiosity and timidity. "I don't consider it an affront," I said. And I didn't, for only from the perspective of how far Kathryn had brought me was I able to appreciate how far I had fallen. I was finally able to see that without Kathryn the pages I had been scribbling for years were destined for a life under my bed.

"I gather all of your projects haven't worked out as well as this one," I said, offering her a beginning.

"'For me, no," she said. "My first husband . . ."

"How many have you had?"

"My first, and only, husband was—is, I suppose—a brilliant man."

"Apparently, your weakness," I joked.

Kathryn then told me how her parents had made a small fortune when they sold their Napa Valley winery but had continued to live in the area. Wanting to stay close to home, Kathryn had chosen Stanford for her undergraduate work.

She looked at me and smiled suddenly. "I've never told you this, but as an undergraduate, I was a liberal arts major. History!"

"From history to marketing?" I couldn't resist. "My God, what caused your fall?"

"The desire for a job," she said, without missing a beat.

"You do know how to hurt a man."

"Yes. Apparently I hurt them by trying to help them. I first met John at a swim meet. It wasn't so competitive back in those days, even at Stanford, so a walk-on like me could join the team and even compete in the meets. I had been swimming since before I could walk and was pretty good at the breaststroke.

"There was an all-comers meet and the swimmers in my heat finished so tightly packed that none of us knew who had won. We all looked up to the officials standing over us and I saw the most gorgeous man I had ever seen above me. He was barefooted and wore bell-bottomed jeans and a denim shirt with the sleeves cut out. His hair was blonde and fell to his shoulders. My God, he was beautiful!"

"I get the picture," I teased.

"'You won,' he said to me. 'Nice race.'"

"'Are you my prize?' I asked him as I pulled off my swim cap hoping that my long, black hair would impress him. To this day I still can't believe those words came out of my mouth.

"'Believe me,' he said, 'I'm nobody's prize.' I should have believed him."

It turned out that John Singleton had been a swimming super-star before failing to register for college classes in time and quickly getting drafted. When he returned from Vietnam and to the water, he could barely complete a single lap. It was not well known at the time just what had destroyed his lungs, but something had. John disappeared from view, save a few random appearances at swim meets.

Kathryn searched for her mystery man, visiting first with the swim coach, which led to a visit to a nearby V.A. hospital. There, she found a woman who remembered John not because of his fail-ing lungs but because of his writing, his poetry, that she described as almost "emotionally unbearable."

The woman had kept some pages and gave them to Kathryn, who found them similarly compelling.

"I finally found John in a dilapidated old trailer near the coast," Kathryn continued. "No one answered the door, but I could hear music inside so I kept knocking for probably fifteen minutes. He finally came to the door and was obviously out of his mind on drugs. I walked inside, cleared a place for myself on a lit-tle bench seat, and began to read aloud the poems I'd brought with me. When I finished, he didn't say a word but he pulled an-other sheaf of papers from a shelf, and then another. For the bet-ter part of three days and nights I read his poetry aloud and even though he listened as if I wasn't there, it was an amazingly inti-mate and spiritual experience. By the time my voice went hoarse, he was sober.

"Not much was known yet about Agent Orange, but I tried to explain to him that something had obviously happened to his lungs while he was in Vietnam. I told him that with just a little re-search I had discovered that there were thousands of others like him. I told him he could make a difference to them through his writing. I told him I would help get him published."

"My God," I said as Kathryn paused for a moment. "You're a serial organizer."

She laughed softly, though there was an admission of truth in her laughter; tears filled her eyes. I did not ask her whether all her projects required sexual intimacy, but the answer was obvious.

"I'm afraid you're on to me, Dr. Harrison," she said. "I should have picked whales to save, but for some reason I decided to save talented writers." She looked at me and smiled. "Talented projects.

"Within three years," Kathryn continued, "John was something of a sensation in northern California literary circles. He had sold his trailer and I had purchased a small duplex not far from my parents' farm where John and I lived. I was working on my Ph.D.—in marketing, thank you very much."

"A terrible loss," I said.

"John and I got married in a weekend civil ceremony. But while I may have saved his writing, I could do nothing for his lungs, and it was hard for me to tell a man in such severe pain not to use his drugs. He became semifunctional. The parts of him that evidently continued to function best were the parts that a hundred young groupies craved, the parts between his legs. His poetry readings drew as many idealistic college girls as they did grizzled Vietnam vets. At some point, I stopped listening to his readings; all I did was watch those young girls sighing and crying and holding themselves as if they were making love to him on the spot. I never knew that would make me so damn crazy, but it did.

"That's where my, well, paranoia began. I couldn't stand the thought that a man I had done so much for might cheat on me, much less that early in our marriage. I suppose it wasn't the wisest coping strategy, but I stopped swimming, started eating, and put on forty pounds within a year. John had his drugs, I had my Oreos." Kathryn sat up and looked at me intently. "I have to work hard to stay fit, Travis. You should know that about me."

"Consider it known," I said.

"You can probably guess the rest," Kathryn said. "My classes were cancelled one day and I came home three hours early. I heard this furious wheezing and raced into the bedroom thinking that John was dying. My God, she couldn't have been fifteen.

"When he saw me, he puckered up and blew me a kiss. 'Honey, I'd like for you to meet Wendy,' he said. Incredibly, Wendy rolled off him, waved to me meekly and said, 'Hi. I've heard a lot about you.'

"I couldn't even speak, but John didn't hesitate. 'I'm going to keep seeing Wendy, honey, until you, you know, get the weight off. I didn't sign up to run a fucking fat farm.' He looked at Wendy and they both laughed."

Kathryn unconsciously pulled the sheet over her exposed hip. "Wendy was just the first that I knew of, but after her, they came like kittens to milk. I managed to keep it out of our house, but that just meant I hardly saw John anymore. I tried to justify it; he was in pain—perhaps even dying—and I had gotten fat. I had invested so much in him that I didn't want to let him go, but he stopped wanting to even touch me. I think that's what hurt so deeply—the comparisons. If he had still found me attractive, I might even have indulged him for a while. But the others were always thinner, more athletic—better fucks!"

Kathryn concluded by telling me how one day she had come home from classes to find him gone. There was no sign that he had ever lived there. Some months later she filed for divorce, and apparently the process servers found John somewhere because it was granted, but Kathryn never again knew where he was, or even if he was alive.

"Even today, I sometimes check obscure poetry sources hoping that he might still be alive, still writing," she said, exhausted. "Not that I want to see him again, only that I wonder what became of him."

*   *   *

Probably half an hour passed in silence before I realized there was no escaping my turn. I began by telling her how happy Helen and

I had been after moving into Preston Street and almost immediately discovering that she was pregnant with Randi. Kathryn placed her hand on my shoulder.

"We bought a scale," I said, "thinking that it would be fun to chart her weight gains as a way of tracking the baby's growth. Over the next three weeks, Helen *lost* five pounds; we knew then that something was terribly wrong."

ELEVEN

THE SMALL garage under the Faculty Club where Kathryn and the Ganzes waited was filled, so I circled the block in order to come around again and turn into the pay lot on the opposite side of the street. To get there, I was forced to turn left on San Antonio Street. Layla's street.

I saw a three-story building of gray composition shingles. It had odd-sized windows, many of them with air conditioning units protruding. The address painted on the front matched the one from Layla's voice mail: 2368 San Antonio.

I reduced my speed to a crawl, tapping my fingers on the wooden steering wheel until a horn honked behind me. I flinched and pulled over as the car passed. Craning my head around, I saw a long steel fire escape in the back of the building. Layla had pointed this out as Enos's preferred method of entry. I turned in my seat to study the building. Six or eight people lingered in the small yard in front, entertained by a mangy long-haired dog that could jump five feet in the air to catch a Frisbee. Layla was not among them. The cluster included four males, none of whom fit my stereotype of Enos.

I leaned my body over into the passenger seat and strained to look up at the third-floor windows. Were Layla and Enos inside one of those windows at that very instant? Was he hurting her? Was she waiting for me to help?

I considered locating her apartment and knocking on the door but then remembered Kathryn and the Ganzes. I thought of calling the police from the Faculty Club and telling them . . . what?

I eased back into the traffic lane, turned the corner, and parked in the pay lot. I sat for a moment, counseling myself on what a slippery slope I might create by lying to Kathryn. I weighed telling her the truth versus telling her a harmless lie and almost laughed out loud when the best lie I could come up with involved my dog, TJ! Surely I could do better than that!

*　*　*

"TJ . . . that damn dog," I muttered as I topped the carpeted stairs inside the building. Kathryn hovered at the top like a mother whose worry over a missing child turns to anger the moment the child is found. She wore a green pantsuit and her gold Mercedes broach, no doubt oblivious to the fact that green and gold were Notre Dame's school colors.

"TJ?" Kathryn asked.

"Yes," I sighed. "He got out. I guess he dug out while I was showering . . . it took me forever to find him. I should have called . . ."

She looked at me suspiciously. "Good thing you didn't have to shower again, after chasing him around and all," she said, noticing that my clothes and hair were perfectly neat. "The buses leave in ten minutes," she said. "I'd like for you to meet Dr. Ganz and his wife before we board." I knew she wanted to grill me on the details of TJ's escape, but time was on my side.

Kathryn took my arm and led me to an elderly couple seated on a satin-covered sofa in the center of the room.

"This must be our bestseller," Norman Ganz said in a gravelly voice as he stood to greet me. A third person, a white-stockinged nurse of sorts, helped steady him on his feet.

"Actually, the book is the bestseller," I said, "but I stand accused of being its author."

Norman and his wife, Olivia, looked at me with equally blank faces and I knew I had made my last attempt at humor. The couple wore matching burnt orange blazers and white boots with longhorns on the toes. Norman also wore an orange bow tie, and Olivia an orange scarf. They both had walkers in the room, and when the party adjourned, they would not go to the stadium but back to their Pemberton mansion to watch the game on television.

"You think Dabs will start H-bomb?" Norman asked. "I think he's crazy if he don't. What do you think?"

"Crazy if he doesn't," I said obligingly.

"That's what I told 'Livia," he said, smiling broadly. "See, honey—I told you. Crazy if he don't."

"Did you go to Texas, Norm?" I asked. The quick, scornful look from both Olivia and Kathryn told me that I had stumbled into messy terrain.

"That's all right," Norman said to both women. "I'm not ashamed I dropped out of high school, not even 'round all you smart people. I didn't have to be the smartest kid on the lot to sell more cars than any of 'em. The people who used to call me stupid, well, today they call me boss. Besides, turns out you can buy those degrees you people work so hard for. I got me a Ph.D. last year . . . just like you, Dr. Harrison."

"From Texas?"

"Yes sir," Norman said. "I got an honorary doctorate, just months after I gave several million to Nevitt's pet project. You see, Travis, he don't care if you can spell cat, unless that's how you sign your checks."

I maintained a thin smile as Olivia quickly turned the conversation back to my book. "The university is lucky to have such a dynamic young couple on its faculty," she said, unable to look up due to the curve in her spine.

I was going to thank her for referring to me as young when an announcement that the first bus was loading startled me. I thought about my options—my responsibility—regarding Layla. A football game that I had looked forward to for a month now loomed as four hours of second-guessing myself if I didn't do something before I got on the bus. But what?

"Crazy, if he don't start the H-bomb," Norman repeated.

When the second bus was announced, I felt Kathryn's hand on my arm. "Are you okay?" she asked. "You seem preoccupied."

"Well . . . it's Notre Dame, and . . . well, I've got to find the men's room before we go."

There was one pay phone near the men's room, but a teenager was using it. She had laid out a napkin full of junk food on the counter beneath the phone; crumbs lay on the carpet beneath her.

I stood as irritatingly close to her as I dared and looked at my watch repeatedly, but the hint had no effect on her. I stepped into the men's room, but when I emerged, she was *still* on the phone, talking and laughing as crumbs of Oreos fell from her mouth onto her dirty blouse. As I paced closely behind her, she finally turned to me and said, "Gonna be a while." She reached into her napkin and produced another Oreo, popped it into her mouth and chewed, open-mouthed, as she faced me.

I turned away, disgusted, and found myself inches from Kathryn, her cell phone in her outstretched hand. "You probably need to call TJ," she said. "Just to make sure he hasn't escaped again. I'll wait for you on the bus."

I felt ten years old. Kathryn knew I had lied about why I had been late, and with the bus serving as my deadline, I didn't have time to rehearse my call. I produced a scrap of paper from my pocket and dialed Layla's number.

* * *

Hi, this is Layla.

My heart jumped until I realized it was a recording.

I'm unable to come to the phone right now. I'm probably either stoned, having sex, or cutting my wrists, so please leave a message and I'll either call you back . . . or haunt you!

The beep came suddenly; I had no choice but to improvise.

"Uh, yes . . . Miss Sommers . . . this is Dr. Harrison from the University of Texas History Department. Our records indicate that you haven't been in class in several weeks and it is, uh, university policy to check on freshmen who might be struggling, uh, with the adjustment and all. I've asked someone from University Counseling to contact you—to visit you—perhaps as early as this evening. I hope all is well."

I ended the call, stared at the phone for a moment, and tried to assess what I had done. The message clearly was more for Enos than for Layla. I suppose I hoped that Enos would leave if he thought someone was coming by. As for Layla, I hoped that I had made it clear, again, that I could do nothing more for her than turn things over to University Counseling.

Only this time, she would eventually find out that I hadn't. All I had done was call her at home, precisely what she had wanted.

* * *

As I got on the bus, I handed Kathryn her phone and sat down next to her.

"Think Coach Knowlton will start the H-bomb?" she asked. It was a sure indication that confessions could come on my own timetable, but I knew that it was a reprieve, not a pardon.

"Crazy if he don't," I said. "This ought to be a good one."

* * *

And indeed it was a good one, at least the half I saw. It was thrilling to see the golden helmets of the Fighting Irish appear for one of the few times in Royal Memorial Stadium. With the latest multi-million-dollar expansion complete (alas, there had been no similar expansion of the history department's budget), there were

92,000 screaming fans to greet freshman Hy Bombgartner as he and his Longhorn teammates took the field. By midway in the second quarter, Hy had launched two "H-bombs" and staked the 'Horns to an early fourteen-point lead.

Kathryn's tickets were in the upper deck on about the 40-yard line. They were good seats, but in September, Texas nights are often steamy, and the walls of bright lights in the upper deck attract crickets by the thousands. These, in turn, attract their share of the millions of cricket-feeding bats that live under Austin's downtown bridges. The result is an almost comical orgy of dodging and swatting by the fans as they sit there, sweating through their clothes.

Despite the distractions, the crowd was raucous until the kick-off following the second score. On the deep-kick return, Notre Dame's Rich "The Rocket" Rodriguez zigzagged 102 yards to make it 14–7. Just like that, the Texas fans suddenly noticed the sweat and the crickets and the bats and fell silent.

In the heart of that silence, I heard Kathryn's phone ring. "I meant to turn that off," she said, reaching down for her purse.

Before she could reach her phone, the crowd cheered again as Hy, back on the field, completed a twelve-yard pass over the middle. On the next play, he dropped back to pass again, and just before being sacked by a blitzing linebacker, he ducked under the tackle, broke away from another one, and raced like a sprinter down the sideline.

The crowd erupted, and I was cheering with them when I looked over at Kathryn. She was extending her phone to me, a perplexed look on her face.

"It's for you," she shouted over the noise. "Layla Sommers."

TWELVE

IT HAD not occurred to me at the time I had called Layla that caller ID would enable her to capture Kathryn's phone number.

"Travis, you shouldn't have called," Layla said breathlessly. "I never wanted you to call."

I resisted the urge to remind her that she had given me her phone number—twice. "I just wanted to make sure you were okay," I said. I sat down with my head between my knees, pressing Kathryn's cell phone to my ear.

"Enos heard your message and recognized your name from the book. He knows your call was a big ruse. That really wasn't all that smart, you know. Enos swore he's going to . . ." Her voice faded out.

"The book? Are you in danger now?" I asked.

"Hell yes, I'm in danger!" she blurted. "What do you think? Why do you think I'm taking the risk of calling you?"

"Is Enos there now?"

"No. He stormed out again. That's his way. He gets in a rage and throws things, then leaves and gets drunk or fucked up, and then comes back and whales on me. He'll be back soon."

"So get out!" I said above the noise, drawing Kathryn's glance, though she was pretending not to notice.

"And go *where?*" Layla screamed. "I don't have any friends or family. I can't afford a hotel. Do you want me to just go sleep on the fucking street? That probably is what you want. I know you hate me."

"I *don't* hate you, Layla!" I looked up at Kathryn, who was standing and applauding. In fact, everyone was standing and cheering except for me and the few lonely Notre Dame fans in the end zone. I felt like an airsick passenger on a jovial Vegas junket. Kathryn looked down and shook her head in a surprisingly sympathetic gesture.

"You can find somewhere—"

"Oh, shit, he's back," Layla interrupted, her voice shaking. "I hear him on the fire escape."

She sounded as terrified as I have ever heard a human. "Layla, call 911!" I shouted. "Or I'll call them."

"*No!* I called them once and Enos beat the shit out of me. Whatever you do, Travis, don't call the cops."

I heard a thick, oily male voice in the background. "Who d'fuck you talkin' to? C'mere—"

"Layla! *Layla!*" I screamed over the noise that erupted with what could only have been another Longhorn score. I pressed the small phone to my ear so hard that it hurt. Even so, I could barely make out the few fading words from Layla.

I stood abruptly and bumped my way down the aisle, a domino of knees rippling before me, a legacy of Coke-stained purses and binocular cases trailing behind. I climbed the short stack of stairs and exited through a narrow tunnel into the outdoor concession area of the upper deck. As I dialed 911, I could almost see Layla's apartment in the distance, though it was at the farthest possible point across the enormous campus.

I told the operator that I had just received a distraught call from a young woman whose life was in danger. I gave her my name, and she assured me a patrol unit would arrive at Layla's apartment in a matter of minutes.

For the first time since my chance meeting with Layla Sommers two weeks earlier, I felt I had done something right. I vowed to myself to continue this trend with a full confession to Kathryn, who just then emerged from the narrow tunnel.

Standing against the concrete wall, dodging crickets, I told her everything, from the inscription in the book to the incident involving the security guard to Layla's e-mail. I even used the word *aroused* and detailed why I had been late to the Faculty Club, thus absolving TJ from blame. I was worried, of course, that the very presence of a young woman in my life was going to summon up Kathryn's own demons. To my surprise, all I got was a pleasant hug and the words, "I guess you'll never learn."

I didn't understand what she meant by that, but I didn't pursue it. We stayed along the wall, staring at the vast campus for the entire halftime, listening to the echo of the bands in the background. Having delegated my responsibilities concerning Layla to the Austin police and with UT leading Notre Dame 28–7 at half, I was beginning to think this might be a decent evening after all. I was even starting to look forward to my weekly ritual in Kathryn's bed.

That was before Kathryn's phone rang again. Reluctantly, I answered it.

"The police came," Layla said. She spoke with a calmness and serenity that was in some odd way more unnerving than her prior panic.

"Good, good," I said, greatly relieved. "I'm sure you feel better." She laughed and I heard bath water running.

"Oh, yeah," she sighed. "I'm feeling a *whole* lot better. I'm soaking in a hot bath, just drifting away. I love hot baths."

"A hot bath? Well, good for you," I said. Kathryn glanced at me. "You deserve it. You've had a pretty tough time. And Layla, I want you to call that counselor . . ."

"Oh, I won't be needing that now," she said.

"Now that Enos is gone?" I asked. She laughed and I heard the bath water stop. "Did they say how long they could hold him?"

"Hold him? They didn't even see him. He was out the kitchen window before they could make it up the stairs. The cops told me that unless I wanted to press charges for assault, there wasn't really anything they could do. *Oh God*," she groaned. I heard the clink of a bottle or a glass.

"Are you okay?" I asked.

"Almost perfect," she said. "Everything's very peaceful. I'm in a hot bubble bath with a bottle of red wine, some pills, and a brand new razor blade. What could be more perfect than that?"

My face fell and must have turned ashen white as Kathryn grasped my arm.

"Layla, please . . . I'm calling 911 again."

"Travis, if the cops or paramedics show up at my door again tonight, I'm going to slit my fucking throat before they get to this tub . . . and it will be *your fault*." It was uncanny how calm her voice was. "Do you understand that?"

"But why, Layla? Are you afraid that Enos is coming back?" I said.

"He *always* comes back, Travis. He'll be back tonight to find out why the police came by and to mess me up good. Only this time, I'm not going to give him the pleasure. This time, I'm going to do it for him. I'm going to do it for you . . . get rid of that little girl that you don't have time for . . . that nobody has time for. That nobody gives a shit about. I'll simplify everyone's lives. *Oh, God . . . ohhhhh . . .*"

"Layla, what's happening?"

"I just took a razor and cut the inside of my arm."

"*What?*"

"The blood is just beginning to trickle out, popping out in little bubbles. It's so dark—like the wine. It's pretty, really . . ."

"*Layla!*"

"Remember when you said my name was pretty? Before you hated me?"

"I don't hate you!"

"Well, you don't like me."

"It's not that I don't like you, Layla—I simply don't know you."

"And you don't have the time to get to know me. That's what you said. *Oh . . . ohhhh. Jesus Christ!*"

"Layla, stop it!"

"Are you saying that maybe we could, like, still be friends?" Her voice was notably weaker.

"Yes, of course!" I said urgently. My eyes were shut and my head faced the sky. An agonizing moment of silence followed; I hoped she hadn't passed out.

"We just need some time," I continued. "Please, stop what you're doing. We'll talk. We'll get together. *Can you hear me?*"

"How do I know I can trust you?" she asked. "I asked you to call me a few weeks ago, and you had some stupid bitch call instead. I asked you not to call the police, and you called them anyway. How do I know you'll find time for me?"

"How can I prove it to you?" I asked.

"Come over. I want you to come, Travis."

"Now?" I asked, looking at Kathryn helplessly. She was brushing a cricket from her hair.

"Of course, now," Layla said. "Unless you're too busy. *Oh, Jesus,* my wrist is bleeding like crazy. I hope I haven't . . . I don't really want to die. Are you coming?"

My eyes were on Kathryn as she swiped away the last of the crickets. "Yes, I'm coming," I said.

"Now?" Finally, a lilt returned to her voice.

"Now," I said.

"You are so sweet," she said. "And, Travis, just in case you're, you know, a little late, could I ask one small favor?"

"I won't be late," I said. "Put a bandage on your wrist."

"Please . . . the favor."

"Yes, okay. Name it."

"Tell me that you love me," Layla said. "*Oh God,*" she moaned, and for the first time, she began crying. "I can't make it stop, Travis!"

"I'll be there in five minutes," I said. "Stop hurting yourself!"

I heard a splash as her phone apparently hit the bath water. I snapped Kathryn's phone shut, grabbed her by the hand and together we hurried down the seemingly endless series of ramps. Since the game was only in the third quarter, there were plenty of idle cabs out front and not much traffic on campus. Even so, it was the longest five minutes of my life.

*   *   *

When we arrived in front of Layla's building, Kathryn paid the cab driver while I sprinted inside and took the three flights of stairs two stairs at a time. Seeing number 303, I hit the door hard and fast with my shoulder, not even considering that it might be unlocked. I tumbled into a room that was eerily quiet.

"Layla!" I shouted as I entered. Not seeing her, I moved toward the corner, where a bathroom was wedged between the tiny kitchen and a shoebox closet. I turned sideways to enter and groaned at the sight.

If the tub had been any longer or deeper, I suppose she would have drowned. As it was, the sheer space constraint had prevented her mouth from slipping below the sudsy-crimson water line. Even so, her body was limp and I could not tell if she was alive or dead—the life had been drained out of the freckle-faced, copper-headed girl. Instead of a glowing, honey-skinned beauty with alluring brown eyes, she looked like a pallid corpse with sunken cheeks and wet, matted hair.

I squatted down and reached both my arms, tweed jacket and all, into the water, placing them under her and lifting her out. Like a fireman would carry an infant, I eased her through the door and laid her on her bed. I reached for two nearby T-shirts on the floor and patted them lightly across her body to remove the bloody, watery residue and reveal the sources of the blood. She was bleeding most profusely from her right wrist. I wrapped one of the T-shirts around it and held it tight. The other wounds seemed less serious.

One was on the inside of her forearm, another across her midsection. Still another was a slit of about an inch along the length of her cleanly shaven labia.

As I held her wrist and looked for any other wounds, I suddenly felt a debilitating pain rip through my chest. As if a current of electricity had been forced through my body, my knees buckled and I fell backward onto the floor. The sickening sweet smell of blood filled my nostrils and lungs, and I became lost in a dark shroud of swirling redness.

I had been there before. I heard Randi's voice.

Daddy?

THIRTEEN

"DADDY, can we go swimming as soon as we get to Lubbock?"

At that point, Randi had caused so many delays in our departure that I wasn't sure we would *ever* get to Lubbock. She had spent an hour packing her suitcase for the one-night trip; every item was perfectly folded and neatly sorted. She had spent the hour before that curling her hair with Mattel curlers that were heated with a 40-watt light bulb and thus had no genuine effect. She had also cleaned her room, which she had long ago turned into a Barbie paradise that could have served as a model for advertisements. She had pink Barbie bedding, Barbie pillows, Barbie cars, baby carriages, chests, four-poster beds, and innumerable Barbie outfits. She had once taken it all down when a friend had told her that nine was too old to be playing with dolls. A week later she told me she didn't care what her friend thought and put it all back to the way it had been.

Finally, after endless goodbyes to TJ, who was staying in Puddy's yard next door, we departed. I was already doing the math in my head and worried about being late when five miles later Randi broke into tears over the matter of having forgotten to give TJ his stuffed armadillo. We turned back.

"I'm a little late for my meeting, Randi," I said as we left Preston Street yet again. "I think you're going to have to go with me and wait while I interview. We probably won't get to swim until after dinner."

"Boring," she said.

"Yes, very boring."

*   *   *

Randi entertained herself in the back seat, mostly by playing with her dolls, but still managed to ask me an unending string of questions as I tried, quite unsuccessfully, to mentally prepare for my interview. As a diversion, I got her started on the ABC game, finding the alphabet letters on road signs, and the out-of-state license-plate game. I even explained to her what the white and yellow lines in the middle of the road meant, only to be victimized by a hundred miles of "Now we *can* pass . . . now we *can't* pass . . . now we *can* pass . . ."

I admit that by the time we were within thirty miles of Lubbock I was wrung out. And I was late.

"Look at that, Daddy," Randi said. From the back seat, she leaned over the front passenger's seat and pointed out through the windshield.

"Randi! Get back there and get your seatbelt on—right now!"

"But look at that!"

Ahead of us on the horizon was a broad red streak. It hardly seemed threatening, except that I had never seen anything like it before. It was as if we were looking at a photograph touched up with a brilliant crimson stripe across it. Like me, most of the cars and trucks had been speeding, and most continued toward the red streak, apparently unconcerned. Some, however, began to slow and even to pull over. The sky above us was brilliant blue, and I couldn't fathom why those cars were stopping. I looked at my watch and realized I still had an outside chance to make my interview on time.

Deciding that truckers were the best judge of things, I nestled in between two eighteen-wheelers; we were doing about eighty.

"Daddy?"

Suddenly, it was as if we had entered another universe. A thick veil of red dust, hurled by hurricane-force winds, subsumed us. I was instantly blinded. Randi began to cry and again clambered over the seat. Even though I was born in West Texas and had seen dozens of dust storms before, I had never seen one of such biblical proportions.

"*Randi, no!*"

"Daddy . . . Daddy . . . ?"

I knew if I tried to pull over, I risked hitting a car that may have already parked on the side. If I slammed on the brakes, the eighteen-wheeler behind us would tear us to shreds. And if the eighteen-wheeler in front of us slammed on its brakes, we'd have our heads sheared off underneath it.

I tried to use my right arm to push Randi back into the rear seat. "Get your seatbelt on, damn it!" At that second, I saw the brake lights of the truck in front of me, inches away. I jerked the car to the left, hoping I could stop it in the median and that no cars would be coming the other way. But one was. It was a plumbing truck that we hit at about a fifteen-degree angle to head-on— just enough to save my life, but not enough to save Randi's. With a closing speed estimated at some 140 miles per hour, she was ejected through the front windshield.

I didn't learn the details of the crash until I came out of my own coma eleven days later. There by my side was Ben Frizell, who told me what he had learned from police, paramedics, and the coroner. Randi had died instantly, he assured me. There was nothing I could have done.

Ten years later, it took seeing Layla Sommers soaking in her own blood to reveal that Ben had been wrong.

* * * * *

Something about the sight—and smell—of Layla's blood had taken me back to Randi's death. But why? If Randi had been ejected and

80

her death had been instantaneous—if I had been unconscious—why the association with blood? Why had I heard her voice?

I looked at Layla lying limply on her bed and berated my own hesitation, my incompetence. I struggled to my feet, heartened to hear footsteps on the stairs outside. I turned, prepared to admonish the EMS for their slow response, but instead saw a thick young man in a loose-fitting San Diego Chargers jersey and baggy jeans. His hair was black and slick, and his fists were like anvils attached to Neanderthal arms. I could see tattoos curling out from beneath his jersey sleeve and up onto the back of his neck.

"What da fuck did you do to her?" he demanded. I recognized the voice as that of Enos. Enos the Penos. He looked exactly as I had imagined.

I did my best to ignore him and moved to Layla's side, wondering where in the hell the paramedics were. Kathryn had called them as we raced across campus and was waiting out front to show them the way. I repositioned the T-shirt around Layla's wrist and leaned close, placing my ear over her mouth; I could not detect a breath. I reached two fingers into Layla's mouth to clear it for CPR, and at that instant Enos tackled me with the ferocity of an NFL linebacker. He knocked me backward and my head smashed against a bedside table, knocking the lamp onto the floor with a crash. He then placed one knee in my chest and hit me hard just above my right eye with a broad, powerful fist.

"I asked you a question, dumb ass," he said.

Sparks flew beneath my eyelids, but I managed to turn my head and capture his next several blows with the back of my skull. I could taste the thick salt of blood in my mouth, felt it flowing profusely from my nose.

I struggled to throw him off, but despite my surging adrenaline, his strength and agility were overwhelming. Though growing frantic about Layla, I had little choice but to cover up.

I was not aware that others had entered the apartment until I heard a loud voice say, "Cool it, Vasquez," as Enos was torn from my body with the force of a catapult and thrown face down on the hardwood floor by two large policemen. One of them crammed a knee into his spine and I heard him scream. His thick wrists were quickly cuffed behind his back and he was dragged into the hall just outside the door, where several other officers were arriving.

A gray-haired paramedic with a mustache cradled my head in his latex gloves and placed gauze compresses in both of my nostrils to stanch the bleeding. "You're a mess," he said.

"Don't worry about me," I said, but as I looked up at Layla, three paramedics had already surrounded her; she seemed to have changed colors again, from the milky white of moments earlier, to an even more disturbing ashen gray.

Kathryn entered the apartment cautiously and approached me. She knelt and placed her arm around me. "Oh, Travis," she sighed, leaving me unclear whether her reaction was one of sympathy or disappointment. She reached out a hand and helped me to my feet.

After what seemed like an absurdly long time, the paramedics placed Layla on a gurney and carried her out, a variety of intravenous needles in her arms. Her eyes never opened and they talked only in medical speak, so as they wheeled her out, I hadn't a clue whether she was alive or dead. From where Kathryn and I stood, we could see Enos squatting in the hall, his hands cuffed behind him. Incredibly, he seemed to be sharing a joke with one of the cops; he seemed to be laughing. Never in my life had I wanted to hurt someone so badly.

The police officer who was sharing the laugh with Enos looked at me and then came toward me. He was dressed in black civilian clothes—expensive Italian clothes, I would guess. On his belt, he wore a silver badge and small revolver. He also wore a silver chain around his neck and a silver loop in one ear. His black head was shaved bald.

"I'm Captain Smith," he said. "Tommy Lee Smith. I understand you found the girl."

"He fucking *killed* the girl," Enos shouted from outside the door.

"Shut up, Mr. Vasquez," Tommy Lee said. "Besides, the girl ain't even dead. Yet."

"Too bad," Enos laughed.

I felt my face flush and I pointed my finger at Enos. "You come near her again and I'll . . . I'll . . ."

"You'll what, you stupid ol' fuck?" Enos egged me on.

"Somebody shut him up," Tommy Lee said calmly.

"Stay away from her!" I shouted.

"Oh, ain't that sweet?" Enos said. "I guess Layla found her a sugar daddy. Thing is, the stupid ol' fuck don't know what he's got into with her. He don't see 'cause he wants to fuck her so bad his eyes hurt. Can't say I blame him," he said, sneering at Kathryn.

I suddenly didn't care about Tommy Lee or myself, I just wanted to hurt the crass young punk sitting on the floor outside the door. With a quickness that surprised even me, I ran the three steps to the door and kicked Enos in the face, the toe of my shoe landing just below his eye socket with a resounding thud. He groaned in pain as the two officers quickly—and soundly—restrained me.

"I'll kill you, motherfucker!" Enos said. Because of the handcuffs, he was unable to wipe away the trickle of blood that now rolled down his face. I smiled at him, feeling strangely empowered, even as the police held my arms uncomfortably behind my back.

"Hurt Layla again," I said, shaking with anger, "and I'll kill *you*."

"Travis!" Kathryn said.

Tommy Lee grabbed me by the arm and pulled me away from the officers and back into Layla's apartment. In the hall, two policemen jerked Enos to his feet and began taking him down the stairs.

"You think *I* hurt *her*?" Enos shouted back to me as he left. "You don't know nothin' 'bout that girl. I tried to take care of her, man, but she won't let you. She's always pushing you just a little further with her freaky games, making you do psycho stuff. For her, there always has to be a risk. She'll turn on you, too, old man."

The cops led Enos out of sight, leaving Kathryn, Tommy Lee, and me alone in the apartment. He took some basic information and asked me what had happened. "That girl tried to kill herself because she was afraid of what he was going to do to her," I said urgently. I heard the siren of the ambulance containing Layla sound loudly and then fade out of range. "He's hurt her before, Captain, and you have to do something about him."

"I'll talk to Mr. Vasquez," Tommy Lee said with resounding indifference. "Of course, the only one here tonight who could press charges against him is you—for assault. Problem is, now that you've kicked him in the face—while he was handcuffed, I might add—and threatened to kill him . . . well . . . sounds a bit like a jealous fit, doesn't it?" He winked at Kathryn and then turned back to me. "You and Ms. Sommers got something going on?"

"Am I free to go?" I asked. "Or are you planning to continue to insult me in front of my fiancée?"

"Travis!" Kathryn scolded.

"You can go," Tommy Lee said. "Go take care of your face. But, Harrison, unless you want to press charges, we got nothing on Mr. Vasquez except a dubious resisting arrest charge. Even if we decide to book him, he'll be out by morning, and I strongly suggest that you stay away from him. I strongly suggest that you not get involved."

I held out my arms, showing Captain Smith and, less intentionally, Kathryn, the residue of Layla's blood on my tweed jacket.

"Sure, Captain," I said. "I'll try not to get . . . *involved.*"

FOURTEEN

As KATHRYN was driving me to Brackenridge Hospital, the same hospital to which Layla had been rushed, I stretched out my arms and could have sworn that Layla's limp and naked frame was still in them. As I stared at my hands, tears began to well in my eyes.

"Are you okay?" Kathryn asked. "I can't believe the way you talked to that police captain."

I feared if I spoke that my voice would crack, and I suddenly felt weak. Finally, I inhaled deeply and tried to form my words carefully. "I don't want Layla to die."

She kept her eyes on the road. "Of course you don't, Travis, but you did everything you could. You seem to be the only one who has done anything kind for that girl. I wish you had never met her, but I love you for who you are."

"Kathryn," I began, "before Enos arrived at the apartment, I heard a voice. Randi's voice. I hesitated . . . those few seconds may have cost Layla her life."

I could see from Kathryn's face, even in profile, that she swallowed hard and her eyes narrowed. As part of our premarital disclosures to each other, she knew about my depression after Randi's death. And while I had not been overly explicit, I had even

85

told her there had a come a time when I wasn't sure I wanted to go on living.

"Things are different now, Travis. That's all behind you. You're future is so bright. Don't go back."

"How could I have heard her voice, Kathryn, if she died instantly? The voice said 'Daddy?' as if she was calling out for me."

"Oh, Travis, don't do this to yourself," Kathryn said. "Don't do this to *us*. No good can come of it."

"Of knowing the truth about my daughter?"

"Of dredging up old wounds. You don't hear me complaining about John anymore, do you? We all have our crosses to bear. Why don't you let me set you up with a good therapist?"

I raised my hand to cut her off. I knew her wounds were deep, but I was in no mood to compare the infidelity of a grown man with the tragic death of a little girl. *My* little girl.

We rode the rest of the way to Brackenridge Hospital in silence.

*   *   *

At the hospital, a harried old nurse made it clear to me that on a busy Saturday night my puffy lip and split right eyebrow, both of which had been expertly bandaged by the paramedics, were not high priorities. "There's a minor emergency center only seven blocks from here," she said in a poorly hidden attempt to get rid of me.

"I'll wait," I said. "Can you tell me about a patient named Layla Sommers?" She looked disgusted but flipped through several pages of a clipboard. "She's in the ER. There's a waiting room there if you want more information."

The air conditioning in the ER waiting room droned loudly, forcing PA announcements to be broadcast at full blast. I filled out paperwork as doctors and nurses scurried in and out of the wide double doors marked ER STAFF ONLY. Every time they swung open I strained to see inside but never got a glimpse of Layla.

Several hours passed before a different nurse came by to suggest again that I might want to visit the minor emergency clinic nearby. I did not. Having sat quietly all of that time, Kathryn weighed in that she also thought that was a good idea and offered to drive me. I told her I preferred to stay at Brackenridge, and we both knew why.

I suppose two more hours passed before I was finally led into the ER, where a doctor who seemed the age of my students put four stitches over my eye. Kathryn told him to make them tight so I wouldn't have a scar. When I asked him about Layla, he said he hadn't heard anything but that he had just come onto his shift. I asked the nurse who was summoned to give me my care instructions if she knew anything about Layla. She was tall and dour looking, and she studied me as if I were up to no good.

"Friends of hers?" she asked, glancing at Kathryn. "They've been trying to find someone who knew her."

I groaned slightly and my expression must have revealed my worst fear. Kathryn reached out for my hand.

"No, no," the nurse said, suddenly sympathetic. "I'm sorry, I didn't mean to imply—Ms. Sommers is hanging in there, but it will be a few more hours before she's out of the woods. Stopping the bleeding was easy enough, but the pills she took are still problematic."

The look on my face must have said it all. "She's a . . . student of mine," I said.

"I'll keep you posted if you want to remain in the waiting room," she offered.

"Why don't you go on, Kathryn," I said, hoping to give her an out.

"Why don't you come with me? I think you've done enough for one night."

"I've got to stay. I just need to know for sure that she's going to be okay." I settled into my chair, picking up the day's newspaper, which I had long since read. It occurred to me that I didn't even know the final score of the Notre Dame game. It also occurred to me that I couldn't have cared less.

"I'll stay," Kathryn said, sitting down beside me. She pulled out a PDA and pecked away at it with a stylus.

I slumped farther into my vinyl chair and finally dozed off, only to jerk awake when I felt a hand on my shoulder.

"She's sleeping and weak but out of the woods," the tall nurse said quietly. "She's going to make it. You two can peek in on her if you want."

"That's all right," Kathryn said quickly, putting away her PDA and standing to leave. "We just wanted to know that she was going to be—"

"No," I interrupted. "I want to see her." I looked at Kathryn. "Just to make sure . . ."

"For God's sake, Travis . . ."

"She's in room 215," the nurse said. "Don't stay long."

*　　*　　*

Kathryn and I took the elevator to the second floor and made our way down the shiny hall. A few nurses and doctors moved about, some of their rubber-soled shoes squeaking as they walked. I felt my heart rate soaring as I counted down the doors: 221, 219, 217. . . . The large door to room 215 was ajar. I knocked softly and slowly pushed it open. Kathryn followed me in.

The form under the sheets was a mere bump within the metal-frame bed. Layla was lying in a fetal position, so we could only see her dull, matted hair and pink face above the sheets. Tubes snaked into her arms and nose. She was sleeping.

I moved closer to her.

"Come on, Travis," Kathryn whispered. "You've seen her now. Let's go."

I was aware that Kathryn had done everything one could ex-pect under the circumstances, and she was right: it was time to leave. But as I was turning to do so, a razor-thin opening appeared in Layla's eyes, and her left hand extended between the metal bars on the side of the bed. Her fingers wiggled slightly as if she was asking for something.

I looked at Kathryn, who folded her arms and looked away. "I'm going now, Travis," she said. "Are you coming with me?"

"I need to stay a bit longer," I said. "Just until she knows that someone was here."

Kathryn zeroed in on Layla's beckoning hand. "I'll be at home. Call me if you want me to come pick you up. And remember, Travis, no more strays."

"No more strays," I said, hugging Kathryn. As soon as she had left, I slid a chair close to Layla's bed and settled in. I looked at her hand, her fingers rhythmically flexing . . . then I took her hand in mine. It felt cool and soft and frail. Within minutes, I was overwhelmed with fatigue. I took several deep breaths trying to force myself to stay awake but soon fell into a deep, unintended sleep.

* * *

When I awoke, it was with a shudder; I was sopping wet with sweat. I looked around the hospital room, trying to recall where I was and how I had gotten there. Earlier events slowly drifted back to me. I looked at Layla and wished she would open her eyes. I wanted to tell her that everything would be okay.

After a time I saw her squinting in my direction. She spoke and her words were slurred, but they were clear enough.

"Thank you," she said.

I felt a rush of adrenaline or some chemical mix within me that would, I think, have made heroin seem mild by comparison.

* * *

The head of psychiatry at Brackenridge Hospital is Dr. Peter Bernard, a remarkably handsome man with olive skin and wavy black hair. Tall, with a chiseled jaw and obvious intelligence, he is the kind of man who intimidates others even though he makes every effort not to.

I was heartened by the fact that Dr. Bernard took a personal interest in Layla's progress. Each day, he would ask me to leave the room while he spent nearly an hour with her. And when that hour had passed, he would find me roaming the halls or grading papers in some stiff chair and ask for my insights. Since I was not related to Layla, he was hesitant to share too much with me, yet as the only responsible party to have appeared in her life, he was equally hesitant to remain silent.

He told me as early as the second day that something *very* disturbing had obviously happened to Layla in her past, almost certainly in her childhood. He said that professionals often describe such a trauma as a "primal scene" and that no matter how hard he tried, Layla wouldn't let him near it. Until that event could be unearthed and dealt with, it was unlikely that Layla's suicidal behavior would change.

As for her physical health, Layla improved rapidly. I had never planned to stay beyond that first day, but each time I made a move to leave, her limp arm would fall in my direction, and I would let her outstretched fingers take my hand. By the third day, I found myself casually stroking the blonde down on her forearm or leaning forward to brush a strand of copper hair from her face. These acts were largely unconscious, often performed with one hand while I held reading materials in the other. As I look back, however, I realize that as early as the second day Layla had come to rely on my touch as an integral part of her recovery, reaching out for my hand during her waking hours as instinctively as TJ might rest his chin on my knee.

I had left the hospital as necessary to teach my classes and to tend to my dogs. Usually by the time I got home there was a phone message from Layla, wondering when I was going to return. And when I did return, her smile would light up the room. With the buoyancy of youth, the shine had quickly returned to her copper hair, the glow to her honeyed skin, and the glint to her deep brown-flecked eyes.

Though I didn't keep track, I suppose I averaged six hours a day at Layla's bedside, often grading papers while she slept. Enos's name did not come up, nor had he tried to call or visit. In fact, no friend or relative of Layla's visited, and she received no phone calls while I was there. It seemed clear that there was not a single person in her life who either knew or cared that she had tried to kill herself—and had very nearly succeeded. That, more than anything, was why I spent so many hours there; I just couldn't stand the thought of her being alone.

Kathryn came to the hospital once; she even brought Layla two magazines—the sort of entertainment fluff that Kathryn would have been embarrassed to purchase for herself. But Layla had slept through the visit—or pretended to sleep. Her eyes remain closed, but her thin forearm flopped through the metal bars and her fingers groped for my hand. I denied it to her while Kathryn was there, fooling no one. Kathryn and I also spoke by phone at least once a day, but the unresolved issue of Layla forced us into awkward and superficial dialog. She gave me a few updates on various wedding details and informed me that she had secured a company to handle my move from Preston Street into her house. But even Kathryn, with all her directness, avoided asking the obvious question: Just when did I plan to leave the side of Layla Sommers?

Ben, too, came to the hospital once, not to see Layla but to have lunch with me in the cafeteria. "Maybe you should marry Kathryn and adopt Layla," he laughed. As for him, he had already found one angel of mercy who had come to his office and had then invited him to her apartment for dinner to discuss her paper on love. "You remember that girl from the Cactus? Marie Patton? A fucking miracle worker if ever there was one. *Good stuff!*" Ben had managed between deep laughs.

* * *

On the fourth day, Dr. Bernard found me near the nurses' station after his meeting with Layla.

"It's a little quieter over here," he said, escorting me to a small break room. He paused and leafed through a thick file folder that he carried. He then studied me in a thorough way that suggested he was measuring his own level of trust.

"In the understatement of the century," he began, "Layla needs professional help. She needs to be institutionalized for a while."

I suppose the shock on my face showed; Dr. Bernard put his hand on my arm and said, "It's not as bad as it sounds. At least it doesn't have to be. There are some fine facilities in the state with some wonderful professionals.

"Regrettably," he continued, again referring to his file folder, "there are also some deplorable ones. One of the worst was a state facility here in Austin that was shut down about two years ago. It was rife with fraud, unlicensed therapists, experimental drugs, and abuse. Women suffered the most." He looked at me as though he had asked me a question.

"Layla was there?" I asked.

"For two years—from the time she was fifteen to the time she was seventeen. I was able to locate her files, which indicated she had tried to kill herself several times in her hometown of Deridder, Louisiana, but the last time was while living with an aunt in East Texas, so they sent her to Austin. Predictably, the records are almost worthless in terms of diagnosis, but I think it's safe to say that her experience was neither productive nor pleasant."

"Her primal scene?" I asked.

"No. She had already attempted suicide several times, and her great trauma almost certainly occurred before she was ten. The problem Layla's experience in an institution causes me is that no matter how fine the place I might send her, she's certain to fight it."

"What are the alternatives?" I asked. "Could she make it on her own?" I thought of Enos Vasquez, a problem I had previously mentioned to Dr. Bernard.

"No. I think we've seen what she'll do if left on her own. I really can't risk that. As things go, she needs at least a month of stability before we can even consider other options. She needs group therapy during that month."

"Surely she could handle a facility—a reputable one—for just one month."

"Well, I asked her about that," Dr. Bernard said. "She said that if I commit her—something she understands is completely within my power to do—she will be 'dead before they roll me out the door.' My concern is that she has both the will and the ingenuity to do just that." He leafed aimlessly through his file, again as if he had asked me a question.

"So what are you going to do with her?" I asked, my frustration showing.

"Well," he said calmly, "Layla had an idea I'm prepared to consider."

"Which is?"

"She said she'd be willing to move in with you."

FIFTEEN

KATHRYN detailed for me the debilitating ripple effect that canceling her scheduled lunch would have before asking one last time if I still wanted her to do so. When I said yes, I could feel the tension through the phone. It was the morning after I had agreed to let Layla Sommers move in with me in lieu of Dr. Bernard's committing her; I planned to tell Kathryn over lunch.

I chose her favorite place—a trendy, vegetarian café inside a trendy natural foods grocery store—but as I stood there waiting for her, I found it cold and noisy. From my second-floor vantage point, leaning over the railing of the café, I looked over a sea of organic wines below just as Kathryn entered. There was a grim determination to her walk.

I hurried down the stairs and intercepted her. "It's too crowded," I said, nodding upward toward the café.

"It turns over pretty quickly," she said, craning her head to see through the rail at the top. "It doesn't look that bad."

"Kathryn, please. I need a quieter place."

They were terribly chosen words, of course, and her face tightened with newly minted anxiety. I took her by the hand and led her out the front door toward the neighborhood bookstore next door. Though I had not noticed it before, the marquee over the entrance read:

Book Signing: October 4.

Dr. Travis Harrison

Reelect Tom Jefferson

"Showing off?" Kathryn said as she saw the marquee.

"Of course," I said, seizing on the slightest hint of levity. "Did I tell you that Knopf is thinking of expanding my book tour to twenty cities? If I reach the top five on the *Times* list, they'll bump it to thirty and pull out all the stops to try and boost it to number one. I can't believe I'm even talking about such things."

"I never doubted you, Travis," Kathryn said as we entered the store. At once, I felt more comfortable. Classical music played lightly in the background and the smell of paper mixed with that of coffee. Only one booth was taken in the small coffee shop; we took the one in the corner. Kathryn set her purse down, and together we went to the counter where I ordered a scone and a Diet Coke. She stared in the small glass display and asked twenty questions about nutritional content before settling on a heart-shaped cookie and an espresso.

"So much for lunch," she muttered.

We sat quietly for a moment, each of us pretending to be busy with our forks, napkins, mugs.

"How have you been?" I said at last. It had only been a few days since she'd visited Layla's hospital room, and we had talked on the phone since then, but my question made it sound as though we hadn't seen each other for months. In a way, that's how it felt.

"Well, I like being chairman," she said.

I picked at my scone with my fingers. Every pause in the conversation seemed interminable.

"Was there anything in particular that you wanted to discuss?" she said, glancing at her watch.

"I think we should talk about Layla," I said.

"Yes, of course," she said, lowering her head and stirring her espresso mindlessly. "Let's talk about Layla."

"Psychologically, she's a pretty messed-up kid," I said.

"I guess the slit wrists were a hint," Kathryn said, and then flicked her hand in a gesture of subdued apology. "What did the doctors say?"

"A man named Peter Bernard is the chief psychiatrist at Brackenridge. A very impressive man. A good man. He's taken a personal interest in Layla."

"Well I'm glad someone other than you is also interested in Layla, but have they found any family members yet? Any friends at all?"

"Aunts, uncles, second cousins twice removed?" I added, laughing quietly. "I know, Kathryn, I know. The goal is to find *anyone* who can take care of her."

"Anyone other than you," she clarified.

Another awkward moment of silence passed. Kathryn stared at the wooden table. It was as if she knew.

I told her everything that Dr. Bernard had told me as to why he was afraid to commit Layla. "I know I suffer too greatly from guilt," I said, "but it's as if he told me that I had to watch over her, or else—"

"Watch over her?" Kathryn said, sitting up straighter in the booth. "What in the hell does that mean?"

"Supervise her for a month. Make sure she sticks with her group therapy. Make sure she has a safe place. After a month, Dr. Bernard will reevaluate her case in hopes that she'll be able to go it alone, perhaps with a carefully chosen roommate." I saw Kathryn's jaw tighten. "She doesn't have anyone in her life," I said. "Not one single soul."

"Except for you," Kathryn said quietly, not looking at me. "Except for Travis the Savior."

I reached across the table and took her hands in mine, squeezing them firmly. "I don't want her in my life; I want you.

But what choice do I have? This starving animal could have picked any doorstep in the city, but she picked mine. I can't just turn her out—"

"So what's the plan, Travis?" Kathryn said, pulling her hands free and making an abrupt transition into business mode.

I took a deep breath and did not avoid her stare. "The plan is for Layla to move in with me," I said.

Kathryn's mouth fell open as she unconsciously formed the word *no*. "*What?* Move in *where?* You're going to be living at *my* house two weeks from now. Or have you forgotten?"

"I'm going to have to ask Flo for a little more time before closing on my house."

"Oh, Travis, no . . ."

"There's nowhere else for her to go, Kathryn. It's just for a month."

Kathryn's face was stone. "There must be some alternatives. Before we agree to this, we have to consider all the options. I can't believe I'm saying this, but perhaps we could move her into one of *my* guestrooms."

The look on my face must have betrayed the truth.

"Oh, wait . . . I see . . . ," she said. "This decision has already been made." She threw her head back and laughed, falsely. "You're not *asking* for my opinion or my input, you're simply informing me."

"Dr. Bernard has to move her out of the hospital today; it's either a state hospital or me. I had to make a decision. Besides, I didn't think it would be fair to get you involved."

"Fair?" Kathryn snapped. "Wait, please. Let me make sure I've got this straight. A needy, suicidal nineteen-year-old girl whom you scarcely know is moving in with you, a skinny thing who worships the ground you walk on . . . who's going to share your small house, your tiny bathroom . . . who's going to sleep ten feet from you, *one hopes*...at the same time as you were supposed to be moving in with me, your fiancée . . . and you say you're concerned about what's fair to me?"

"There will be strict rules, Kathryn. You can help me write them if you'd like."

"You know, Travis, when it comes to the man in my life and his young women friends, I've wanted only one rule: *no fucking!* But for some reason, that hasn't carried much weight." She looked off into the distance, and I was certain she was seeing her first husband, John, in bed with his young friend.

"You're not talking to Ben Frizell," I said. "For a very short period of time, I'm going to try to help her, just like I've done with stray dogs over the years. I've always been honest with you, Kathryn, and I always will. I love you too much to lie to you."

"Really?" She couldn't refrain from sarcasm. "So tell me, Travis, just how many of your strays have you found new homes for?" She took a sip of her espresso and looked away again in thought. After a moment, she sighed and nodded, as if she had come to an agreement with herself.

"One month?" she said.

"Not a minute longer," I said. "Layla may not be ready by then, but I will be, and I will tell that to both her and Dr. Bernard from the outset. You and I will continue to see each other as we always do, and she'll be a memory by the time of our wedding."

This time Kathryn reached for my hands. "I wonder," she said, "if part of what makes you attractive to me is how little you know about women, for I assure you that Layla Sommers has ideas very different from your own.

"Travis, if anything happens between you and that girl, I will not suffer as I've suffered in the past. I love you, but I do not have the energy left to fight for you under those conditions. Please don't expect me to."

"Trust me, Kathryn, nothing is going to happen. There will be rules."

"What about her boyfriend, Enos?"

"He hasn't called or come to see her in the hospital. She hasn't mentioned him since Saturday night. I wouldn't call him her boyfriend, and I doubt I'll ever see him again. At least I hope not," I said, lightly touching the bandage over my eye.

A better guess for when I would next see Enos would have been about eight hours.

SIXTEEN

LAYLA moved in that afternoon with little more than her half-empty blue backpack.

Dr. Bernard hadn't wanted her to return to her apartment just yet, but I took her by to pick up her car, a rusted blue Escort. As I turned onto Preston Street, I remember watching her following me in my rearview mirror. She caught me several times and waved.

I parked on the street and walked up to the front porch to my house. Layla got out with her backpack and surveyed the neighborhood.

"Beautiful roses," she said, admiring the fall blooms in Puddy's garden next door.

"Yes. You'll have to meet Puddy."

"You're selling your house?" Layla asked as she walked past the CONTRACT PENDING sign in the yard.

"Sold it, actually," I said.

"When are you moving?"

"Not for a month or so," I said, making a mental note that I needed to call Flo Landers first thing in the morning and delay the closing.

Layla joined me on the front porch and walked through the door, which I held open for her.

"So this is home," she said. "I sort of, like, imagined it was bigger."

Though many large homes had been built in the popular neighborhood called Hyde Park, my house was typical of the original cottages. It had two small bedrooms with tiny closets, a formal living room, a study, and a small kitchen. There was just one small bathroom in the hall between the bedrooms, and that, I knew, would be problematic.

"No, it's just this big," I said.

TJ sauntered up to Layla and sniffed her in an approving fashion.

"What's your name?" Layla asked as she scratched TJ under his chin with long, unpainted nails. As I saw the dog's neck stretch out and his eyes roll back lazily in his head, I realized that long fingernails were tools TJ would come to appreciate.

"That's TJ. He's got five friends out back that I'll introduce you to later."

"You've got a lot of books," she said, observing the hundreds of volumes stacked on shelves and piled up in corners on the floor.

"Never enough," I said.

Layla walked toward the door frame leading to the bedrooms; the bathroom door stood open in front of her. "Is that the only bathroom?" she asked, staring into the small, ceramic closet.

"Yes, I'm afraid so," I said. "We'll just have to set up some rules, perhaps a schedule."

"A schedule?" she laughed. "I'm going to have to crap on schedule? Prunes for breakfast, I guess."

I forced a thin smile and decided I would need to add proper language to the list of rules I was planning to draft.

She stepped into the bathroom and took in every fixture, every row of tile, and every line of grout. Her fingers traced over them as if tracing invisible topographical lines. "You have plenty of hot water, I hope."

"I've never had a problem with it."

"I've got to have my hot baths," she said. "They're, like, the most healing thing in the world. Late at night . . . burn a little incense . . .

fill the tub up as hot as I can stand it, and the world just melts away." She sighed and looked at me. Through the intensity of our silence, we were returned to the night that I lifted her weight-less body out of her own tub, the water still warm and red-tinged with her blood.

"Your room is there," I said, pointing. She lingered a moment longer in the bathroom and then drifted down the short hall, tak-ing in every surface of my house as she passed it. She ran her hands over the wall surfaces as if she was trying to divine some-thing from the texture.

The room, of course, had been Randi's room, and I was strangely and powerfully moved to see Layla, this girl who re-minded me of Randi, enter it.

"Could use a woman's touch," Layla said.

The room was, indeed, barren. There was a canopy bed with plain white sheets and a brown blanket, and a desk and chest, both of which were empty. The walls were bare, covered only with pinholes and the remainders of Scotch tape; they had once been covered with Randi's art.

"What's in the boxes?" Layla asked, noting the dozen or so brown book boxes that were stacked along the far wall.

"Nothing, really," I said. "I've been meaning to put them in storage for years. I'll move them in the next day or two."

"So whose room was this? I'm getting sort of a weird vibe. Do you have an ex? Kids?"

"I have neither," I said. "Not any longer. This was my daugh-ter's room, but she died some time ago."

Layla's face fell as much in disbelief as in sympathy. "Oh, Travis . . . How . . ."

"I'd rather not go into it just now if that's all right with you."

"Of course. I understand," Layla said as she continued to drift around the room, eventually sitting on the bed. She patted the mat-tress with her free hand. She smiled coyly, her sympathetic mode having quickly passed. "Are you going to tuck me in at night?"

"Let's finish the tour," I said. I led her to the study, telling her that this was where I read and she was welcome to study there. I then showed her the kitchen. "Are you a coffee drinker?"

"Not really," she said. "Keeps me awake during class."

"I get up around six and put on a pot. Then I read the local paper—I save the *Times* for the evening. After that, I may write in my journal or read for a while, have some cereal, shower, and head to campus around 8:30. I spend most of the day on campus, even if I don't have a class to teach.

"I usually get back home around four to walk the dogs or jog a couple of miles. Then I read the *Times,* pick up something for dinner, settle down to read a book—maybe with a glass of wine—take a shower, and retire to bed around eleven. That's it. Do the same thing the next day. Think you can work around all that?"

"Wow," she said without emotion. "Sounds . . . predictable, or whatever."

"You mean boring?" I joked.

"That'll work," she said.

*   *   *

The next few hours crept by slowly with her in her room and me in my study. The only evidence that the other was in residence was that we had each used the small bathroom once. I know this be-cause flushing that toilet created an unfortunate roar that burst through the thin walls of my house like something from a Holly-wood disaster movie.

Preparing for bed was especially awkward, as I didn't know ex-actly what to wear, whether to say goodnight, when to shower. Clearly, we were going to have to communicate, something I had spent years learning to avoid.

I let TJ in for the night, suffering the jilted looks of his com-panions, especially Madison, who simply couldn't believe that I didn't want to throw the slobbery ball that he rolled over in his

103

mouth. I went through my nightly ritual of locking doors and turning off lights, leaving only a small orange-tinted nightlight plugged into an outlet in the hall near the bathroom.

Having returned to my bedroom, I thought of offering Layla the shower first but decided I didn't want to knock on her door since she might be asleep. I opted for a first-come, first-served rule instead. Sitting on my bed, a precious few feet from the bathroom door, I thought for the first time in my life that I wanted a robe— a long, thick, terry cloth robe.

In the interim, however, I opted for nylon jogging shorts and a T-shirt I had received from a 5K run. It had turkeys on it. I was just barely out of my bedroom door when I heard Layla's door creak open. We were at opposite ends of the short hall, both of us still and silent like gunfighters waiting for the other to make the first move. She was naked.

She finally moved forward, sullenly, the orange night-light casting a glow over her like sunset on desert mounds. "I'm going to take that hot bath now," she said.

"Oh, okay," I said. "Fine." I tried to speak calmly, as if a completely naked nineteen-year-old girl in my house was the most ordinary thing in my day. I tried not to stare, but I can't deny she was an exquisite thing to view.

She walked past the bathroom door toward me and took both of my hands in hers. "Letting me stay here," she said, "is the kindest thing anyone has ever done for me."

She inched closer still as I kept my eyes trained on hers. She didn't blink; her deep brown eyes sent chills down my spine.

"Layla, we shouldn't . . ." She took my right hand and placed it on her breast. "W . . . what are you doing?" I asked, pulling back my hand.

"Shhhh," she said, placing a finger over my mouth. Then she knelt in front of me and started to reach her hand under my nylon shorts.

"Layla!" I said, pulling away suddenly. She lost her balance and fell backward onto the floor. Even in the pale orange light I could see that her face was instantly red.

"What do you think you're doing?"

"You don't *know*?" she said. "I was just trying to make it easier for both of us to get the tension out of the way."

"The tension? Layla, that is not why I brought you here!"

"Do you expect me to believe that you asked me here for a month and we're not going to have sex?"

"Sex? Is that what you thought? My God! How could you think that? I'm trying to help you, not take advantage of you. I'm old enough to be your father. I'm engaged, for God's sake!"

She slowly stood. Even as tears welled in her eyes, there was not a hint of modesty, no attempt to cover up. "You are a different sort, Travis. I'll give you that much because that's a first for me. Layla on her knees and the man isn't interested. Pushes her onto her ass instead. Oh, yeah, that's a first."

"I didn't push you . . ." I started to protest, but she quickly stalked the few steps to her room and slammed the door shut. I paced the short length of the hall several times trying to decide what to do, but in a matter of minutes, she emerged from her room dressed in her tattered jeans and white T-shirt. Saying nothing, she walked toward the front door.

"Where do you think you're going?" I demanded. "I can't let you leave the house tonight. You're my responsibility."

"And just how are you going to stop me, Travis?" she taunted. "Are you going to tie me to the bed? Like Enos does?"

"I'll call Dr. Bernard if I have to."

"Fine, call him. I'll call him too. I'll tell him that the exalted Dr. Harrison tried to seduce me on our first night together. Felt me up and forced me onto my knees."

I shook my head, confounded. "Why are you doing this, Layla? Do you realize the sacrifices I'm making in order to—"

"Oh, spare me," she said as she opened the front door and ran down the steps to her car. I stood there, my body shaking with frustration.

* * *

"I told you not to get involved, Harrison," Captain Smith said. Tommy Lee Smith had not been on duty that evening, and it had taken much persuading on my part to get them to track him down. I was eventually forwarded to his personal cell phone and could hear the booming bass of a home entertainment system in the background.

"And I told you that I already was involved, Captain. I'm even more involved now, and I need to know where Enos Vasquez is."

"He's wherever he wants to be. Nothing happened to Mr. Vasquez. He wasn't even charged. That girl has really got under your skin, hasn't she? Listen, Harrison, those little Romeos and Julians are just doing what kids do, and they're legally old enough to do it. Ain't none of my affair—or yours."

"*Juliets*," I corrected, to his utter lack of interest.

"Leave 'em alone, Harrison," Tommy Lee said, "or you'll be the one I'm snappin' the cuffs on. For your information, Vasquez ain't all that bad. He moved here to get away from the gangs in East L.A. He's a kid tryin' to get away from trouble, not find more of it. And by the way, I probably shouldn't share this with you, but I ran a quick search to help out the doctor over at Brackenridge, and found a man in Deridder, Louisiana, who we think is Layla's father. His name is Darryl Sommers. He's only been outa jail for a couple of years after servin' time for manslaughter. Seems he killed his wife in the heat of passion."

"Killed his wife?" I asked, dumbfounded. "When did that happen?"

"You're not as dumb as you act, Harrison," Tommy Lee said. "I think you get the picture. He killed her about ten years ago. Your little friend, Layla, would've been about nine at the time. Nine years old when Daddy killed Mommy. Gotta wonder if she saw it."

SEVENTEEN

I DROVE my Wagoneer to Layla's apartment. Her Escort was parked in front, and I parked a block away. As I got out, I stepped on a three-foot-long piece of steel rebar about as thick as my index finger. I picked it up and took it with me.

I was reluctant to knock on her door. If Enos was there, I could predict the results; I still had stitches over my eye from our first encounter. I walked around back through a small parking lot and saw the fire escape that Layla had mentioned in her voice-mail message. The area was dark and quiet, and though I was aware it was a crazy idea, I used the trust Dr. Bernard had placed in me as an excuse to begin climbing.

As I reached the second floor, someone below me got into a car. I froze, but they did not seem to notice me. I continued upward to the third level, my heart pounding faster with each step. At the landing at the top, I set the steel bar down, placed my palms against the walls and slowly raised my eyes to the level of the small window. From where I was, I could see the corner of Layla's bed bathed in incandescent light. There was dried blood on the covers; it had not occurred to me that someone had to clean up after such gruesome events as her attempted suicide. I moved as far to my right as I could to improve the angle of my view.

There, seated on the side of her bed, shirtless, elbows on his knees, was Enos Vasquez. He looked directly at me with a dumb, drugged look, but it was obvious that he could not really see me. A dense dragon-like tattoo wrapped around his arm. He lifted a clear bottle—vodka, I suspected—from the floor and washed down a handful of pills, shaking his head like a wet dog.

A slim arm appeared over his shoulder and pinched his nipple, which was pierced with a gold ring. He leaned his head back and howled. He handed the bottle over his shoulder to Layla, and she took a long, hard slug. She was wearing his oversized San Diego Charger jersey. He offered her pills, but she declined. As I watched, I could literally see Enos's face slacken as the drugs and alcohol took effect.

He stood at last and turned to face her. She got to her knees, placing her hands in front of her like the paws of a begging bear. She was laughing. She then stabbed at him several times with an extended index finger, poking him hard in the stomach, ribs, and chest, as if she were taunting him, chiding him. Perhaps even belittling him.

Unlike the eager and even playful Layla, Enos's body language spoke more of uncertainty and reluctance. Then, without any warning, she slapped him hard on his face—a slap so hard that his head twisted and his hand went to his jaw to feel out the damage.

As if this had completed some electronic circuit, he pushed her back onto the bed, twisted her onto her stomach, and placed his knee in her back. I heard her scream sharply and instinctively wedged my fingers under the small kitchen windowsill, but the window was stuck.

Enos leaned over, opened the drawer in the bedside table, and removed four pieces of nylon rope. He grasped Layla's right wrist and tied it tightly to the right bedpost with one of the nylon cords. Her legs still free, she began to kick at him with little effect as he quickly secured her other wrist and then her ankles.

He then got off the bed and retrieved the vodka bottle again; he paced the floor, looking at Layla between gulps.

I picked up the steel rod and tried to pry it underneath the windowsill as I thought hard about my options. I even tried to convince myself that Layla had brought this on. Perhaps they were just a couple of Romeos and Julians. I continued to press upon the steel bar with my full weight; the window opened an inch or two.

Inside the apartment, Enos stumbled across the floor. He made his way to the bedside table again and sifted through the contents of the drawer. Layla continued to squirm, and her body suddenly tensed as she turned her head sideways to watch him.

Enos threw things out of the drawer with an increased sense of urgency until he finally produced something that caused Layla to shut her eyes tightly and turn her head away.

I couldn't see exactly what it was—it appeared white and reflective. With the window now cracked, I heard her shout, "No, no . . . I've changed my mind. Enos, please . . . I can't handle this tonight . . ."

He grinned as he kneeled over her, the white object in his left hand. With his right hand, he grasped a handful of her hair and pulled her head back toward him. She screamed sharply, but with a quick, efficient motion, he placed the white object—a plastic bag—over Layla's head. The bag had a built-in yellow cord around the opening, and I saw the muscles in his deltoids bulge as he pulled it tight and wrapped the excess length of the cord around her neck, twice. He tied the cord in a triple knot and threw the empty bottle of vodka in my direction, where it broke into pieces on the floor beneath me.

I froze for a moment, then pressed hard on the steel bar that served as my lever but could not get the window to budge any farther. Layla's body began squirming, her legs kicking and her back arched. She tossed her head from side to side, and I could see her fingers, long and outstretched, clinching and releasing the bedposts in a rhythm that had its own sickening eroticism. I put both hands on the lever and placed the entirety of my weight on it, lifting my body off the fire escape. The bag over Layla's head expanded and contracted more and more rapidly in front of her nose and mouth, as if she were trying to swallow it. Or desperately trying not to.

As I jumped up and down to apply maximum force to the lever, Layla's body suddenly went limp, as did the bag on her head. She had stopped breathing.

One more jump, and the window finally gave way and burst open with a loud slam. I held onto the steel bar and forced my head and shoulders through the narrow opening. As my hips cleared, I placed my free hand in front of me to brace my fall onto the kitchen floor but I could not avoid the shards of glass from the vodka bottle. One shard sliced into my palm and I stifled a scream.

"Just rip the goddamn bag!" I shouted as I struggled to my feet, wielding the steel bar like a baseball bat.

Enos charged me, but this time given his drugged state I easily stepped aside and shoved him to the floor. I sprinted to Layla's side, grabbing the bag on her head and ripping it open. I turned again, ready to fend off another attack from Enos, but he was still on his hands and knees, vomiting onto the hardwood floor.

I turned back to Layla and untied the ropes as fast as I could. I rolled her over onto her back and placed my ear to her nostrils as I studied her chest for the slightest movement. There was none. She was not breathing. *How many times must I go through this?*

I grabbed a white sock from the floor and clinched it in my fist to staunch the flow of blood from my palm. With my free hand I pinched Layla's nose shut and covered the entirety of her purple-rimmed mouth with mine, delivering two full breaths. I tasted the vodka remnants of her saliva; the expansion of her chest temporarily gave me hope, although of course the air filling her lungs was mine alone.

I checked her carotid artery in the side of her neck with my fingers and found no pulse. I placed my open hand and my clinched fist squarely over her heart and pumped vigorously fifteen times.

I administered more breaths, having to stop twice to clear away a trickle of vomit from her mouth, and mine. At last . . . a weak pulse . . . a shallow breath. *Oh, God, please.*

Her body was cold and clammy, but her pupils were not dilated and her pulse rate increased; she was not in shock. Finally, she coughed and rubbed her throat. Within five minutes, she was smiling weakly.

"What are *you* doing here?" she whispered, her voice slurred, her hand wrapping around mine.

"I've come to take you home, Layla," I said. "To my home. And you're not leaving again for a month. And there are going to be some rules. And you are not going to break them. Got it?"

"Yeah, I think I've got it now," she said.

Enos never stirred from his kneeling position. I picked up the steel rod near him and wondered what it would sound like crashing against his skull. I also imagined the joy that Tommy Lee Smith would take in arresting me, so I dropped the rod on the floor and took Layla home—for the second time in our first day together.

EIGHTEEN

Dear Layla,
In an effort to make your stay here mutually enjoyable, I believe it incumbent upon us to observe certain standards of propriety, to follow certain rules . . .

No. THE start of my first draft sounded far too legalistic. I would need to adopt a more casual tone. As I lay in my bed, my pencil poised for another try, I heard Layla's door creak open and mentally traced her footsteps into the bathroom. It was just past ten on her second night in residence. She had slept the entire day with only the occasional roar of the toilet to confirm that she was in my home.

I tried to concentrate on my writing, but it was hard not to track her progress through the paper-thin walls: the bath water ran, then stopped. Then there was another quick fill, probably an extra measure of hot water. I heard the gentle slosh as she got in, the periodic slapping of water against the side of the tub. Another shot of hot water.

I turned my attention back to my draft but then heard a sharp moan. Instinctively, I got out of bed and stepped toward the door. *Not in my tub!* But just then I heard the drain being pulled and the water spinning out of the tub. I got back into bed and recollected my pencil and pad.

> *Dear Layla,*
> *As you may have discovered, the walls in my house are very thin.*
> *Last night during your bath . . .*

Ridiculous. Sounded as if I'd been eavesdropping.

> *Dear Layla,*
> *Given that you are a guest in my house, and that I am engaged to be married . . .*

It took forever for her bath water to drain—the gurgling, whirling sound resonated throughout the house. I then heard water running into the sink; she brushed her teeth for an eternity and spat out globs of toothpaste. She turned on my hair dryer but turned it off almost as quickly. I wondered if she was worried about the noise waking me. She opened the door and walked out. I wondered if she was wearing any clothes and, yes, the vision of her standing naked in the hall came to me in all of its perfection. I heard her bedroom door shut.

> *Dear Layla,*
> *Here is the first draft of the rules that I mentioned to you.*
> *I think this will help both of us to enjoy our time together . . .*

I started four more drafts, none of which satisfied me, before finally setting my reading glasses and writing pad aside and drifting into a light sleep.

Like many old houses, mine could produce a symphony of comforting sounds. There was, for example, the pleasant creaking of the hardwood floors, the turbine-like whine of the A/C compressor outside my bedroom window, and the plaintive creak of the joists in the attic when the temperature changed. Sometimes, these would be accompanied by the scratching of squirrels or raccoons sprinting across the roof and, at other times, by howling dogs in the neighborhood, including my own.

But a new noise—the sound of Layla's door creaking open again—awakened me. TJ approached my bed and looked at me curiously. One of the most distinctive sounds of my house was the clicking of his untrimmed nails across the hardwoods. When I ignored him, he made his way to the door and whimpered softly. It was then I realized that he had heard what I had not—Layla was on the move again. Focusing more intently, I heard the suction of the refrigerator door opening, followed by the rustling of aluminum foil. TJ also heard the foil; his whimpering became louder. I told him no and pointed to his bed at the foot of my own. Again I wondered if Layla was wearing clothes and silently chastised myself for that thought.

She soon left the kitchen, and though I could not track her whereabouts exactly, it was clear that she was making a complete tour of the house, occasionally opening a drawer or cabinet. I suppose it was fifteen minutes before she returned to her room.

Just as I was drifting off to sleep again, I heard a digital voice say, "Welcome!" Though I had not heard her leave her room this time, she had evidently logged on to the computer in the kitchen. I could hear the light clicking of keys, not unlike the sound of TJ's nails on the hardwood floors. TJ again moved to my door and whimpered, and again I hushed him sternly.

I turned on my bedside lamp, put on my reading glasses, and picked up pencil and pad again.

Dear Layla,

Since I work for a living and have to get up early in the morning . . .

She stayed online for the better part of an hour, alternating moments of silence with periods of frenetic typing. I was relieved, at last, to hear the AOL voice say, "Goodbye," followed by the sound of her bare footsteps back to her room.

By four, I was sleeping as soundly as one can whose alarm was set for five and who was determined to complete a set of rules for Layla before leaving for campus.

When my alarm rang, I tried to focus on the pad on my bedside table; it gradually dawned on me that I still had work left to do. Nevertheless, I got out of bed, threw on a warm-up suit, and started the coffee. The morning papers had not yet been thrown, so with no diversion at hand, I penciled out two more drafts of the rules.

At around 8:30, having heard nothing from Layla's room, I placed my opus on the dining room table and left for campus.

Dear Layla,

I hope you slept well. Please feel free to ask for anything that will make your stay more comfortable. I feel that we are now off to a good start. However, here are the first few rules that I would like for us to adopt:

1) Nudity (full or partial), should be restricted to the times you are either in your bedroom or in the bathroom and, in either case, when the door is shut. I am planning to purchase a robe soon. I have left my Foley's charge card nearby and encourage you to purchase one for yourself as well.

2) I am generally not comfortable with swearing, at least not in mixed company. Let's try to keep our language clean. The English language is beautifully expressive when used properly.

That's it for now. Only two rules . . . not bad! Have a great day, don't forget your group session at 3:00, and please call if you need anything.

Travis Harrison

I drove slowly down the Drag on my way to campus, past the Catholic church just south of Barnes & Noble. I stopped long enough for my homeless friend Dale to come to my window and collect a five-dollar bill. He still hadn't heard from Shawn.

With no classes to teach that day, I holed up in my office with the door shut, at times fighting to keep from nodding off in my chair. Kathryn had gone to Dallas to give a keynote speech at a meeting of telecom executives, and Ben was working from home, though I did get an e-mail from him begging to know the particulars of Layla's first two nights.

Of course, I could have sent Ben reeling with a description of Layla in my hall, but I decided to keep certain things to myself. I suppose hiding things from Ben should have been an early clue that I was heading into unknown and dangerous territory.

The truth is, I got almost nothing accomplished on campus that day, finally giving in to a forty-five-minute nap in my leather chair. By the time I got home, however, the benefits of that nap were gone and the frenetic barking and leaping of my dogs confirmed that I would not be able to escape my duties. Though Layla's car was gone, I was not overly concerned as her group session was supposed to last two hours. And truthfully, I was a bit relieved to know that I would have a few moments of solitude to read the *Times* and sort through my mail.

As I entered the house, however, I was struck by an unfamiliar scent, pungent and fruity. There, on an end table in the living room, I saw the source—a small crystal bowl filled with potpourri. I leaned closer to smell it, setting my satchel down nearby.

I looked around to see if anything else had been added and noted that the mail had been neatly sorted on the breakfast room table. Magazines were in one stack, bills in another, and personal letters in yet a third. Also on the table was a large box from Foley's department store, and next to that the legal sheet on which I had written Layla's note. She had written on the back:

Dear Travis . . .

NINETEEN

Dear Travis,

I didn't think you'd have time to get a robe yet, so I picked one up for you. Got one for myself too. And a few other things for the house, and I couldn't help picking up a few things for myself—just a shirt, a pair of jeans, and some panties. I hope you don't mind . . . I'll pay you back. Oh yeah, and some bath oils. Also, I thought we could use a rug for the bathroom . . . hope you like the color. And a wrap-around mat for the floor below the toilet. (Your aim seems a little off!) And your shower curtain was kind of gross . . . moldy . . . so I figured it would be okay to replace it. We can talk about your rules this evening.

Layla

OF COURSE, the purpose of writing the rules down was so that we would not have to *talk* about them.

I opened the box expecting to find the thick, long terry cloth robe I had envisioned. Instead, I found a silk Oriental robe, red with ornate gold trim. I held it up in front of me; it stopped well short of my knees. My white legs would have stabbed out from under it like a cadaver's. Of course I would never wear it, but I knew I couldn't tell that to Layla. Even that early on, I knew that hurting her feelings was not a risk worth taking.

* * *

Layla returned a little after seven that evening. I was sitting in the study reading the *Times*. I was already wearing a gray warm-up suit as I planned to walk the dogs and perhaps jog a mile or two. I leaned just far enough around the corner to acknowledge her presence with a slight wave.

"How was your session?" I asked.

She walked to the breakfast table, gathered up the rules I had unfortunately left there, and joined me in the study. She was wearing new jeans (made to look old) and a yellow T-shirt with red piping on the sleeves. She sat cross-legged on the sofa across from me. TJ immediately ran to her side and her nails curled into an unconscious scratch of his chin.

"So, number one is nudity," she said, ignoring my inquiry and studying the rules.

I let the paper fall into my lap. "Actually, it's *no* nudity," I corrected.

"Why does that bother you? Are you one of those religious freaks who think the human body is sinful? Or are you just a prude?"

"Those are the choices?" I asked. "Well, I do not consider being a prude negative, if that's what you're implying. In my family, we called that *propriety*. So I'll take number two, prude."

"I'll bet you were an only child," Layla said. I was, but I wasn't ready to reward her intuition quite so quickly.

"Why do you say that?"

"When I was growing up, I shared one small bathroom—about the size of yours—with four brothers and two parents. Prudishness or even propriety were not options for us. We ran around naked all the time, never even thought about it. We used the bathroom with the door open while talking—"

"Yes, yes, thank you—I get the picture," I said as firmly as I could. "But there are only two of us here, it's my house, and these are the rules."

"Jesus," she said disgustedly. "Travis the dictator."

"I don't mean to sound dictatorial," I said. "I want you to have equal input into our . . . cohabitation."

"We're cohabitating?" she smiled.

"As I understand the word, yes. But as to Rule Number One, please keep in mind that I am engaged to a wonderful woman."

"Oh, yeah, that wonderful woman you sicced on me at your book signing." She twisted her face as if she had tasted something sour. I had told Layla about Kathryn and our engagement during one of our hospital conversations.

"I did not sic her on you, and it would hardly be fair to her if a young woman went nude around my house."

Layla smiled and her eyes sparkled as if she had just been handed something of unimaginable value. "I won't tell if you won't," she whispered.

"But I *would* tell. That's my point. You wouldn't be here if Kathryn didn't trust me completely, but none of us are immune to jealousy—it's a natural and painful emotion. As I recall, it was *you* who told me that Enos threatened to *kill* you over the most superficial act on my part. That's the power of jealousy. So, while Kathryn is far above that level, I will not betray her trust by having you parade nude around my house."

"Parade? Is that what I did?" she laughed. "Doesn't what's-her-name *parade* around nude when she's here?"

"Her name, as you know, is Kathryn, and as you will discover someday, people often become more discreet with age." I instantly regretted that I had responded at all, but it was too late. Layla's mouth and eyes flew open at the conclusion she drew.

"Discreet? You don't *see* each other naked? What do you do, fumble around in the dark like a couple of cave frogs?"

"Excuse me," I snapped, my patience at an end. "This conversation has ventured into inappropriate territory. It is now over."

"Oops. Better write that down," Layla teased, pretending to lick the tip of an imaginary pencil and write across her palm. "Rule Number Three: no talking about cave frogs."

Suddenly, even as I stifled a smile, a month with Layla seemed as long as Mt. Everest is high. In fact, for a moment I thought seriously of calling Dr. Bernard the next morning and reneging on the deal. But as I would learn so often and so painfully, Layla had an uncanny knack for knowing how far she could push me and when to back off.

"I'm sorry," she said with apparent sincerity. "That was out of line."

"Then you agree to the no-nudity rule?"

"Yeah, sure. But I've just got to ask, does it really do that much for you?"

I looked at her, perplexed and suddenly tired. "Does what do what for me?"

"Nudity. Does it get you off just to see a girl naked?"

"My God, Layla, do you speak that way to everyone? The reasons for the rule are respect for Kathryn and a commonsense approach to propriety. I think we have adequately covered the subject."

"I was just curious . . ."

"Look, I am prepared to discuss current events, great works of literature, not-so-great works of literature, world history, philosophy— even your past and future if you wish. But our conversations should not be intentionally provocative."

"Provocative?" She laughed a spontaneous, screeching laugh that I had not heard from her before. It was so raw and so genuine that I could not refrain from smiling. "This conversation has been provocative?" She laughed even harder until she saw my smile evaporate and my face harden. Her face then fell as quickly.

"I'm sorry," she said softly. "It's going to take me a while to learn all these rules."

"Yes," I said wearily, "and we're still on Number One."

"I'll try, Travis. I really do appreciate your help. I'm not here to fuck up your life."

"Which brings us to Rule Number Two," I sighed.

"Oh, yeah, I mean I'm here to *mess* up your life," she said, staccato.

"No, no," I corrected. "You're *not* here to mess up my life."

"What?" she asked.

"You said that you *are* here to mess up my life."

She sighed. "Shit, this is going to be harder than I thought. Maybe we should create a list of banned words—shit, fuck . . ."

"Thank you, yes. Perhaps we should." I lifted the *Times* in hopes of signaling an end to our first great deliberation. She stood and turned toward her room, took a few steps, and then stopped. I held the paper as long as I could before peeking over the top. Soft alligator tears were easing down her face. "Now what's wrong?" I asked.

Her ripe lower lip was quivering. She wiped tears from her eyes, straightened her posture, and looked hard at me, though her voice was weak. "Was it really superficial?"

I was lost. "Was what really superficial?"

"You said that Enos threatened to kill me over the most superficial act on your part. I guess you were referring to your inscription in my book. Was it really superficial?"

I knew to handle Layla carefully, but I wasn't prepared to completely abandon all truth. "Yes, it was, Layla. I didn't even know you. I had met you that morning for the first time, and I had signed a hundred books before yours. Though I wrote *best wishes* in most of them, those inscriptions were also superficial, by definition.

"But things have changed now, Layla. I have now pulled you bleeding out of your tub, gotten my face pummeled on your behalf, sat by your side in the hospital for the better part of a week, and invited you into my home for a month. You may not challenge me on superficial grounds."

Her tears flowed more freely, but her body language was instantly altered. The tears had somehow shifted from those of hurt to those of relief. She walked confidently to where I was sitting and knelt next to me. She touched my bandaged eye and then laid her head in my lap, wiping her tears on my cotton warm-up pants. "You poor man," she said. I laid my hand hesitantly on her cool copper hair, which seemed to have a magical, calming effect on her. And on me. After a moment, she stood and gave me a hot, tear-stained kiss on the cheek. A smile came back to her face and I was again stunned at the speed with which her emotions shifted.

"Do you want me to sign something?" she asked. "You know, agreeing to the rules?"

"I'll take your word for it."

She nodded and then said, "Hey! I almost forgot—don't you just love your robe?" Her face was radiant.

"Well, it's not exactly what I would have selected . . ." I watched as her shoulders drooped and her expression began to go limp. "But it is very beautiful," I added quickly. "I look forward to . . . beautiful, really."

She perked up instantly. The physical effect that mere words had on Layla was nothing short of shocking. It was also curiously powerful.

"Want to see mine?" she asked excitedly.

"Perhaps later," I said, but she was already running to her bedroom. She quickly returned wearing a robe over her shirt and jeans. It was a red silk robe with gold trim—a robe identical to the one she had purchased for me. In her stocking feet, she gathered up a running start and slid halfway across the hardwoods, stopping only inches in front of me.

"His and hers!" she said, beaming. "Cool, huh?"

"Very cool," I said, trying not to grimace as I imagined myself in the robe.

"Want to see my panties?" she asked.

"Layla, *please!*"

"The new ones I bought today. They're hilarious."

"Maybe later—"

Too late. She quickly skated back to her room, pushing off walls or pieces of furniture when her momentum slowed. Again, she returned quickly, this time dangling from her bony fingers three pairs of white cotton panties. Printed in random spots on each pair was the word *No*. The only difference between the three was that *No* was printed in a different color on each—blue, green, and red.

"Very nice," I said, repositioning my paper in front of me as yet another hint of the conclusion of our meeting. I suppose I did do a double take on the panties, however, if only because they looked impossibly small hanging from her fingers. I didn't see how they could possibly fit *on* her. Inadvertently, I found myself thinking that Kathryn couldn't have gotten them over one leg . . .

"No, no—you don't get it," she said.

She walked to the far wall and flipped off the overhead light and then walked back toward me, placing one pair of panties a foot from my face. She leaned over me, her stomach resting on mine for a moment, and turned off my reading lamp. As my eyes adjusted to the darkness, the words printed on the panties changed. The *No* had disappeared, replaced by a glowing, fluorescent, *Yes!*

"Isn't that, like, hilarious?" she demanded. "When the lights go out, *No, No, No* turns into *Yes! Yes! Yes!*"

"Isn't that *like* hilarious, or isn't that hilarious?" I asked.

Her look was one of utter confusion. "What?"

"You—your generation—you're always saying that things are *like* other things. 'He was *like* crazy . . . it was *like* awesome.' I don't understand that. Someone is either crazy or he's not. Something is either awesome or it's not. Hilarious, or not."

"And I gather this is not," she said.

"It's very clever, Layla," I said, turning the reading lamp back on and folding my paper with a loud snap.

"O—*kay*—I can tell you really enjoyed that," she said as she stuffed the panties into the pocket of her robe. "I'm going to take a bath."

"Layla, don't be upset," I said, as she walked away. "I'm glad you found something you like. I guess I'm just more interested in what's going on in the world right now, like the problems in the Congo, than the latest technology in female underwear."

She stopped, turned, and pointed at me with the lecturing finger of a parent. "You definitely are different," she said. "You see, the men I've met before, given a choice, would sort of, *like*, be more interested in panties than the Congo, wherever the fuck that is. But you're just the opposite. Maybe that's why I love you."

"The Congo is in Africa, you just violated Rule Number Two, and you don't love me."

"I don't love you?" she said. "With what you're doing for me?"

"That's appreciation, not love," I said.

She shook her head and laughed. "You're a trip." She took several sliding steps toward me and kissed me on the cheek again. "I appreciate you! I am in appreciation with you. You are the appreciation of my life. Should we add *love* to our list of banned words?" she asked, poising her mock pencil over her palm again. "Crap, get off, shit, fuck—and love."

"Go bathe, Layla," I said, honestly exhausted. "And yes, of all of the words on our list, I'd rank *love* at the top."

"Sounds like a topic for another night," she said.

"Oh, please, no," I pleaded with a heavy sigh.

"You're going to love having me here," she smiled as she slid away toward the bathroom, pushing her feet outward as if she were on skates. The water soon began running.

I no longer had the energy to walk the dogs, much less to jog. One day would hardly matter, but in terms of exhaustion an evening with Layla Sommers had seemed the equivalent of a marathon run.

I wondered if anyone had ever survived thirty marathons in thirty days.

TWENTY

FOR THE next several nights, Layla and I settled into my study, and conversation became easier. She would generally start by asking if I liked the things she had added to the house. I had not reclaimed my credit card after the purchase of the robes and was soon the proud owner of a fully stocked spice rack, assorted dish towels, a menagerie of pot holders in the shape of various farm animals, a woven, peach-colored runner that lay in the hall between our bedrooms, and nearly a dozen small potted plants that dotted the front porch. Candles had sprung up like mushrooms in every imaginable size, color, and scent.

In return, I would ask about her therapy, and she would provide me with just enough detail to confirm she was at least attending the sessions. She told me she thought I would like the group leader, a man named Nicholas Nickemeyer. Layla described him as a "long-haired nut" who wanted to write a novel. I did not seek to clarify just why she thought that would appeal to me. Though she had dropped her university courses, she brought books and magazines into the study each night and spent a fair amount of time reading them.

I had not left her another written note, nor had I proposed any more rules, though several had occurred to me. One issue I considered addressing was the laundry. Though she had purchased a new pair of jeans and an assortment of T-shirts, she still had so little clothing that I didn't mind throwing the items she left near the machine in with mine. At least not until I found myself handling her undershirt, flimsy white bra, and cotton panties that were so minute I could scarcely fold them. The word *propriety* had come again to my mind.

But I did my best and placed them neatly on top of the dryer. They were gone the next day and my hopes grew that we were establishing a nonverbal system of communication.

When Layla had first settled into the sofa in my study, I admit that I had been apprehensive, wondering if I would ever get another bit of work or reading done. At first I considered it a major interruption when she commented about her readings, a fact I tried to convey by simply nodding instead of looking up. But she paid no attention to my subtleties, and by the third night of our joint study sessions I found myself actually encouraging her interruptions as well as offering comments from my own readings. I don't know what I had expected, but I found her to be surprisingly intelligent.

She expressed a growing curiosity about current affairs, and asked me again why I was interested in the Congo, which, despite continued genocide, was again being ignored by the world. Even more surprising, one evening she commented that she thought it was sad that a man of Thomas Jefferson's intellect would stand no chance of winning office today. I was flattered that she had made some effort to read my novel.

We eventually worked our way around to our favorite movies, bands, and meals. I told her about the Blue Fox, a restaurant in San Francisco where I had eaten the finest meal of my life—beef tenderloin and au gratin potatoes, washed down with a spectacular Lafite Rothschild Cabernet.

Her favorite meal? "A number 9 from the Taco Bell on the Drag." We both laughed.

* * *

By the end of the first week, I admit that I had come to look forward to our evenings together. Of course I still talked to Kathryn at least once a day, and we had eaten lunch together on several occasions on the benches outside Garrison Hall, but I didn't call her in the evenings as I had so often done in the past. Not even just before going to bed.

Kathryn had asked several times if the two of us could at least have dinner together and then run by her house for "obvious reasons." But my agreement with Dr. Bernard, I told her, demanded that I spend every evening at home to make sure Layla was also there. I floated the idea of Kathryn's joining Layla and me for dinner one night, but given their brief unpleasant encounter at the Barnes & Noble signing, the idea went over poorly. Kathryn argued that it would feel too awkward, if not downright hostile, to confront Layla again and that we had best stick to our lunches outside Garrison Hall. I protested that *hostile* was too strong a word but respected her position.

What I did get both of them to agree to was that on the last night of Layla's residency, Kathryn would come by for a celebratory toast. That was also the night on which Kathryn was to be honored at the chancellor's house, so it seemed to me an ideal opportunity for the three of us to end our unlikely beginning and move forward toward our respective futures.

I did not know then that that would also be the night on which Layla would try to destroy me and I would be charged with the murder of Enos Vasquez.

* * *

By the time I sat in my study on the Sunday that ended the second week with Layla, both of us had grown comfortable in our routine.

Sunday has always been a special day to me, a day to plan the week ahead, catch up on my letter writing, and to reflect on life in general. I often drank a bit more wine than usual on Sunday evenings, and though not sentimental by nature, if I was ever to let my mind wander, if I was ever to let myself get lost in a particular song, or photograph, or memory, Sunday would be the night.

By the time Layla returned that Sunday evening with Chinese food, I had put on a CD of classical favorites and was already sipping my third glass of Chardonnay.

"Are we eating at the table?" she asked from the kitchen as she prepared our plates. We had yet to cook a meal at home.

"I'd like mine in the study, if you don't mind," I replied.

"Am I invited?"

"Of course," I said, putting my journal aside.

She handed me a plate of chicken fried rice and stopped on her way back to the kitchen to light some piñon incense and half a dozen candles.

"Do I get wine?" she shouted from the kitchen. It was the first time she had asked.

"That would be up to you," I said.

"Oh, I thought there might be some rule covering that." She appeared momentarily with her white rice and steamed vegetables and a crystal wine glass filled with Chardonnay. She set the wine glass on the end table and sat down at her usual spot in the corner of the leather sofa, tucking her bare feet up beneath her. She wore khaki shorts and a khaki shirt as if preparing for a safari. She also wore the leather hat, which I had not seen on her in days.

Layla had asked me several times if I wanted my credit card back, but her spending was not excessive and she needed some new clothes. Admittedly, I also found it entertaining to locate the knickknacks she added to the house.

We ate quietly for a few moments, picking at our plates and sipping wine, commenting only that the food was good. Finally she broke the silence with a deep breath and looked at me pointedly. "So, how long have you been single?" she asked.

"Single?" I repeated. "That's a curious word. For a man my age, it sort of conjures up images of leisure suits and gold chains, doesn't it? I don't really think of myself as single, nor do I like the term *widower*."

"Your wife is dead?" Layla said, looking shocked.

"I told you that," I said.

"No! You told me that your daughter died. I assumed you were divorced. My God, Travis, did you lose them both? Together?"

"Not together. Randi, my daughter, died in a car accident about ten years ago. Helen, my wife, almost twenty."

"They both lived in this house?" Layla asked, looking around the room.

"Helen and I moved into this house before you were born."

"Time goes fast, doesn't it?" she said.

I laughed and wiped a trace of wine from my mouth before taking another sip. "And what might Layla Sommers know about the ravages of time?"

She just shrugged, stood, and took my plate from me. From the kitchen, she said, "How did your wife die?" She returned with the bottle of wine, refilling both our glasses and setting the bottle on the coffee table in front of her.

"We probably should keep that cool," I said, nodding to the Chardonnay.

"Or just drink real fast," she said. "Your wife . . ."

I studied the golden hue of my wine as I swirled it around in the glass. I took another sip. "Helen and I met in high school in Colorado City, Texas. Population 750. I was the—"

"You were the quarterback and she was the homecoming queen."

"Close enough," I said, raising my glass to her insight. "In the interest of full disclosure, however, I should note that I was the quarterback only because, out of the thirteen boys on our team, I was the only one who could memorize the 150-page playbook.

Our coach—Moose, we called him—had just been run out of college coaching for some sort of scandal and was determined to start a dynasty in high school. We won one and lost nine that year and Moose quit coaching forever."

"But let me guess," Layla said. "You and Helen had great sex in the backseat of your dad's car!"

I blushed so brilliantly that Layla put her hands over her mouth to stifle a laugh. "I'm sorry, Travis. I know there must be a rule somewhere about you and your significant others—and sex."

I waved off her apology. Even though I was blushing furiously, for some reason in Layla's presence I wasn't really embarrassed.

"Helen and I both went to Texas for college. She majored in education, I majored in American history." I told her the rest of the story—how Helen had given up on having a child and how we were preparing to leave Austin when I got a job, bought a house—this house—and Helen became pregnant with Randi. I told her how happy we had been and how optimistic. And I told her how we had purchased a scale to chart the growth of Randi inside of her mom.

"We put the scale right over there," I said, pointing to the narrow wall outside the kitchen. "I got a sheet of graph paper, and we marked Helen's weight—118 pounds on the day we bought the scale. A week later, it was 116, and a week after that, 112.

"Helen also became exhausted." I sighed deeply and took another sip of wine. Layla was silent, her deep brown eyes burrowing in on me, demanding that I continue. "Her obstetrician made an emergency appointment with an oncologist . . .

"To this day, I'm not sure what was wrong with her. Lymphoma, leukemia, Hodgkin's, Waldenstrom's—we heard them all. But there was no doubt that it was an aggressive cancer . . ."

"Oh, Travis . . ."

"The doctors insisted that she abort immediately so that they could begin a level of chemotherapy that would destroy the fetus but possibly save Helen. Because of the difficulty we'd had conceiving, Helen refused. She told me she knew that she would never conceive again and that she was not giving up our child.

"She became weaker and weaker. When she reached the fourth month of her pregnancy, the doctors tried to convince her that the fetus could probably survive the treatment that was necessary to save Helen's life. They pleaded with her; I begged her. She wouldn't hear of it. She refused to jeopardize the baby in any way.

"Helen held on until they took the baby seven weeks early. It was a tiny girl we named Randi; she was just a little over four pounds. My God, Layla, you should have seen her tiny little fingers and fingernails . . . she had a little tuft of red hair, like her mother's." I looked at Layla, but did not tell her that within three years Randi's hair had turned precisely the color of hers.

"They immediately began massive chemotherapy on Helen, but it was too late. She held on for a few weeks until she knew that Randi was going to make it. She died in my arms."

"And you were left to raise an infant alone," Layla said, her eyes wet with tears. "Do you have pictures?"

I went to the bookshelf on the far wall and pulled a haggard photo album out from a bottom shelf. I sat down on the sofa next to Layla, who sat up straight and put her arm around my shoulders as easily as a sibling. I began leafing through the pages of the album. There was one picture from high school of Helen in her cheerleading outfit, a short skirt with alternating blue and gold panels. Her red hair was long, her cheekbones high, and her limbs lithe.

"You were right," I said, lost for a moment in that picture. "The sex in the backseat of my dad's car *was* incredible." I couldn't believe I had said it, but Layla scarcely noticed.

There were also pictures of our college graduation, the two of us in our caps and gowns beneath the landmark Tower on the Main Mall. Layla laughed at my long curly hair and generous sideburns.

I flipped to a photo of Helen in a hospital bed, smiling bravely. A tiny infant tightly wrapped in a cotton cloth was lying on her chest.

"Helen and Randi," Layla said as she took the album from me. She flipped through the book until she came to the very back, where she found a single, loose Polaroid. It was a black-and-white picture of Randi as an eight-year-old girl. A bit of a tomboy, she held a bat, wore a New York Yankees uniform, and freckles dotted her flushed face.

"She's beautiful," Layla said.

"Yeah. I didn't know that was in here." The picture bothered me. For some reason, pictures of a three-pound baby wrapped in cotton cloth seemed remote enough from my own reality, but when I saw pictures of Randi as a little girl, even a decade later, it was still too fresh.

"Do you have other pictures of her?"

"Somewhere, probably," I said, closing the album abruptly and returning it to the cabinet. I shook my head as if that would remove the last image of Randi from my mind.

"Where are they?" Layla asked. "You should blow them up and frame them—hang them up."

"It took me a long time to get over Helen," I said. "Maybe I haven't gotten over Randi yet. I just haven't wanted the daily reminders."

Layla nodded her understanding, though I could tell she was less than convinced. She leaned over to pour the last of the wine and seemed poised to ask another question.

"So, what happened to Randi?"

Yes, what happened to Randi? I suppose that was the question Layla Sommers forced me to answer. For ten years, I had held one belief, but the moment after I pulled Layla from her bloody tub, the moment at which my knees had all but collapsed and I had heard Randi's voice, I knew differently.

"What I know about Randi's death I learned from a man named Ben Frizell. You'd like Ben, I think. I *know* he'd like you." I told her about Ben's accident and how, wheelchair bound, he had traded God for Nietzsche and other atheists. I told her about how

Ben had come to Lubbock, and how he had sat with me for eleven days, about how he had pieced together the details of the accident, and about how Randi had died.

"I raised Randi with no help; it was before being a so-called single dad was fashionable, and without Helen's income I didn't have a lot of extra money for nannies or maids. After too many years of being passed over for tenure at Texas, I realized I'd have to get a new job. The best chance I had for quick tenure was at Texas Tech in Lubbock."

I told her about how Randi and I had gotten off to a late start that morning and how I was speeding when we first saw the red stripe on the horizon.

"Randi began crying but I couldn't turn around. I told her to stay where she was, to make sure her seatbelt was tight, but she took it off and started climbing into the front seat to be with me."

Randi, no!

Daddy?

I told her the rest of the story, as best I knew it, and when I finished tears were streaming down Layla's face.

"How did she die?" Layla asked.

I gave her a wounded look. "What do you mean, how did she die? We hit a truck almost head-on at seventy miles an hour. She was ejected from the car. She died instantly."

"That's what Ben told you," Layla said calmly, dabbing at tears with the sleeves of her shirt. "That she died instantly."

"Ben got the whole story from the paramedics."

"But Ben wasn't there when it happened," she said. "Neither were the paramedics. You were the only one who was there."

I reached for the bottle of wine and silently cursed its emptiness.

"Did you see her again? Did you see Randi's body?"

"*Of course not!* I told you, I was in a coma for eleven days. They didn't know if I would ever come out of it. Helen's parents arranged for a funeral for Randi and buried her next to her mother in Colorado City."

Layla studied me intently and asked the one question I didn't want her to ask. "Have you been to her grave?"

I walked toward the kitchen, intent on opening another bottle of wine, but stopped short. "Where are you going with this?" I asked.

"I'm not *going* anywhere," she said. "I just think it's sad that you lost a beautiful daughter that you raised and loved and yet you didn't get to tell her goodbye, you didn't get to see her body, and you haven't been to her grave. I guess I'm worried about something my shrinks would call *closure*."

The bottle of wine I sought was wedged into the rack inside the refrigerator door. I cursed it, yanked it free, smashing my thumb on the rack above, and then opened it clumsily, splitting the cork into pieces and cursing that as well.

"You don't remember anything at all from that day?" Layla asked.

I hurried back into the study, the wine bottle in my hand. "Layla, believe me—I have tried." I took a deep breath and set the bottle of wine down. My hands were shaking. "I think we had better change subjects," I said, my face glowing crimson. "You don't know what you're talking about."

"Yeah, well, one of us certainly doesn't," she muttered under her breath, pulling her knees tightly into her. A few minutes later she shook her head and walked out of the room. A minute after that, I heard bath water running.

I had two more glasses of wine in her absence and remained in the study for over an hour. I was angry with myself for dismissing her, as she had taken me precisely where I needed to go. I shut my eyes. Heavy with the wine, my mind filled with images of Randi, clearer than I had ever seen before. I saw her in my rearview mirror as she unbuckled her seatbelt. *Randi, no!* I heard the distinctive click, but I couldn't afford to keep my eyes off the road for long. I felt one of her hands glance off my shoulder as she tried to climb over the seat . . .

Daddy?

I saw the brake lights of the truck in front of us. They were inches from my windshield. I stomped on the brakes; the silhouette of a small girl sailed past me. My chest was crushed by the steering wheel, the sound of breaking glass and twisting metal roared in my ears, deafening me . . .

I was upside down when the car finally skidded to a stop. I unbuckled my seatbelt, falling to the ceiling of the car and then climbing out through a small opening. I was on the grass median and began crawling. Though I could see nothing through my own blood and the smoke and dusty red shroud, I could smell gasoline and smoke, and I heard someone screaming.

"Daddy!"

"Randi!"

*   *   *

The bathroom door opened just as I let out a painful wail.

"Did you say something?" Layla asked as she peeked around the corner, holding her robe closed.

"No," I said. "Nothing at all."

135

TWENTY-ONE

ONCE WE had passed the midpoint in Layla's scheduled residency, I sensed a growing anxiety in us both. It was as if a bomb of unknown explosive power had been placed somewhere in my home and was ticking quietly but steadily.

Layla dealt with her increasing anxiety by simply buying more and more things for the house. Though I had finally reclaimed my credit card, she discovered that I had an account at an upscale pharmacy nearby that required no card. She purchased a ceramic Labrador puppy and placed it next to the fireplace. She had, quite artistically, painted a collar on its neck, and "TJ Jr." on the collar. There were other statuettes on the front porch, and I noted the addition of a dozen or so straw baskets, some filled with porcelain eggs of various colors, others with wooden fruit, and one with seashells. Candleholders of infinite variety continued to be a favorite; I once counted twenty-three actually lit. I suppose the risk of a Layla meltdown prevented me from taking control of her spending habits.

She also made changes to the house that did not require purchases. One day, the bench swing on the porch was newly painted. On another, the leather sofa in the living room—the one in front of the fireplace—was angled forty-five degrees. Two tall brass lamps in that same room were moved and appeared to have brighter bulbs.

Paintings disappeared and were replaced by others that I hadn't seen in years. On the lighted spot over the mantel, for example, she had replaced a print of Monticello (as drawn by Jefferson himself) with a wild and colorful print of an ocelot by Leroy Neiman. It was a print Helen had purchased and loved. In fact, many of Helen's favorite things—small framed paintings, beaded pillows, throw rugs—had made their way from closet shelves back into the main of the house.

And there were always more plants. Layla loved to transplant ivy, so one plant quickly became a dozen. She had also planted blooming plants in clay pots, dotting the porch with rich blues, purples, and reds. One day I saw her through the front window as she hung onto every word of advice that Puddy gave her about roses. I watched as she took the pruning sheers and followed the old woman's directions, and then, inexplicably, I saw the two of them laugh like girlfriends sharing secrets about boys.

*   *   *

It became somewhat like a game for me to arrive home and attempt to determine what changes had been made that day. The day after I had watched her and Puddy laugh, perhaps symptomatic of my own anxiety, I purchased a gift for Layla.

When I entered the house that afternoon with a huge sack, I was as nervous as if I had arrived for the senior prom, corsage in hand. I set the sack down inside the door and quickly searched for the day's changes.

I did not immediately notice anything new other than a few small potted plants, and I admit to feeling a little disappointed. That is, until I reached the study. There, a dozen or so books had been removed from the center bookcase, the one just at eye level. In their place was a simple wooden frame, 8" x 10". Rays of light from the nearby window shone upon it. In the frame was a black-and-white photograph of a freckle-faced Randi in a New York Yankees baseball uniform. A bat was slung over her shoulder; her face was flushed from her effort. With the enlargement of the original

Polaroid, it was also evident that two of her teeth were missing. She was the most beautiful thing I had ever seen.

I moved slowly to the frame and picked it up. I breathed deeply and fought back tears.

"You like it?"

I had assumed Layla was home, but her voice still startled me. I dabbed at my eyes with my sleeve and turned to face her. "I like it very much," I said. "You were right. It's something I should have done a long time ago. Thank you."

She came toward me quickly and gave me an enormous hug. "You look tired," she said, as her hug lingered. With Layla in my arms, I could still look over her shoulder at the picture of Randi in my hand. I remembered putting her to bed at night, the long stories and endless questions. I remembered holding her, feeling the bones in her body, the silky smoothness of her skin.

I let Layla go, and as she stepped back, I saw that her eyes were also filled with tears. I brushed some strands of hair from her face.

"Hey, I've got something for you too," I said.

Her face lit up and her eyes grew wide. "You have something for *me?*"

"Yes. Wait here," I said as I hurried to the front door to collect the oversized sack.

"That giant sack is for me?" she said as I rustled back into the study.

"I couldn't really wrap it. And really, it's no big—"

"Give!" she said excitedly, reaching for the sack. She tore into it, pulling the contents out with the tenacity of a toddler who prefers the unwrapping to the gift.

"Oh . . . my . . . God! You have got to be kidding." She held the large plastic bag before her. As described on the package, the bag held sheets, a comforter, two pillowcases, and shams. The decorative theme was roses against a green background of leaves and thorns. The roses were petite but plentiful and bloomed in every imaginable color.

"I love roses!" Layla gushed. "You know, I've been learning a lot about them from Puddy." Tears streamed from her eyes and down her cheeks. She made no effort to capture them, and with apologies to Shakespeare, I was quite sure that no rose had ever bloomed more gloriously. "I'd like to plant some roses in our yard," she continued, sniffling, "but Puddy says we should probably wait a few months."

A moment of awkwardness followed as we both registered the fact that Layla would not be there in a few months. Neither would I.

"Oh, Travis . . . these are beautiful." She dropped the bag and hugged me again, bringing the side of her wet face into contact with my neck, her profile tucking perfectly under my chin. I could feel the warm wetness of her tears on my skin. I could smell her salty fragrance. Oh, yes, Ben, I could smell that freshman.

"They're just sheets," I said, realizing that the emotions that had been pent up inside both of us were about more than just bedding.

"I don't deserve this," she said. "I don't deserve you."

"As of now," I said, "I'm introducing a new rule: you will not put yourself down. Look at all you've done for this house. I think a beautiful young woman deserves to spend a few nights between roses instead of threadbare sheets."

She pulled away suddenly and looked at me with abject confusion. I had a moment of panic thinking I might have said something wrong and she was about to melt down.

"You think I'm beautiful?" she asked, as if it were the most far-fetched possibility she had ever entertained.

"Very," I said. "Very beautiful—and *very* young."

"Too young for you, I suppose that means," she said, smiling.

"Sometimes, Layla, I feel that Rome is too young for me."

* * *

We didn't speak much more that evening, but every now and then she would go to her room to look at her new bedding. When she returned, she would look at the picture of Randi and ask, "You like it?"

"Yes, I like it very much."

She finally excused herself to bathe. When I heard the water running, I knew from experience that it would be a good twenty minutes before she was finished. I picked up my journal, but curiously, soon after the water had stopped running, I heard the bathroom door open. I sat quietly in my leather chair.

I speculated that perhaps she had left her towel or her robe in her room, yet I heard no footsteps. Nor did the door close again. It was as though she was just standing in the hall, waiting.

Waiting for what?

That question was answered in a flash as a vanilla phantom, wearing nothing but a film of soapy bubbles, rounded the corner and came at me like a rocket. My eyes grew wide; I did not even have time to close my journal before she jumped into my lap, her knees straddling me. Water dripped off her and soaked me and my journal. Covered with soapy bubbles, she threw both arms around my neck and pulled my head toward her, kissing me first on one cheek, and then the other.

I was speechless. My mouth hung open and my heart raced. She placed her soapy forehead against mine, looked me deep in the eyes, and said, "Sorry, Travis, but sometimes you just have to break the rules. I love the sheets!"

As quickly as she had appeared, she was gone, leaving a trail of soapy water on my hardwood floors.

From all the times I've recreated that incident in my mind—and they are innumerable—I've concluded that Layla was probably in my lap no more than fifteen seconds. Maybe as few as ten. But in those precious few seconds, she had not just broken the rules, she had shattered them.

*   *   *

Kathryn and I had lunch several times in the days following. She avoided asking about specifics of Layla's visit, and I avoided giving them. There was no scenario under which Kathryn would find humor in Layla's soapy, naked attack, and such knowledge would only have reversed Kathryn's growing hopefulness about our wedding. She too had a countdown clock of sorts, which she voiced with NASA-like precision, saying it was "T minus 13" days until Layla's departure. She continued this, ending each of our lunches or phone conversations with a reminder of how many days Layla had left. T minus 11 . . . T minus 8, T minus 7 . . .

Kathryn had also repeated her offer of dinner and *dessert,* making clear by her tone what the latter implied. As the fourth week began—Layla's last week—I finally accepted Kathryn's offer, not because I so craved "dessert," but because I was becoming uncomfortable about the so-called celebration I had arranged for Layla's last night, the one in which I had initially envisioned the three of us toasting our respective futures.

As that final evening drew near, even though Kathryn was growing optimistic and Layla was doing well, it occurred to me that having dinner—and sharing a bed—with Kathryn a few days prior to the celebration might be a good idea. My thinking was that this might reduce the tension level for Kathryn and me. And telling Layla that I was going to see Kathryn prior to that final night might smooth the transition for her emotions as well. An interim step, so to speak.

The problem was how to tell Layla. I sensed an opportunity the very next day when Layla asked if she could jog with me. Ordinarily I tried to run two miles and Layla never ran at all, but that day the conversation flowed between us and we had no difficulty going four. Though I had begun with the intent of telling her about my dinner with Kathryn, just two nights away, she managed to get me somewhat off track.

During the early portion of the jog, while I was enlightening her with the importance of hydration to runners, Layla blurted out, "Is that why you pee so often at night? Because of all your— hydration?"

Only two weeks earlier I would have blushed purple at the thought of discussing my bladder with a nineteen-year-old girl, but for reasons I still do not quite comprehend it seemed utterly harmless with Layla.

"No, it's not from hydration," I said, "it's because of my prostate."

Layla stopped in her tracks, digging her fingers into my arm as she jerked me to a halt. There was shock in her eyes, her hand covered her open mouth. "You have cancer?" she asked.

"No. *No!*" I said, placing one hand on her bare arm for reassurance.

"I thought prostate problems were a cancer thing."

"They can be," I said, "but mine is not. The prostate is just a little gland that tends to become enlarged with age, even if benign. It sort of, like, constricts the flow of things—makes it feel as if you need to go all the time. Especially at night."

"It *like* constricts the flow?" she asked. "Or does it constrict the flow?"

"Constricts it," I said humbly, unable to repress a smile.

"How do you know it's not cancerous?" she said, unwilling to give up too easily on this impending crisis.

"I just had a physical two months ago. There are a couple of tests."

"Oh, that's good," she said. I sensed her relief but also her ongoing curiosity. I started jogging again and she stayed with me.

"Blood tests?" she inquired.

"That's one of them, yes." We ran another block in silence.

"What's the other test?" she asked.

I hesitated but couldn't resist. "It's called a digital exam."

She looked at me curiously. "They examine your digits?"

"No. They, uh, use their digits to examine you."

She skidded to a stop again and waved her hand before her face as if she was feeling faint. "Details, please," she said, excitedly.

I took a deep breath and soaked up the childlike wonder in her brown eyes. "The prostate gland can be accessed with—how shall I say—" I extended my middle finger.

She shook her head and mouthed the word *"No!"* She smiled as if someone had just told her she had won the lottery. "Bullshit," she said, reverently. "You can't be telling me that when a grown man goes to see some Harvard M.D., he gets a finger, like, up his ass."

"Trust me," I said, it's not *like* up his ass—"

We both laughed and said in perfect harmony, *"It's up his ass!"* She gave me a sweaty hug as if that was part of the laughter. She felt so alive in my arms. Our shorts touched as she pressed close, too close, yet I didn't want to let her go. What was this girl, this woman, doing to me?

"And he charges $350 for the privilege," I added, pulling away from her.

We stood there in the middle of the street and laughed until we cried. Why was everything that I had previously considered disgusting or embarrassing suddenly so silly and wonderful in her presence?

As we picked up the pace again, Layla's smile remained wide. I could almost hear her mind whirring, and I couldn't help but think that somewhere in the future, some unsuspecting man was going to get a sudden physical from "Dr." Sommers.

"Enough about me," I said at last. "Let's talk about you."

"Ask me anything," she said.

"That skimpy undershirt you're so fond of—"

"My wife-beater?"

"That's what it's called?"

"Yeah. Just an old Southern stereotype, I suppose, about the men who wear them." Layla's expression suddenly went stone cold. "So what about it?"

The change in her demeanor made me leery to ask my question, but it was too late. "I was just wondering if you knew that when you're wearing that shirt . . . well . . . it's just that it's a little transparent."

She put her hand over her mouth as though shocked. "You don't mean to tell me you can see through it?" she said.

"Well, yes . . . a little bit."

"And you're wondering if I *knew* that? If I *knew* that my nipples were on display to the world?"

"Yes."

She looked at me sympathetically and shook her head in mock disbelief. "Of course, I know that, Travis! What woman doesn't? Women always know what they're doing to men."

If only this man had known.

TWENTY-TWO

HAVING failed to inform Layla that I would be dining with Kathryn, I had only one more night to do so. I decided to take the direct, almost nonchalant approach.

"Layla," I began. "I'm going to be gone for a short while tomorrow evening."

We were in my study. I was reading the *Times,* and she was on the sofa opposite me, her knees tucked under her chin as she worked her way through a stack of magazines she had purchased that day. I didn't recognize any of the titles, but they all had nearly naked celebrities on the cover. She was eating a peach.

She looked up from a magazine and mindlessly took a huge bite out of the peach. A trail of juice trickled down her chin. "Dokker B'nard won like that," she said with smiling eyes and a full mouth.

"I'm sure he wouldn't mind if he could see how wonderfully you're doing. I'll be gone from about seven to ten."

She opened her mouth wide so that I could see the peach in her mouth. "Where y'goin?"

I took a deep breath. "Kathryn has offered to cook dinner for me. Beef tenderloin—my favorite."

145

She shut her mouth, puckered up her lips, and pressed masticated peach out in a narrow string.

"You look like a baboon," I said.

"C'mon, haf sum," she said, puckering her purple lips and extruding more orange strands onto her shirt, her wife-beater.

"That's gross," I said. "Now you look like a defecating baboon—"

She was on me in a second. She charged with amazing quickness, the masticated peach dangling out of her mouth and dripping down her chin. She jumped, knees first, into my lap and tried to force her mouth onto mine. I grabbed her by her shoulders and bobbed my head from side to side to avoid the thrusts of her fruity face. She feinted and faked with her mouth like a boxer dodging blows and ultimately managed to scrape her lips across my head, leaving a slug-like trail of peach at the corner of my right eye.

Thinking that my groan of protest had sufficiently acknowledged my defeat and that the game was over, I released my defensive grip on her shoulders. She seemed to relax but then thrust forward again and forced her peach-laden tongue into my mouth.

"*Oh, yes!*" she roared with laughter as she scurried back to her sofa, wiping her forearm across her mouth and chin. As she looked back to gloat, I sprung from my chair and lunged for her, but she was too quick. She jumped over the sofa before I could catch her; I raced around it. Both of us sock-footed, we skated around the dining room table three times and then through the kitchen and living room before she finally hit a dead end in the hallway near the bathroom.

Pinning her against the wall with one arm, I used the other to grab the tail of her undershirt and spit out the peach I still held in my mouth. "You are terrible," I said unconvincingly.

"And you love it!" she sang.

"I do not."

"And you love me," she said.

I looked deeply into her copper-flecked eyes.

"Be sure and tell that to Kathryn tomorrow," she said, smiling. "It's time she knew about us."

TWENTY-THREE

THAT NEXT evening, I was already a half-hour late for dinner with Kathryn when I arrived home to change clothes. Dean Schramm, of all people, had stopped by my office in Garrison Hall with several VIPs and had asked that I sign their copies of *Reelect Tom Jefferson*. As I walked up to the front door of my house, hoping to be showered, dressed, and on my way to Kathryn's as quickly as possible, I wondered with some anxiety what Layla's state of mind would be. It didn't take long to find out.

The dining room table was set with blue and gold china that Helen's parents had given us as a wedding present. I hadn't seen it in over a decade. Wouldn't, in fact, have known where to find it. A dozen candles of various colors and fragrances flickered. I did not see Layla, but as I neared the table, I leaned over and grasped the bottle of red wine from it. It was a label I had never seen before—Lafayette. It was made in Louisiana, but I had little doubt that Layla had confused it with the Lafite Rothschild, the fine French wine that I had told her was the best I had ever tasted.

I then noticed the smells emanating from the kitchen—most notably the deep, wooden vapor of well-seasoned beef. I crept there silently, looking for Layla around each turn. I opened the oven door and studied the string-wrapped tube of brown beef floating in its own juices, surrounded by freshly cut vegetables.

On the cooktop above, covered with aluminum foil, was a glass dish. I peeked under a corner of the wrap—au gratin potatoes. Beef tenderloin and au gratin potatoes—my favorite. Lying open next to the glass dish was a cookbook.

* * *

"Surprise!" Her voice was tenuous.

I turned slowly to face her and my heart jumped. Though she wore her customary faded jeans, she also had on a pair of black suede boots and a red blazer with a white turtleneck underneath. The ensemble gave her something of a fox-hunting look. More startling was her hair. I was not sure if the proper term was a bun or beehive, but it was spectacular. Only a few rebellious tendrils curled out of the tall nest, though more threatened to topple with every move of her head.

The combination of boots and tall hair made her seem not only taller but slimmer if that was possible. Her neck and jaw line, unobscured by her hair, drew attention to a face of absolute symmetry and perfection. Her lipstick (her nails were *always* the same color as her lipstick) was a brilliant red—just the color of her blazer. Her lips were full, and I admit that at that instant, I wanted nothing in the world so badly as to kiss them.

I remember that vividly because, despite what Ben Frizell or Kathryn or even Layla might have imagined in their own carnal minds—despite what so many others would later callously assume—that moment was the first moment at which I had an abject physical longing for Layla Sommers. It was also the first time I fully realized the power she held over me. Perhaps it had always been there, somewhere in my subconscious, but at that moment, my back to the oven, I remember wanting nothing so much as to kiss those red lips.

Was that twisted? Perverted? Wanting to kiss this girl who reminded me of my daughter, for God's sake?

Perhaps. But she was not Randi. She was a woman whom I was beginning to realize I needed in some powerful but hidden way. She was a person I had come to feel comfortable with in my study at night, who brought vitality into my life. She was a woman in whom I could confide things. *Anything.* She was a woman I could laugh with and who, as Kathryn had warned, seemed to worship me. Was that such a bad thing? If it was, then bad things can feel very, very good.

Of course, she may also have been a woman who was trying to seduce me. However, in that effort, she would fail. No matter how much I wanted to kiss her, I was still a rational man, and I was not going to throw away a comfortable lifetime with Kathryn for a moment of ecstasy with Layla.

Layla stood like a prom girl wondering whether her dress-up effort looked adult or absurd, simultaneously craving and fearing my reaction. "I'm sorry I've never cooked dinner for you before, Travis," she said hesitantly. "It's your favorite . . ."

"So I see," I began. "This is really unbelievable. But you do re-member that I'm seeing Kathryn . . ."

"You can *eat* first, can't you?" she asked.

"I told you that Kathryn is cooking . . ."

"How stupid of me not to cook for you before."

"Layla, I never expected you . . ." I could tell by the redden-ing of her face that a meltdown of Chernobyl proportions was but a word away. "Of course, I'll eat," I said. "How could I resist this fabulous meal?"

She smiled broadly and ushered me to my seat, refusing to let me help with the serving. Though she claimed to have little expe-rience with cooking, she balanced the timing of heating, serving, and pouring remarkably well. Before we began eating, she even proposed a toast. Her voice quavered, and the raised glass of Lafayette in her hand shook ever so slightly as she spoke:

Our lives may be short, or they may be long,
They may be here tomorrow, or they may be gone.
All we can hope for in the end,
Is to say that we made at least one friend.
To my friend . . .

The meal was delicious, though we found conversation awkward. What was there to talk about? My evening ahead with Kathryn? The fact that Layla would be moving out on Sunday? The fact that I would be moving out only two weeks after that? That Preston Street would be a memory?

"Dinner was wonderful," I finally told her. "Now I've *got* to get over to Kathryn's."

"Sure," Layla said. "I'll do the dishes and take care of the dogs. You'll be back by ten?"

"Yes," I promised. "We'll talk when I get back."

"Are you sure you wouldn't just rather spend the night at Kathryn's?" she asked. "I mean, Jesus, I'll be fine, and you guys haven't spent a night together since I moved in. You guys must be horny as hell!"

"We should probably not discuss that—"

"Are you reinstating my gag order, Travis?"

Her jaw tensed and she bit her lower lip. The signs were unmistakable; just like that, she was ready to implode.

"Layla, please don't do this, not tonight."

"I'm just saying I don't want to be the one who prevents Kathryn from getting laid. God knows she could probably use it. God knows *I* could!"

"That's enough, Layla! Stop it right now."

"My God, Travis, it just occurred to me that while I'm here doing your dishes and feeding your goddamn dogs, you'll be fucking another woman! How would you feel if those roles were reversed?"

"How would I *feel*? Layla, you and I are not—Please, *please* stop this. Things have been going so well."

She stood and yanked off her red jacket. She pulled a linchpin from her hair that sent it splashing down over her shoulders like a copper waterfall.

"Say, I've got an idea," she said, her voice suddenly tinged with bitterness. "Why don't you fuck me before you go?" Her eyes flashed pure hatred. "That way, when you're fucking Kathryn, you can compare the two of us—"

"Godammit, Layla, why are you doing this?"

"Careful, Travis—Rule Number Two." She turned abruptly and strode to her room, throwing her red blazer through the doorway in front of her, slamming the door behind her.

"Layla!" I shouted, following her. Loud music erupted from her room. "Don't shut me out!"

*　*　*

I quickly threw on some clean slacks and my blue blazer before knocking on Layla's door. The music still resonated and she offered no response. Finally, having long run out of time and patience, and my anger rising, I turned the knob of her door hard and pushed. To my surprise, it was unlocked.

My heart sank when I saw her room. In a gesture of privacy, I hadn't looked in there since the day she had moved in, and in stark contrast to the meticulous job she had done in keeping the rest of my house neat and orderly, her room was a disaster. Her clothes were strewn across the floor along with newspapers, textbooks, dirty towels, fast-food wrappers, and Styrofoam containers. Her sheets and comforter (the rose pattern I had bought for her) were piled in disarray on the floor in the corner. In the middle of the mess was a wooden frame identical to the one in the study containing the picture of Randi. I walked over the clutter to the center of the room and picked up the frame.

The picture in it was of me.

"I'm engaged to the woman," I said, quietly, laying the frame down. Layla lay face down on the bed, sobbing. "She's invested four years in me. She agreed to let you stay here. I *owe* her one dinner and you simply have to learn to deal with that."

She slowly turned her head toward me. Her face was tear-stained. Though I was prepared for one, there would be no further attack. "I didn't mean to pick a fight," she said. "I just wanted to cook for you . . . I'm so sorry, Travis."

I stepped over more debris and sat down on the edge of her bed. I put a hand on her shoulder. "Apology accepted," I said, and in some way, I thought we had crossed an important hurdle.

I started to stand but she gripped my arm forcefully. "Travis, what if I'm not ready to leave on Sunday?"

"Look," I said, "you've got to start building a life of your own and the sooner the better. What I want you to understand—for your sake and mine—is that the only way I'll be able to remain a part of your life is if you and Kathryn can find a way to coexist."

She released her grip and dried her eyes with the hem of her shirt. "She's still coming over Saturday evening?"

"That's the plan, and it's very important that you make a good impression."

"I will," Layla said. "I'll make an impression."

"A *good* impression, Layla. We'll talk when I get home. I won't be late, I promise."

I leaned over and picked up a stuffed lop-earned bunny from the floor. Bringing it close to my face, for a moment I was jarred by the familiar smell—Randi. I handed it to Layla, who pressed it close to her face.

The phone rang, and we both knew it would be Kathryn wondering why I was running late. Layla looked at me, bit her lip, and nodded bravely.

* * *

Halfway to Kathryn's house, an unwelcome memory shook me. The last time I had seen that lop-eared bunny was after Randi's death when I had packed all of her belongings into boxes.

Right after I had tried to kill myself.

TWENTY-FOUR

AFTER waking from my eleven-day coma, I remained in the hospital in Lubbock for another two weeks. Ben had returned to Austin but called every day. Helen's parents came from Colorado City several times to visit. They never asked about the accident, and they told me that Randi's funeral had been a beautiful affair, presided over by Reverend Banks, the same man who had married Helen and me, the same man who'd buried Helen. They told me that Helen and Randi were now side by side, both in God's green Earth, and in Heaven. They presumed I would be visiting the cemetery as soon as I was able.

On the day of my release, Ben arrived with his van. He talked the entire way back to Austin, telling several stories two and three times. I remained silent, trying desperately to be strong, yet aware of the inevitable collapse I would suffer when I walked into my house on Preston Street and found it empty and void of Randi's presence.

I was too weak to help lift Ben and his wheelchair up onto my front porch, so he had to sit outside as I made my way into my house. "Thanks for everything," I said as I handed him a glass of iced tea. "But I think I need to be alone for a while."

At that moment, however, Puddy came over with a dozen red roses and Randi's puppy, TJ. TJ raced across the floor and into Randi's room, up onto her bed as if he was looking for her.

"I've got to go," Ben shouted from outside.

I went out front and wheeled him to his van.

"Travis," he said, "it took a long time for me to learn to deal with my losses. There were some very, very tough times. You're going to experience the same. The key is not to be alone when you're at your lowest. You know what I mean?"

"I'm not going to kill myself, Ben, if that's what you mean."

"If you even have that thought, even just a flash, even if the thought is that you *won't* do it, call me. Call me that second. Okay?"

"I'll be fine, Ben. I just need some time alone."

Puddy was sitting on my living room sofa when I went back into the house, and she gave the impression that she was planning to stay.

"I think I need to rest now," I said to her, offering her a hand.

"You shout if you need anything," she said.

* * *

Moments after Ben and Puddy left, I found myself standing in the middle of Randi's room. Her bed, her Barbie sheets, were still unmade from the morning we had left for Lubbock. The lop-eared bunny's head lay on her pillows. Her crayon drawings lined the walls, and Barbie paraphernalia covered the floor. Even so, at that moment, I thought of Helen as much as of Randi. No, I guess what I was doing was thinking of them both, and no matter how sorry I felt for myself, I felt sorrier for them not having known each other. I wondered whether the joy Helen would have felt during Randi's life would have been worth the pain of losing her.

I sat on Randi's bed. TJ, following a burst of energy, was sound asleep on the floor, his legs splayed. It was suddenly quiet and I felt utterly alone. It was the first time in my life that I had ever asked the question of myself: Why would I want to wake up in the morning? No one would be there with me. No one was depending on me, needing me. I had no one to hold, no one to love. And the task of ever getting to that point again with someone—with another woman or another child—seemed impossible to fathom.

This may sound melodramatic, but to me it was a purely objective assessment of the energy I had left, the effort I was willing to make to rebuild a life worth living.

Without a lot of conscious thought or agonizing over the details, I walked down the short hall to my bedroom, opened the drawer in the bedside table, and pulled out my father's .38 caliber revolver. It seems odd, but even then, even as I returned to Randi's room, I wasn't frantic or angry. My actions were matter-of-fact, and the sole question before me was whether I wanted to try to rebuild or whether that effort exceeded what remained of me.

As I entered Randi's room, TJ lifted his head slightly but quickly went back to sleep. I stood in the center of the room and placed the barrel of the revolver against my head, and inexplicably, tears began flowing. I suddenly saw Helen in all her beauty and remembered the day we'd made love on the hardwood floors and gushed about her pregnancy. Then, just as suddenly, I saw Randi in all her brilliance, and I felt an amazing sense of tranquility, of peace. A deep sensation of warmth spread throughout my body.

I pulled the trigger.

I heard a click.

The gun didn't fire.

*   *   *

I staggered back to Randi's bed, weak in the knees. I lay down there for a while—hours, I think. When I awoke, I was disconcerted. What was I doing in Randi's room? Why was my gun on her bedside table?

The picture finally came into focus, and at that moment, I was glad to still be alive. I thought at the time that I would turn my energy toward my writing. I also remembered that my father had once told me, "To avoid accidents, always leave the first chamber empty. That way you'll have to pull the trigger twice if you *really* want to kill something."

I got off the bed and returned the gun to my bedside table. I went to the garage and collected two dozen empty cardboard book boxes into which I placed every crayon drawing, every Barbie doll, and every Barbie sheet—even the lop-eared bunny.

*   *   *

As I punched in the codes to gain access to Kathryn's gated community, I wondered what else Layla had found in those boxes.

TWENTY-FIVE

KATHRYN looked lovely, if a bit overdressed for an evening at home. She wore a long skirt with boots peaking out from under and an evening jacket over a sleeveless brown sweater. She also wore several necklaces and bracelets, and a gold and diamond butterfly brooch. In fact, I was struck by just how much *stuff* she wore. Her hair was perfectly coiffed, as always, but not without the coarse effect of extensive spraying.

When she had called, I had said I would be at her place in fifteen minutes; surprisingly, she made no inquiries about the reason for my tardiness.

After an awkward minute of silence, she said, "We'll have to get you a new jacket for the wedding parties." I nodded. Even I could admit that my blue blazer's best days were behind it, and I decided not to mention that the dry cleaners had been unable to get Layla's bloodstains out of the tweed jacket.

As we settled onto her white leather sofa, I noticed a fine line at the top of Kathryn's forehead where a layer of some sort of makeup stopped. I also noticed a bit of cruddy material lodged between her eyelashes and silently cursed myself for noticing. As I smelled the rich French fragrance she wore, it occurred to me that

I had no idea what this woman whom I was about to marry actually smelled like. The actual woman. I knew what Randi had smelled like. In fact, that smell still swirled around in my brain from having picked up the lop-eared bunny from Layla's floor. Every parent knows the smell that rubs off like magic dust on pillows and stuffed animals.

I also knew what Layla smelled like, but Kathryn's presence always brought a potpourri of smells from lotions, perfumes, shampoos, hair sprays, laundry detergents, bathroom deodorizers . . . Was that simply a function of age? Are the smells and jewels and layers an attempt to cover up or distract? Cover up what? Distract from what?

I fought to banish those thoughts from my mind and concentrate on Kathryn. I knew better than to compare her with Layla in any way; it was both unfair and deadly to the purpose of the evening.

I also knew that such comparisons would play directly into Kathryn's great wound from the past. I was not going to allow my mind to participate in that crass and grossly unfair game. Then again, try telling someone *not* to imagine a polka-dot elephant! The very effort of avoidance only serves to sharpen the image.

Even as I studied Kathryn, I was aware on some level that my thoughts were also self-reflective. Why does our generation try so hard to stay young? Why are we so loathe to admit that every generation gets a turn in the sun and that a long shadow was inexorably falling over ours?

Yet observing her—observing me—I had no second thoughts about marrying her. The evidence was overwhelming that she was good for me. Still, as the day of our wedding approached, what I'd have to leave behind loomed larger. Foremost among them was that I was going to miss my house on Preston Street. Preston was the place of all of my memories, wonderful and tragic. It was the house that had seemed so full of promise during those first days of Helen's pregnancy, until the devastating news. It had been the place of my efforts to properly raise Randi—hard but infinitely re-warding work. I had initially thought that my losses could only be eased by selling the house, but every time I had let an agent put a sign in the yard, I found myself taking it back down.

And then, there was the matter of my dogs . . .

Kathryn was right, of course. We would have to move into her house. Mine was too small, too crowded with books, and had only one tiny bathroom. Kathryn's house was over 4,000 square feet, newly constructed, and had several bathrooms the size of my study.

*   *   *

Kathryn retrieved a silver wine cooler containing a bottle of cham-pagne. She opened it with a pop and filled two glasses. She sat down next to me and placed her hand on my thigh.

"What are we celebrating?"

"T minus 3," she said. "Here's to Saturday and Layla's last night." Kathryn lifted her glass for a toast.

"Indeed," I said with mixed emotions as our glasses clinked.

Kathryn's mood showed little of the wariness one might have expected after our infrequent visits over the past three weeks. It was as though she didn't want to ask how things were, so much as to make them the way she wanted them to be by sheer force of will.

She proposed a few more toasts—one being to Flo Landers, who had persuaded the buyers to reschedule the closing on Pre-ston rather than sue me. She also shared some wedding details, such as the fact that a particular string quartet she wanted had come available. It was, she had said, just an omen as to how great things were going to go from that point forward.

When she asked me if I was hungry, I saw no way out but to explain what had happened with Layla. I left out most of the de-tails, but even so, Kathryn shook her head and said of Layla, "What a pathetic young thing."

After her third glass of champagne, the fact that her dinner would go uneaten didn't seem to bother Kathryn; it became clear there was only one thing remaining on her mind. She clung to me tightly, acting a bit more intoxicated than I believed to be the case. Though we hadn't made love in almost a month, I suspected her urgency was as much a confirmation of our future as it was a physical need. It was as if the mere act of my making love to her would vanquish any doubts she may have conjured up about Layla and me. I had never before considered that making love to a woman might bear such profound proof; it was a dispiriting thought.

Kathryn grasped my arm, laid her head on my shoulder, and smiled up at me. I was struck by the weight of her head. I also noticed how thick her fingers were as she wrapped them around my arm. I had never before thought of Kathryn as a "big" woman, though I knew of her weight battles from the past. But as she nestled up to me, I couldn't help thinking about the diminutive cotton shirt and microscopic panties of Layla's, which I had folded. I remembered holding them up, looking at them, unable to envision how they could fit onto the girl who owned them.

A physical comparison of the two—my promise to myself of not going down that slippery slope was quickly disintegrating—would show Kathryn to be about 5'6," and about 155 pounds. Layla, I would guess, is about 5'8" and 120 pounds. Were they really so different?

I knew they were, for I had held them both in my arms, and that's what didn't make sense to me. Layla had the lightness of a bird to her frame, as if her bones were hollow so that she might take wing. Her skin literally glowed. Kathryn was solid. A land animal, grounded. Her skin was cloudy, the exposed portions often powdered.

Why was I doing this to myself? Why was I contemplating the ravages of time?

Kathryn kept her head on my shoulder as she pulled me farther down the leather sofa. The crispness of her sculpted hair scratched the side of my face. She sat up for a moment and grasped a remote control device from the table nearby. Instantly, the room was filled with a Kenny G. love song. I've always hated Kenny G., but was not unaware that throughout my somewhat laughable dating life he had become an unwitting ally. Kathryn unbuttoned two buttons on my shirt and slipped her hand inside, massaging my chest and plucking lightly at scattered gray hairs.

"I've missed you," she said, turning my head with her free hand and kissing me heavily on the lips.

"I've missed you too," I said when she finally allowed me a breath.

She placed a hand on my crotch. "And we're about to find out just how much you've missed me, aren't we Dr. Harrison?"

The devastating thought suddenly hit me: What if I couldn't perform? The thought was exacerbated by the fact that, tonight of all nights, Kathryn would take my failure personally and undoubtedly blame it on Layla's presence in my life. The fallout from that, I knew, would be disastrous. This was not a helpful train of thought.

"It's been a quite a while, in case you haven't noticed," she said. "You have noticed, haven't you, Travis?"

"Of course," I said. "That's why I may need to take it . . . a little slow. The motor has been turned off for a while."

"I'm sure I can find a key," she smiled, squeezing. She then stood and reached her hand out to me. "Come with me, Dr. Harrison." She took my hand and led me into her bedroom.

Like most new lovers, Kathryn and I had acted out our Hollywood roles at the outset of our relationship—romancing, seducing, teasing, taunting, undressing the other. But as we had moved closer to marriage, perhaps in inevitable preparation for the future, all of that had given way to a mechanical make-ready that seldom ever varied. We would undress ourselves instead of the other, and would do so as quickly as practical—in the dark—before plunging under the covers, where hugs and pats and pecks would eventually satisfy.

But that night, as I stood there in her bedroom, it was evident that Kathryn had a return to romance in mind. "Undress me," she ordered as we stood beside her bed. There was a crack of light from the bathroom, enough to prevent our stumbling. We had both left our jackets in the other room, so I began by pulling her sleeveless sweater over her head and her outstretched arms. I tossed it onto the floor as she reached around her neck and released her several necklaces. She also removed her earrings as I began negotiating her cumbersome black bra. She had trained me on both front and rear catches, but in the dim light, I was not certain which type this was. I began fumbling (yes, like a cave frog!) at the back where a broad swath of elastic was overlapped at the edges by small rolls of flesh.

"In the front," she whispered.

But of course. Acting on this information, I popped free the three-latch contraption and held her bra—a medieval-like combination of fabric, elastic, and metal ribbing—in my hand. From what I could tell, Layla only owned one bra and seldom wore it. It had shown up in the laundry one week; I could have stuffed it in a shot glass. And there I was, thinking of that as I held Kathryn's bra aloft like a proud hunter holds a dead pheasant.

I caressed Kathryn's breasts (more ample, it seemed, since her return from Germany), while contemplating the removal of her remaining clothes. With the concentration, if not the dexterity, of a safecracker, I unlatched and unzipped her skirt in the back and let it fall to her feet. She stepped out of it, kicked it aside, and removed her boots, tossing each in an opposite direction. I was humbled to see that there remained an imposing array of silk garments, held in place by still more buttons and intricate hardware. She wore a black lace thong and a black garter belt with garters attached to matching hose. I'm sure the word she had in mind for all this was *erotic;* the word that came to my mind was *daunting.*

I kneeled and successfully popped free the four fasteners on each leg, pulling her individual stockings off one leg at a time. All that remained was her garter belt and thong, but when I placed my thumbs inside the waistband, her hands clamped down to stop me.

"Your turn," she whispered. I stood, my knees cracking loudly, and she began to undress me.

She removed my shirt and stroked the hairs on my chest. I bent over and took off my shoes and socks; she removed my slacks. I was left standing there in white boxers. She hugged me tightly, pressing her lone remaining article of clothing against mine. She reached her hand down, and when she had confirmed that there was more work to do, she continued to hug, to gyrate, to rub.

I began to sweat.

As I watched her toil in the dark, it struck me that I could describe Layla's body more accurately than Kathryn's. After all, I had held Layla's naked body in my arms and had stanched cuts on its various parts, including her shaved labia. I had allowed my hand to be briefly placed on the firm perfection of her breast and had felt her soft, soapy nakedness in my lap. I had seen her copper hair covering her bare shoulders and nothing else.

As I put my arms around Kathryn and rubbed her back, for a moment I recalled holding Layla. I didn't mean to—I didn't *want* to, it just happened, and I knew I had let the most unwelcome of guests into Kathryn's bedroom, and I knew at that instant that the evening was doomed. Kathryn, regrettably, did not yet know, as evidenced by the unending minutes that followed during which she knelt and attended me with the determination of an ER doctor resuscitating her own child.

"I'm sorry," I said at last, backing away and leaving her on her knees. The light from the bathroom reflected off beads of sweat on her brow. "It must be the stress of all that's going on."

"Goddamn you, Travis," Kathryn said almost under her breath. "I can't believe you're letting that girl do this to our lives." Even as she railed at me, she offered her hand and I helped her to her feet. We sat on the edge of her bed.

"I'm not letting her do anything to our lives," I said. "I just have so much on my mind. So many questions."

"Really?" Kathryn said. "I only have one. Have you screwed her?"

"Of course not," I said.

"Has she tried to seduce you?"

"No. Well, maybe she has. But I'm not available, Kathryn. I'm engaged to be married to a woman I love. I understand how good we are for each other and I'm not about to sacrifice that for a short-sighted act of idiocy." She said nothing.

"But I can't deny that Layla has tapped into something deep inside of me, something I shut down long ago. I'm afraid that if I try to shut it down again it will destroy me."

Kathryn looked at me quizzically. "You're talking about Randi?"

"Yes. Ever since I first heard her voice again that night in Layla's apartment, bits and pieces of the accident have been coming back to me. I know now that before I lost consciousness I managed to crawl out of my car." My voice started cracking, and Kathryn put her arm around me. "I cried out for Randi and I heard her voice. I crawled as fast as I could through the red dust and smoke in her direction." Kathryn pulled me closer, but her touch was stiff.

I stood and paced in front of her bed, running my hands through my hair and shaking my head with uncertainty. "Do you ever feel old?" I asked her. She looked at me as if confused. "Do you ever feel as if the best is behind us?"

Kathryn pulled a quilt over her and turned on a dim bedside lamp. "I suppose I should resent that question when issued by a man who is about to marry me," she said, smiling. "I think, Travis, that the best times are those in which we feel most ful-filled, and I see no age limitations on that. I thought your writing served that purpose."

"I thought so too," I said. "Until the memories of Randi resur-faced. Nothing else that I've done compares to the fulfillment I felt at being a father. Nothing comes close.

"Do you remember when you said that you wouldn't fight for me?"

"I didn't mean that—"

"No, you don't need to explain. My point is that you said you didn't have the energy left to go through that again. That's what I mean when I ask about feeling old. I mean, do you ever think that you just might not have the energy to rebuild?"

"It's been a decade, Travis," Kathryn said. "I will never ask that you forget about Randi, but I think you must come to terms with her. For yourself, if not for us. If Layla has stirred this up in you, then perhaps it's for the best. The question is, what will you do with it?"

"There's something about the accident," I said. "Something my brain just refuses to allow me to see." I looked at the clock on the bedside table.

"You'd better go on," Kathryn said. "Tomorrow is T minus 2."

I got dressed, kissed her on the forehead, and left.

TWENTY-SIX

WHEN I returned home, I parked my car on the street behind Layla's car and sat quietly for a moment. Humidity blanketed the streetlights in yellow shrouds, and a few neighborhood dogs barked.

When at last I entered the house, TJ was waiting patiently for me inside the front door. I rubbed his ears and asked him where Layla was. I went straight to her door to tell her I was home and knocked softly. "Layla?"

"Come in," she said.

I opened the door. My mouth fell open.

It was Randi's room.

Every Barbie doll was in its place, including those who rode in cars or busily prepared meals in Barbie houses. Stuffed animals were arranged along the foot of the bed, as if they were holding a meeting. The lop-eared bunny was front and center. Posters of butterflies and rabbits were in their original places on the walls, next to the many crayon drawings of Randi's. There were photographs of Randi, of Helen, and of me. The bed was covered with a Barbie comforter, under which I was quite certain there were Barbie sheets.

There was also a picture of Randi standing in her room, the room that Layla had re-created. In the picture, a puppy was at her side. TJ.

The boxes that had held all the items were closed and neatly stacked in a corner. Layla sat cross-legged on the floor in her red and gold silk robe. She looked up at me in a way I had never seen her look before. She appeared to be in some degree of pain, but her look was more a reflection of my pain. She was sending a look of aching sympathy.

She stood and started weeping. "I can't believe you lost her," she said.

I felt as if I had been hit in the chest by a sledgehammer as I sat on the edge of her bed. I clasped my fingers behind my neck, trying to catch a deep breath. Layla sat down next to me and put one slim arm around my shoulder. She said nothing, but at the moment of her touch I, too, began to sob.

"Randi was everything to me," I choked on the words I had waited so long to say. I had no choice now—I couldn't stop myself. I saw a stack of photographs on the floor and picked one up. It was Randi playing with TJ as a puppy. Randi was lying on the ground holding TJ upside down on her stomach. His legs were splayed, displaying his fat, spotted pink tummy. Randi smiled a toothless grin, her reddish hair and freckles framing her beautiful face.

"We could have been sisters," Layla said.

I groaned, but of course, she was right. "I know. She would have been just your age."

"I've been looking at you like a man I'm attracted to, and you've been looking at me like a daughter. No wonder all the weirdness. That helps my ego a bit."

"Randi was so smart," I began, fighting back more tears. "Funny too. Funny even to adults, you know, a very adult sense of humor. Witty. Yes, she was an incredible wit. Very talented at music too . . . and Scrabble . . . jigsaws . . ."

Layla began to massage my shoulders and neck.

"It took some time, but I eventually got over Helen, as much as was possible. I know that sounds clinical, cold even, but the death of an adult can eventually be rationalized. But nothing eases the death of a child. I grieved for Helen for years, but the day finally came, with the exception of holidays and anniversaries—things like that—when I could deal with it.

"Randi has been so much harder. I raised her, gave her everything I had. For the first few years after her death, I would park across from schools and observe the kids her age. I would read parenting and child development magazines and think about all the things she would be doing. All the things *I* would be doing. I tried to imagine how she would have changed, how she would have turned out. What she might have looked like."

I took a long hard look at Layla. At that moment, she demanded nothing of me and was not going to patronize me with easy answers where there were none to be had. She seemed willing to be whatever I needed her to be. Do *anything* I needed her to do. I knew that, but at that moment all I needed her to do was to listen.

"You were right, Layla. Randi didn't die instantly." It was becoming clear in my mind even as I spoke. "She suffered." Layla's hand gripped my shoulder. "I heard her cries and crawled to her side before I lost consciousness. For all these years, even while not acknowledging that consciously, I guess I've been wondering deep inside if I could have saved her, if I should have done something differently. Consciously, I've always taken Ben's word for it until—until I pulled you from your tub."

"It reminded you of the accident?"

"Yes. Your blood on my hands, the smell, the pressure of not knowing what to do."

Layla stopped massaging my shoulder, moving her hand to my chin. She grasped it lightly and turned my face toward hers. She pressed her wet lips against my lips.

I'm not even sure I would call it a kiss. Neither of us moved our lips—certainly not our tongues. We weren't twisting our heads and necks like soulful young lovers. There was no move-ment at all, just a warm, healing touch, an intimacy that neither of us wanted to end.

Finally, I pulled away from her slightly and took a deep breath. "What are we doing, Layla?" I asked quietly, looking around the room.

She wiped away tears that had escaped down her cheeks. In a choked voice, she said, "We're resurrecting Randi."

*　*　*

We sat silently together on the edge of her bed. Then, after a time, she arose and peeled the Barbie comforter and top sheet back, and nestled into bed. She curled up in a parenthetical posture, facing me. She blinked hard as I studied her.

There was no doubt in my mind that my relationship with Layla had just changed forever, even though I couldn't have imag-ined the consequences. She was the only other person on Earth who knew the truth about Randi and, therefore, the only person on Earth who knew the truth about me. More revealingly, she was the only one who I wanted to know. Our bond was powerful and sobering. I would say it was a bond at least as intense as sexual in-timacy, but in truth, it may have gone beyond that. What I was feeling for Layla at that moment was not genital but umbilical. In my awakening, a connection between us was silently established that was as nurturing as that conduit of nutrients that curls out of a mother's womb and into her child.

I got on my knees beside her bed and rested my forearms on the mattress. I pulled the comforter snugly over her. I breathed deeply, and my eyes pinched shut. "I miss Randi so much," I moaned, words so long unexpressed. "I loved being her father!"

Almost instinctively, Layla cradled my head with her hands.

She placed her hand on my blazer and tugged slightly. She threw the covers back with her other hand and patted the mat-tress, encouraging me to get off my knees and lie down beside her.

I worked my way under the comforter and lay facing her, our fore-heads, knees, and feet touching, her breasts lightly touching my jacket through her silk robe.

She wrapped her arms around me tightly and we held each other and sobbed in unison, as if drawing on a single pair of lungs.

"I held her," I said at last, pulling away from her slightly. "I crawled through the smoke and fire and red dust and found her and held her. She was crying and saying over and over, 'Daddy, please make it stop hurting.' I wrapped my arms around her as I screamed for help, but my hand disappeared into a gaping hole in her back.

"'I love you, Randi,'" I said, "knowing those were the last words she would hear. She died in my arms."

Neither Layla nor I spoke after that. I placed my cheek against hers, my stubble beard against her satin softness, and as we held each other tight, our faces were so warm and moist that it was im-possible to tell which tears were hers and which were mine.

*   *   *

I awoke the next morning to yet another warm, wet sensation—TJ's tongue. I opened my eyes and stared into his black nose, yellow-gray muzzle, and deep brown eyes, inches from my face. I stared at my watch until the numbers came into focus; it was a few minutes after seven. I thought of going back to sleep for a while but decided instead to get out of bed for some coffee and the morning papers.

I slid my legs over the side of my bed, only to realize that it wasn't my bed. A lithe arm draped across me.

I sat up abruptly, looking behind me to see Layla's eyes peep open. I stared down at myself; my blazer and pants were a wrin-kled mess, but at least they were *on*.

"You know there was nothing you could have done," Layla said groggily. "For Randi, I mean."

"Yes, I know that now," I said.

"At least she died in your arms, knowing she was loved."

"Yes, at least that." I walked quietly away from Layla's bed but stopped in the doorway. I turned again to face her. "Layla," I said. "Thank you for last night."

"And you don't even have to send flowers," she smiled, pulling the lop-eared bunny tight under her chin. "You see, I'm good for you, Travis."

I pulled her door shut behind me, showered, and made coffee. I made an effort to read the morning papers, but I could not clear my mind of two debilitating thoughts: Saturday night would be Layla's last in my house. And, she was right. She *was* good for me.

Which is what made it so hard for me to understand why she was about to destroy my life.

TWENTY-SEVEN

AT THE Cactus Café, I stared at Ben as he sipped on a martini and rolled an olive between his fingers. This time, we were there at my invitation, as neither of us had business on campus that Saturday. I was seeking words of wisdom prior to the night's celebration.

"Castration, did you say?" Ben laughed.

"Celebration," I defended meekly.

I told him that Layla's psychologist, Dr. Nickemeyer, and Dr. Bernard, had agreed that Layla could move back into her old apartment. I had paid to have it cleaned.

"I've told her that she can call me anytime," I said, "but also that it is crucial she make a good impression on Kathryn tonight."

"So the wedding is *still* on?"

"I think so. I hope so."

"Do you really? Try not to sound so excited."

"Ben, marrying Kathryn will be good for me. It will be a comfortable and healthy life."

"So Kathryn is sort of like—broccoli. Good for you."

I smiled. "I thought for sure you were going to say like a peach."

"And Layla?"

"I don't know. She gets so low and then so high, and often I feel like she's starting to take me with her on that same wild ride."

172

"Like heroin."

"Well, I wouldn't know, but perhaps."

"So it's broccoli or heroin."

"Ben, there's no choice to make, but I can't just cast Layla aside. She has forced me to see some things. Ben, Randi lived for a while after the accident. She didn't die instantly. I made it to her side, but I couldn't help her. I don't just want to help Layla, I *need* to help Layla."

I told him the details about Randi and watched as compassion flooded his features. He shook his head in disbelief and seemed as though he wanted to apologize for having gotten it wrong, but I waved off that absurd idea.

"The three of us will share a little toast before Kathryn and I go to her reception at the chancellor's house. Then, I'll return home and spend a late night talking with Layla and wishing her well. On Sunday, she'll move out."

"The lamb and the lion together," Ben said somberly. "Damn thing is, I'm not sure which is which and neither, I think, are you.

"We'll be together for less than an hour," I said. "Just a quick toast. Surely we can make it through that."

"Dr. Harrison's two women in the same room. That's rich," Ben smiled. "Thousand bucks to be there!"

TWENTY-EIGHT

As KATHRYN approached the front porch, her big Mercedes hogging the curb, she stopped abruptly. I leaned over in my tuxedo and peered out the front window to watch her. She studied the porch and the neatly tended flowerbeds surrounding it. She craned her head upward and took in the hanging baskets. She looked at the newly painted bench swing and small statuettes.

In retrospect, of course, it does seem like evidence of my insanity that I thought Kathryn and Layla could coexist, even for a minute. Somehow that crystallized as I watched Kathryn outside my house shaking her head in disbelief. I turned with a sudden new sense of anxiety toward the bathroom where Layla had been ensconced for an eternity.

I scanned the inside of my house and blanched.

It was only because of the stunned look on Kathryn's face that I suddenly realized how radically my house had changed in only four weeks under Layla's care. In addition to those items out front, there were innumerable plants inside. There were new leopard print pillows on my brown leather sofa, a centerpiece on my dining room table, several small framed paintings on previously white walls, and every book, CD, videotape, and magazine was dusted

174

and perfectly stacked or stored at neat right angles. In front of the fireplace, TJ—the real dog, not the ceramic puppy—rested comfortably on a new dog bed, images of serene green-headed mallard ducks beneath him. There were potpourri and scented candles and the ever-present residue of incense. In the study, in the center of a bookshelf, there was the picture of Randi. And, of course, Randi's room had literally been reincarnated.

I let Kathryn knock but then quickly opened the door and greeted her, kissing her on the cheek. She wore a white formal gown with sequins and an elaborate silver brooch in the impressionistic form of a swan. Her hair looked like a black ceramic beehive. Her glazed eyes looked past me into the living room and beyond, her mouth hanging slightly open. She seemed to be in a state of semishock as she continued to survey the house. "Did you two run off to Vegas and get married?" she asked quietly.

"I thought that letting her have some projects around the house . . . Dr. Bernard felt that . . . she'll probably take most of this stuff with her when she . . ."

The roar of the toilet interrupted me. It was followed by the bathroom door slamming open, and a sudden pain stabbed my chest as it occurred to me that, while I had given Layla some guidance on how to act, I had neglected to give her any on what to wear. I could only hope it was more than her wife-beater.

Kathryn's head spun around; I also turned to face Layla. She wore tight-fitting black jeans with flared bottoms that covered her black suede boots. She wore a black T-shirt that I had never seen before; it had a white dragonlike icon in the center, and it fit tightly, clinging to her slim arms and making it quite apparent that she wasn't wearing a bra.

Her nails—too long and perfect to be anything but false ones—were painted a matching black, and in one of the most curious effects I have ever seen on a woman, so were her lips. I'm not one for omens and symbolism, but as I think back, that would have been the time to get religious.

Layla's hair fell where it pleased, like bronze silk across her shoulders and back, and it occurred to me that, above all else, the gleaming reflections of a young girl's hair must be the ultimate affront to an older woman.

"You remember Layla," I said to Kathryn as Layla eased toward us. It was, of course, a horrible choice of words since, other than the regrettable meeting at Barnes & Noble, the only times that Kathryn had seen Layla were when she had been either unconscious at Layla's apartment or at the hospital pretending to be.

Predictably, Kathryn sidestepped the awkwardness by ignoring my remark and extending her firm hand to Layla. "Kathryn Orr," she said. "I've heard so much about you." I cocked my head slightly, thinking I had just heard an electric pop somewhere in my house. As I looked at the two of them together—Kathryn, in her Glenda-like good-witch dress, and Layla, almost Gothic—I wondered to what extent they had dressed not for me but for each other. Kathryn had chosen to look elegant, in command, successful. Layla had chosen, well, dark and foreboding.

Yes, there stood Kathryn, the consummate professional, so successful in her field. She of our future life together. A wonderful manager of things. A relationship with her would be one of equals, of partners, of checks and balances. And, as had already been demonstrated, it would be one of enormous intellectual productivity. It would be, quite simply, the life that I knew was the proper one for me.

And there stood Layla, a woman—a very young woman—who soared and collapsed with the turn of a phrase, who could be at once crass and tender, furious and compassionate. A woman who appeared to want me in ways I could scarcely comprehend. A life with her would be a life of—what? Roller-coaster uncertainty? Anguish? Emotional chaos?

Or a life of fulfillment and purpose?

As I watched Layla's long black nails slither out of Kathryn's grip, the odd thought struck me that this was Layla's house; Kathryn was the visitor. In an absurd way, it was as if Layla were meeting my date, poised to signal her approval or disapproval, as if Kathryn and I were off to the prom and Layla were holding the camera. I had a powerful feeling of wanting Layla to like Kathryn. I can now only shake my head in amazement when I think back on that desired outcome, wholly impossible in the world as we know it.

Like storm clouds gathering, the magnitude of the mistake I had made was becoming frighteningly apparent as events began to unfold.

"I'll get the wine," Layla said, almost casually. "Why don't you two sit in the living room?"

*   *   *

"Do you think she's ready to move out?" Kathryn whispered as Layla disappeared into the kitchen.

"Does it matter?" I said boldly.

"How often do you think you'll see her?" Kathryn asked.

"That depends on you."

"Travis," Kathryn admonished. "Look around you. You and Layla have made a *huge* emotional investment in each other. That isn't just going to end."

Before I could respond, Layla entered the room carrying a tray with three glasses and a carafe of Cabernet.

Layla poured the wine, and then Kathryn and I sat on the sofa, Layla on the brick hearth directly opposite us. TJ immediately approached her, and Layla stroked the underside of his neck with her long black nails. Kathryn placed her hand conspicuously on my thigh, and I saw Layla's eyes instantly focus on it.

A long minute of awkward silence passed during which Layla looked at me with the longing of a condemned prisoner seeking a pardon through my utterance of a few precious words, *any* words! I previewed a few sentences in my mind, but the best I could come up with dealt with the weather and football, absurd topics that would only have accentuated the discomfort.

Layla stared at her drink and continued to pet TJ aimlessly. Finally, Kathryn broke the ice. "This is good wine," she said to Layla. "What kind is it?"

Layla was no wine connoisseur, but I expected her to at least have read the label.

"The wine? It's red," Layla said coolly.

I knew at that moment that the worst lay ahead; I just didn't know how bad it would be.

* * *

"What time will you be home tonight, Travis?" Layla asked in a manner that ignored Kathryn's presence in the room.

I looked at Kathryn.

"The reception is from seven to ten," Kathryn said.

"Let's say no later than eleven," I said to Layla.

"Eleven or twelve," Kathryn added. "We might want to have a quiet drink afterward." Her hand inched up my thigh and squeezed.

Layla's spine arched. "Oh, I understand," she said. "It's just that being my last night here and all . . . I was hoping to . . ." She mindlessly stared at the wine in her glass.

Kathryn slid closer to me on the sofa, placing her right arm around my shoulders. She kissed me on the cheek. "I haven't had him to myself much lately," she said, looking over at Layla without blinking.

I felt flames erupt from the fireplace, only there was no fire burning, just Layla sitting on the hearth, her face deep red, her eyes piercing. TJ yelped and pulled away as her nails dug into the ear that she had been gently stroking. His tail between his legs, he moved back to his new bed and lay down.

I didn't know what to do. I wasn't about to embarrass Kathryn, but the expression on Layla's face gave me pause for panic; molten lava was bubbling up to the surface.

"It's nice to be so popular," I said desperately, straightening my bow tie in a feeble gesture of humor. I was trying to buy time while in search of a strategy to ward off disaster, but as I struggled, Layla cut me off at the knees.

As she looked up from her glass of wine, I saw huge tears easing down her cheeks—cheeks so flushed that they were purple and looked as though they might physically hurt. It was a frightening effect.

"I can't do this, Travis," Layla said, again speaking to me as if Kathryn weren't there. "I thought I could pretend, but I just can't go through with it."

My entire body stiffened as I leaned forward on the sofa. Though Kathryn remained by my side, she removed her arm from around me. "You can't go through with what, Layla?" I asked guardedly.

"This ruse," she said. "I know I promised you that I could—I really thought I could—but I can't. Not now that *she's* here."

Kathryn looked at me and I could only hope that my perplexed look in some way vouched for my honest confusion.

"What is it that you can't pretend, Layla?" Kathryn asked coldly.

Layla looked down and then directly at Kathryn. "That it's okay with me if Travis sleeps with other women, too."

*   *   *

I was speechless, but Kathryn was not.

"You little bitch!" Kathryn seethed, suddenly standing over Layla like a giant shadow.

For a moment, I thought I might have to break up a fight, but Layla remained seated on the hearth and began quietly crying. I had seen that sort of mood shift in her before and was hopeful that she was on the brink of an explanation . . . and an apology. I was wrong.

"Travis made me promise not to tell," Layla said, looking up at Kathryn, who still hovered over her. "But I just can't lie to you . . ."

Kathryn spun around and looked at me with an ire that only hardened my dumb paralysis. She was shaking, not so much from rage as from the effort it took to contain that rage. "Just tell me that nothing happened, Travis, and I will believe you," she said. "That's all you have to do."

"Of course nothing happened!" I blurted. "Layla, why are you doing this? Why would you want to hurt me?"

"You told me you loved me, Travis, and that you were going to leave her. Now I know that from the time you felt me up on that first night to the night we slept together in your daughter's bed all of that bullshit about caring for me was just so you could use me!" She stood, brushed by Kathryn, and walked quickly to her room.

"That is unacceptable!" I shouted. "Kathryn, she's inventing all of this—twisting things—"

"How dare you!" Kathryn raged. "Both of you!"

I started to follow Layla to her room when I saw Kathryn gathering up her purse.

"Goodbye, Travis," Kathryn said, storming toward the door.

"Kathryn, wait—God, this is a disaster. I can't believe she—"

"It's very simple, Travis," Kathryn said with an eerie calmness. "I'm willing to believe she's lying. She's obviously a very disturbed little . . . bitch! I'm leaving because I don't care to be in the same house with her. Or you."

"I made some mistakes, Kathryn, but I have not had sex with her. I swear."

"Did you touch her breasts?" The tiny muscles in her face rippled in coordinated waves.

"She placed my hand on her breast one time. I had nothing to do with—"

"Oh, she forced you? Forced you to feel her up? Please, don't insult me. Did she also force you to sleep with her?"

"I didn't have sex with her."

"But you slept with her?" Kathryn's look was of utter indignation.

"I fell asleep," I said, but my voice betrayed a guilt I could not suppress.

"In her bed?"

"We had talked about Randi—"

"In her bed? *In Randi's bed?* Was that the other night when you left me alone in *my* bed, Travis?"

I looked at her eyes and saw the hurt, but now was not the time for deceit. "Yes, it was."

"So you went from my bed to hers and cried your eyes out about your daughter."

"Yes."

"Goddamn you, Travis. I think I'd rather hear you tell me that you fucked her. Assuming for the moment that you haven't."

She paused and gathered herself. She looked around the room, and I thought for a moment she was going to calm down and give me a chance to explain. As with everything that night, I was wrong.

"Go to hell, Travis!" Kathryn said as she shoved me out of the way of the door. She lunged down the porch steps, stopping just long enough to kick over one of Layla's potted plants.

*　*　*

I paced furiously in my study for some time before approaching Layla's room. I had not heard a sound from her, and despite my near-zero batting average in predicting the behavior of women, I suspected she would be remorseful. This time, I was right.

I pushed her half-opened door the rest of the way. She was indifferently stuffing her clothes into her blue backpack—noticeably more clothes than she had brought with her a month earlier. "You should wait until morning to leave," I said. I could not find the anger to scold or accuse or debate.

"I think I'd better go now," she said. "I've done enough damage—I just can't seem to help myself. But Travis, what I said, I said for your sake."

"For my sake?"

"She's not right for you. I know it."

"Yeah, well. That's probably for me to decide, Layla."

"I know, I know—of course you're right. I just—I think we're good for each other, Travis. I don't care about the difference in our

181

ages and don't understand why you do. Does it matter what other people think?"

"Please, stay here tonight," I said.

"I don't want to be alone," she said. "Enos has been staying at my apartment for the last few weeks."

"Enos! Jesus, Layla."

"He's not as bad as I made him out to be. I was drawn to him for the same reasons I was drawn to you."

"You're comparing Enos and me?"

She laughed and put a hand on my arm. "You both make me feel safe. I used to get hit on by every man in every bar until I started walking in with Enos."

"But what about, you know—the abuse?"

Layla sputtered a laugh and returned to her packing. "In case you haven't figured it out yet, Travis, I'm sort of a messed-up girl. *Woman.* Some weird shit went on in my house when I was a little girl. You blocked out Randi for all those years, but I remember the things my father did to me like they happened yesterday. I've never told anyone, and now's not the time to tell you, but it would ex-plain a lot."

"You know I'll listen anytime," I said. "Stay here tonight. Don't see Enos. He's not right for you."

"Yeah, well . . . that's probably for me to decide."

*   *   *

As much as any moment, that moment helped to clarify my feel-ings for Layla. Had she been my daughter, I would have been fu-rious at her for seeing Enos and would have prevented it. Had she been my wife, I would have wanted to take revenge on *him.* But what I experienced was more painful than either of those feelings. What I felt was jealousy, which meant that I wanted to punish my-self for letting something I loved get away.

"Just one more night, Layla," I pleaded. "I need to set things straight with Kathryn, but my guess is tonight was the end for us."

"Just one more thing I've destroyed," she said, slipping her backpack over one shoulder. "I'll tell her the truth if you think it will help."

"Thanks, but if she won't believe me, there's not much to salvage."

"I'm sorry for everything." She turned and left.

*   *   *

Through the front window, I watched her get into her rusty Escort and drive down Preston Street.

As I had told Layla, I was almost certain that irreparable damage had been done to Kathryn and me, but I had some profound need to convince Kathryn of my fidelity just the same. More than most, I understood how one's past could cause unbearable pain, and I somehow needed Kathryn to know that I had found enough value in her to keep my word.

I drove to the chancellor's house.

Twenty-Nine

MY TUXEDO served as my invitation, and I quickly found myself immersed in a clutch of similarly dressed men and their sequined spouses. Known as the Bauer House, the University of Texas's chancellor's residence is an unexceptional two-story house with white columns in front, located only a few miles west of campus.

I grew anxious as I looked for Kathryn. I worked my way through the crowd to the pool out back, where at one end, near the diving board, I saw a group of six people, including Kathryn. I walked, head down, to the opposite end of the pool and stood beneath one of the outdoor lights. It was obvious when Kathryn finally saw my profile, though she made no immediate move in my direction. She had not answered my repeated calls to her cell phone, and I had no illusions that she would be happy to see me or that showing up would repair the damage already done. Still, she was a good and decent woman who had done much for me; it was important to me that she understood that.

After what seemed like an hour but was probably only minutes, she excused herself and slowly walked over to me. Neither of us spoke for a moment, and then we hugged. When we finally put enough space between our bodies to look at each other, I saw that her mascara had run. I don't think I'd ever seen Kathryn tear up before.

"Layla's gone," I said quietly. "I'm not proud of some of my actions, Kathryn, but nothing happened between us. That's really all I've come here to tell you."

Kathryn wiped her eyes with the backs of her hands and then studied the dark residue. "Look at me," she said softly. "And I'm supposed to run an entire department? I hope the wrong people don't see me like this and change their minds."

"They won't," I assured her. "They got the best and they know it." I handed her my slightly damp cocktail napkin, and she dabbed at her streaking makeup. "How do I look?" she asked.

"You look great," I said. She took me by the hand, led me into the house, and introduced me to dozens of people. Most of the conversation centered on Kathryn and what an incredible woman she was. But, without fail, Kathryn would deflect the praise to me and my book.

"I hear it's going to be number one on *The New York Times* bestseller list tomorrow," Chancellor Thad Willoughby said while extending his hand for a congratulatory shake.

I guess my perplexed expression spoke volumes, as Kathryn quickly added, "I just got a message from Saul. He said he had tried to call you."

"So you checked your messages?" I teased her gently.

"Some of them," she said.

* * *

The time passed quickly, and it was after 11:00 p.m. when Dr. Willoughby asked if he could borrow Kathryn for a quick business meeting with an important donor. I excused myself and wandered off on a tour of the house.

Always intrigued by home libraries, I was delighted to find the chancellor's. I skimmed the books and judged they were a bit too perfect, somewhat like a volume-by-volume collection of the *Harvard Classics*. I doubted this was where he did his serious reading.

On his ornate cherry desk lay the morning's local paper. A front-page headline read: VICTIM OF SEXUAL ASSAULT FIGHTS BACK. It had nothing to do with Layla, of course, but my mind suddenly filled with fears of tomorrow morning's headlines. COED TAKES LIFE, NOTE BLAMES PROFESSOR.

I sat in a big leather chair with a phone on the table next to it. I looked through the doorway, and when I didn't see Kathryn, I quickly dialed my voice mail service. I was informed there were two messages. The first was from Saul Westberg, my agent. It was the message Kathryn had already relayed. I fast forwarded to the end and saved it, then pressed the key to hear the next message.

Layla? This is Enos. I got your message. You there? Pick up. Yeah, I'm at your place. Come on over. We've got a lot of catching up to do.

* * *

The phone still at my ear and my face growing red with helpless frustration, I turned to see Kathryn leaning against the door frame. Her demeanor was tense, but she still held her usual composure. My God, what was I doing to that poor woman who had done so much for me? Her arms were folded across her chest.

"I just found out that Layla and Enos are getting together tonight," I said.

"Call the police," Kathryn said coolly.

"They think I'm a meddlesome old man who's trying to inter-fere with two young lovers, and to tell the truth, they may be right."

"Then call Layla."

"The phone in her apartment was disconnected weeks ago," I said.

Kathryn looked at her watch. "We've got our own cars here," she said. "Why don't you go on and do whatever it is you have to do."

I reached for her, uncertain of what to say. "Thank you," I said, kissing her on the cheek. "Thank you for understanding."

"I never said I understood," Kathryn said as I walked past her. "But I do believe you and I do appreciate your coming here tonight. It meant a lot."

THIRTY

I SUPPOSE I had told Kathryn what I needed to tell her, but what exactly was it that I needed to tell Layla?

This was my thinking as I grabbed my keys from the valet in front of the chancellor's house and hurried to the Wagoneer. I assumed Enos Vasquez would be at her apartment, but for some reason, that thought did not frighten me. I was starting to think that Enos might not be the demon I had initially made him out to be. Captain Smith had indicated that he was a boy trying to get away from trouble, not to find more of it, and Layla had said she felt safe with him. The fears she had originally expressed were now cast in a highly suspicious light. While I bore the scar of his anger over my eye, I had to consider that, after all, he had discovered a strange man in the apartment of his naked girl. *His* naked girl. His actions may have been rash or stupid, but with the clarity of hindsight, they were hardly indefensible. Even the psychosexual acts now seemed to be more *her* idea than his.

In a strange way, in the distance between the chancellor's house and Layla's apartment, Enos—Enos the Penos—went from being a hated rival to a potential ally in my mind. Enos Vasquez had become the aunt, the uncle, the second cousin twice removed—the *anyone* other than me who could be there for Layla. Who might just keep her from trying to kill herself again.

So as I walked anxiously up the stairs to Layla's apartment, a part of me was actually hoping that I would find Enos. And staring through the half-opened door to Layla's apartment, I did.

Dead on the floor.

* * *

"Layla?" I said as I stepped inside. "It's me, Travis."

Enos Vasquez was face down, wearing the same San Diego Chargers jersey and loose-fitting jeans I had seen him in before. His head was lying in a pool of blood; his hair was wet and matted. I looked around, noticing only that the nylon ropes he had used before to tie Layla up were attached to the four corners of the bed.

"Layla?" I walked slowly toward the corner bathroom and was overcome with grief as I pushed the door open. I could almost see her pale form slumped in the crimson water again. I swallowed hard and entered; the bathroom was clean and empty.

I picked up the phone near the bed, only to be reminded that it had been disconnected. I looked at Enos's body on the floor and thought he might have a cell phone on him. Somehow, I had to call 911. It felt surreal to touch him, but I had to roll his body slightly in order to get the small flip phone out of his side pocket. Moving him ever so slightly also revealed that he was lying on top of a rod, a piece of steel rebar. It was obviously the same rod I had carried in with me weeks ago, and it was covered with blood. So were his head and matted hair.

I flipped open the phone and began to enter the numbers when I heard an army of footsteps outside the door.

"Freeze!" a voice screamed as six uniformed policemen poured into the apartment and arranged themselves in a circle around me. Their guns were drawn. I raised my hands as much out of confusion as fear. Within seconds, my hands were cuffed behind me.

A moment later, Captain Tommy Lee Smith, immaculately dressed in Italian black, sauntered in.

"You just had to do it, didn't you?" Captain Smith said. "I warned you not to get involved, but you've got a thing for that girl, don't you?" He reached into his back pocket and produced a small laminated card. He studied it as he read: "You have the right to remain silent . . ."

THIRTY-ONE

AMID THE subtle smell of urine and the more obvious one of alcohol, I tried to stay as inconspicuous as a middle-aged white man wearing a tuxedo can while in jail on a Saturday night.

Actually, it wasn't jail at first. After riding handcuffed in the back of Captain Smith's car to the Austin Police Department, I was placed into what they called a holding tank. The holding tank is simply a room where everyone who has been arrested is placed together until they can be individually processed. Periodically, a guard would enter and call out a name. That person would leave the holding tank, presumably on his way to a cell.

Two phones hung from the wall of the holding tank, and despite my naïve assumptions about getting *one* phone call, there seemed to be no limit. The problem with this liberal policy was that two men—both weighing at least 260 pounds—monopolized the two phones.

After about an hour, my name was finally called and I was processed. That involved being fingerprinted and having my mug shot taken, as well as trading in my tuxedo for some blue scrubs, a trade I was actually not unhappy to make at the time. From the closet that served as a dressing room, I was told to follow a yellow line that was painted on the floor. It led me through a narrow hallway and up a winding set of stairs. When I arrived at the top, a guard took my identification folder from me and assigned me to a cell.

In the center of that cell, which was about the same size as my bathroom on Preston Street, a man was sitting on a stainless steel toilet, straining.

"Got a roomie for you, Hector," the guard said.

"Good, I make it smell nice for him," Hector said, smiling a gold-studded smile.

"Hector Lopez," he said, extending his hand to me. "Drunk driving. And you—what you in for?"

"A murder I didn't commit," I said, passing on the opportunity to shake his hand at that particular moment.

"Murder?" Hector whistled as he got his pants back up. I looked around and noticed that our cell door remained opened.

"Oh, they leave 'em open if everyone's cool," Hector explained. "Surprised me too my first time. Murder?" He whistled again.

The narrow hallway between the cells was more pleasant than the cells themselves, and there were four more phones. I managed to get to one of them and made a call, but at 2:00 on a Sunday morning, Ben didn't answer. Perhaps an angel of mercy had fallen to her knees before him. I left a message that I knew would forever impact the stories on the first day of fall.

I was struck at that moment that for all my degrees and supposed intelligence, I had absolutely no idea what to do to help myself. Should I call Kathryn? Should I drive one more stake into her heart?

Or perhaps I should call the university president, Rod Nevitt, or Dean Howard Schramm. Surely they knew good lawyers, and surely they were loyal enough to stand by one of their own, even at the risk of public disgrace. The only lawyer whose name I knew was an estate lawyer who had handled the paperwork almost two decades ago when Helen had died. Her name was Marta Wilkinson, and she had been in her sixties at the time. I had no idea if she were still alive, much less how to reach her.

I looked around and noticed that Hector was staring at me while whispering to some of his friends, somewhat like a proud parent. I beckoned him over to the phone. "Who would you call if you were me?" I asked.

Hector smiled his golden smile and said, "Do what everyone does, man—when you in jail, call 444-Gail." I learned later that "When you in jail, call 444-Gail" was a jingle that was omnipresent on Austin late-night cable channels, as well as billboards near the jail.

So I called Gail.

And while I got only an answering service, I did notice an increase in the operator's attentiveness when I told her the charge against me. I didn't understand at the time that Gail's fees were tied to the size of the bail and that mine was going to be memorable.

The operator took down all of my information and assured me that someone would be by to visit with me within four hours. As it turned out, someone was there within thirty minutes, and that someone was Gail.

When Gail's arrival was announced, I was told to follow the yellow line back downstairs and was then led into a tiny closet of a room that I accessed from the jail side while Gail entered from the other. There was only a Formica desk between us, and Gail filled out her side of the closet from wall to wall. She wore an enormous African leopard-print caftan, which covered what was obviously an enormous woman. Her hair was styled in dreadlocks with gold beads woven in, and she wore 1950s-style glasses, pink and pointed.

"Tell me, Dr. Harrison," she said as I settled into a metal folding chair, "just what kind of doctor are you?" Her voice was deep and rich.

"I'm a Ph.D.," I said. "A University of Texas history professor."

She looked disappointed. "Oh, I thought maybe you were a real doctor. Always wanted to represent a real doctor. Oh, well."

"How soon can you get me out?" I asked.

"Don't know if I can, hon," she said. "I have to warn you that this place is buzzing over you. They're going to try and deny you bail."

"You're kidding," I said. "I didn't do anything."

Gail reached into a pocket in her caftan and pulled out a small spiral notebook with Garfield the Cat on the cover. She flipped it open to a marked page. "Why don't you just listen for a while, hon? Then we can see if there's anything to talk about."

I nodded and folded my arms.

"Let's see," she began, "about a month ago, the police say they found you in the apartment of a Ms. Layla Sommers. You know Ms. Sommers?"

"Yes, I do."

"Uh-huh. Now, they say that Ms. Sommers had apparently tried to kill herself and, uh, you saved her, but her boyfriend, a Mr. Enos Vasquez—the deceased—beat the crap out of you. Those are my words, by the way, hon, not the D.A.'s. Is that about what happened?"

"Close enough, I suppose."

"Uh-huh. And then they say that with police officers as witnesses, you threatened to kill Mr. Vasquez if he so much as touched Ms. Sommers again. Let's see," she continued flipping pages. "'Go near Layla again, and I'll kill you.' Does that sound about right?"

"I didn't mean that literally . . ."

"Then, a week or so later, Mr. Vasquez *does* touch Ms. Sommers again, so *uninvited,* you break into her apartment—force your way in through a window, apparently while she and Mr. Vasquez are doing the wild thing—and this time you assault Mr. Vasquez, the deceased, and drag Ms. Sommers to your house." She drew her glasses down over her nose with one finger and looked over the top of them. "Have a bit of the hero in you, Dr. Harrison?"

"I didn't assault Vasquez; he passed out. And I didn't *drag* Layla anywhere. She moved in with me based on the recommendation of a psychiatrist."

"Yours or hers?" Gail asked, laughing. She pushed her glasses back into place with her thumb. "Moving right along, the D.A. maintains that last night, after you became aware that the two of them were going back to her apartment, you went berserk. Those are the D.A.'s words, not mine, hon. You flew into a jealous rage and broke into her apartment, where you found the two of them, well, let us just say in a carnal state, and you killed Mr. Vasquez with a steel bar—"

"I did *what?* Look, Gail, this is insane."

"Well, correct me if I'm wrong, hon, but when the police arrived, you *were* kneeling beside the corpse. And the D.A.'s betting your prints are all over that steel bar. Are they, hon?"

"Yes, but I can explain—wait a minute! Where's Layla?" I leaned forward over the small Formica countertop, coming inches from Gail's face. "Listen to me, Gail. Layla Sommers must have killed Enos Vasquez, and he probably deserved it. She's a very disturbed young girl, but she won't leave me twisting in the wind. She can explain all of this. All we have to do is find Layla."

Gail continued to stare at me as she took her glasses off. Her look turned decidedly sympathetic—the kind of sympathy one has for someone who is trying but just not capable. Who just doesn't *get it.*

"Oh, they found Layla, hon," Gail said. She leaned forward and rested her enormous, fleshy forearms on the countertop. "She's already given the police a statement."

I felt queasy and sat back. "A statement?"

"Oh, yes." Gail flipped forward several more pages in her small notebook. "Miss Sommers says she saw the whole thing. She says that she and Enos were playing a harmless little bondage game when this madman—that'd be you, hon—came crashing through her kitchen window in a penguin suit.

"The police confirmed that the window was open and it looks like someone climbed through, knocking things off the counter and breaking a bottle on the floor. They even found some blood samples on the floor that they're anxious to match with yours. Think they might find a match, hon?"

"Yes, they will, but that has nothing to do with the death of Enos. I cut myself there on an earlier night."

"On an earlier night when you crashed through their window?" Gail shook her head in amazement. "Well, moving right along, Layla says that when you saw her tied up on the bed, you went crazy, and as Enos prepared to defend them, you smashed the rod across his skull. She says you just kept hitting him even though she begged you to stop.

"When Enos lost consciousness, she says you cut her free and told her to get dressed, but she got scared and ran out the door to a neighbor's apartment, where she called the police. The D.A. maintains that's why the police arrived so quickly, in time to find you kneeling beside Mr. Vasquez, making sure he was dead. The door was open when they got there, which they say confirms Ms. Sommers' story that she had just fled moments earlier."

"*Unbelievable*," I said, shaking my head at the absurdity of it all. "So I've been denied bail?"

"I said the D.A. was going to try and deny you bail. It will depend on the judge and your attorney. Whatever it is, you might want to start making of list of rich friends."

"I don't have any rich friends, Gail."

"Guess you should have been the other kind of doctor."

I shook my head as Gail continued. "Look, hon, despite what they're saying about you, and despite the evidence, you seem like a nice man. I'd really like to help you, but your case is out of my league. The circumstantial evidence alone is devastating; the eyewitness is the proverbial slam dunk.

"I'll be honest with you, hon, you've got a hell of a long row to hoe. Unless Miss Sommers suddenly gets religion and confesses, there are no good outcomes for you now. The best-case scenario is a year or more of hearings and trials and hundreds of thousand of dollars spent, followed by either a dismissal, an acquittal—or the rest of your life in prison.

"I don't know how much money you have, hon, but my advice is to spend every last penny of it on the best defense lawyer you can find. That's the best I can do for you, unless there's someone you want me to call. Friends? Family?"

I almost laughed out loud at the thought of Gail calling Kathryn at three o'clock on a Sunday morning and telling her I had been charged with murder. Graveyard humor, I suppose. Of course, whether or not Gail called her, the facts would not change, and I wondered how much the inevitable headlines would hurt Kathryn. It would certainly come out that I had been with her at the chancellor's house the night that Enos was killed. There might even be witnesses called, like the valet, who might well say that I ran out of the house and looked angry. Kathryn herself would no doubt be called to testify as to my state of mind that evening.

One thing for certain was that Gail was right; it was going to get a whole lot worse before it had any chance of getting better. I knew that in the sea of politically correct cynicism, there would be precious few sympathizers for a professor who had invited a vulnerable female student to live with him. There was no doubt it would be spun that way.

"They're pretty generous with the phones around here," I said, "and I've left a message for my friend, Ben, so I guess I'm okay. But what happens now?"

"You'll either find another attorney or have one appointed to you. They'll negotiate bail for you, and if you can't make that bail, you'll be moved out of here to the county jail in a day or two. It's not so bad, but if you can't find your way out of there, they'll move you again, to Del Valle, until your trial. Watch your backside at Del Valle; that won't be fun."

I sighed and stared at this huge woman of whom I suddenly felt very fond. "Thanks for coming down," I said. "At least I'll know from now on, 'If you in jail, call 444-Gail.'"

"Well, hon, I thought you were a real doctor!" She broke into a huge grin, reached over the desk, and gave me a motherly hug. "By the way, that stupid jingle nets me three hundred grand a year," she said, shaking her head in disbelief. "Took me six years after graduating Harvard to get to that level at a big firm in Boston, and they wouldn't let me dress like this!"

THIRTY-TWO

BY 4:00 A.M. I assumed that Ben had not yet received my message. The thought of sleep had not entered my mind, yet neither was I able to process the enormity of what had transpired and what lay ahead. I was just about to call Ben again when a stout little guard summoned me.

"How many lawyers you got, Harrison?" he asked.

"None that I know of," I said, but I was soon proved wrong.

The trip down the yellow line was now familiar; the face across the Formica tabletop was not. Or, I should say, faces, as three men were crammed into the small booth that Gail had previously filled by herself.

"Dr. Harrison," the man in the center said, extending his hand. "I'm Christopher McGowen." Despite the hour and despite the fact it was Sunday, he was crisply dressed in a business suit, freshly shaved, and smelled of cologne. His face was slightly pocked, giving the impression that he had started life poor and battled his way up. I recognized his name; he was one of the top criminal lawyers in the state.

"These are my associates," McGowen continued, as he introduced me to Bruce Epstein, a pudgy gray-haired man in a gray suit with no tie, and Marvin DeLaney, a boyish looking man in a trim-fitting Adidas warm-up suit. "We've been retained to represent you, Dr. Harrison, and you'll be glad to know that your bail has been set and posted. We'll have you out of here in less than an hour."

"Retained by whom?" I asked. "Posted by whom?"

"We've been hired by Dr. Kathryn Orr. A friend of yours, a Ben Frizell, contacted her a few hours ago. You do want our help, don't you, Dr. Harrison? Because I can assure you that you're going to need it."

"Well, yes . . . I suppose. It's just . . . How much might all this cost?"

"I suggest you not worry about the money right now. You've got plenty of other things to worry about. When you're released, you'll go right through that door." He pointed to an innocuous-looking door behind a desk of clerical workers. "Drs. Orr and Nickemeyer are waiting for you on the other side. They'll explain what happens next. Any questions?"

"Hundreds," I said, "but I'm too damn tired to think of them. I'm too damn tired to think at all."

"Well, try to hang in there," McGowen said, "because sleep is going to be pretty far down on your to-do list for a while."

He and his associates filed out while I followed the yellow line back to my cell, wondering if McGowen had shaved and put on a suit just for me. I also wondered how Kathryn had reacted to Ben's call. As for Ben, I knew he had a new story that he could tell endlessly.

*   *   *

Within an hour, I was dressed again in my tuxedo (minus the bowtie, studs, and cufflinks, which I stuffed into a pocket) and released from jail. As I exited into a hallway of the municipal building, I found myself facing Kathryn and a scruffy, almost disheveled man who appeared to be in his late twenties.

Kathryn expressed no emotion upon greeting me. "Travis, I'd like for you to meet Dr. Nicholas Nickemeyer," she said as the man offered me a limp handshake. "As you know, he's been treating Layla Sommers, and he thinks perhaps he can help you."

Kathryn remained cool and businesslike as she explained the plan. "We'll meet over breakfast at the Magnolia Café. Travis, you'll ride with me."

*   *   *

The ride in Kathryn's Mercedes down Sixth Street began in silence. There was very little traffic at this early hour, and a fine mist had begun to fall in advance of the year's first hard cold front.

"How'd you find Nickemeyer?" I asked at last.

"It's been a hectic night—morning," she said. "But once I learned from Ben that Enos was dead, I thought somebody probably needed to check up on Layla. I had Dr. Bernard paged, and he had Nickemeyer call me. I spent about thirty minutes on the phone with him, and he thinks he might be able to help."

"Help how?" I asked.

"I'd rather let him explain that, if you don't mind."

"Kathryn, I'm sorry you got dragged into this," I said at last. "I didn't know Ben was going to call you. I had hoped to spare you."

She drove for another block in stony silence and then whipped the car into the parking lot of an antique store and slammed on the brakes. She turned to me with fury in her eyes. "You hoped to *spare* me? You bastard! You don't even know what love is, do you? I'm trying to *marry* you, and you're trying to *spare* me?" She moved her hand to slap me but stopped herself.

"Can you imagine how you would feel if I were hurt or in danger and I didn't even bother to *call* you?" she continued. "I thought—I thought we had something meaningful, but you treat me more like a neighbor you don't know very well and wouldn't want to *bother* with your little problems—like the possibility of spending the rest of your life in jail."

What she was saying now had obviously been brewing ever since Layla moved in, and though tired and disoriented, I had the good sense to keep my mouth shut and my eyes locked on hers, letting her infuse me with whatever level of rage and hurt she felt. I had earned it.

"You see, Travis, when I commit to someone, it's not conditional. I love you and I want you in my life, and if I have to give up the department chair, teaching, my house—if I have to move to Outer Mongolia to have you in my life, that is what I would do. Not because I feel I must, but because I *want* to. I even believe you when you say that you didn't screw that little—Layla—despite sleeping in her bed, despite—petting. Despite everything, I have to believe in you. Can't you see that?"

She paused for a moment and then continued. "It infuriates me that you seem to want me in your life only when it's convenient, like I'm some sort of holiday ornament to be pulled out when the spirit moves you and tucked back away when the season has passed. When you needed to cry your eyes out about Randi, you ran to Layla. When your career—your life—is on the line, you call Ben. How do you think that makes me feel?"

As if something is missing, I thought.

Her anger faded; her voice returned to its more rational pitch. She adjusted the rearview mirror so that she could see her face in it and then fished a wadded Kleenex out of her purse and dabbed at her damaged makeup.

"I called Schramm and Nevitt," she sighed. "The story won't be in this morning's paper, but I didn't want them to be caught by surprise. It certainly will be on the television news later today. Fortunately, few people watch the local news on Sunday." I was relieved that Kathryn was returning to operational mode. "They're both understandably concerned, and at least for now, they're committed to hearing your side of the story."

"There is only one side of the story," I said, and then looked at her sternly. "Mr. McGowen said that his fees and the bail had been taken care of. I can't let you do that."

"Travis!" She turned and placed her finger firmly in the middle of my chest. "I thought we just had this conversation. Unless you're going to tell me that you would not do the same if our roles were reversed, then I suggest you shut the fuck up!"

I thought about that for a moment and took her advice.

*   *   *

One of Austin's few twenty-four-hour restaurants, the Magnolia Café, was only modestly crowded for five o'clock on a Sunday morning. As we walked up to the front door, the rain began falling hard, and the temperature had plummeted during our short drive from the jail.

Dr. Nickemeyer had arrived moments earlier and was waiting for us in a corner booth. He stood as we approached, and Kathryn and I slid in opposite him. He hadn't shaved in days and looked as if he hadn't cut or combed his hair in years.

We ordered coffee and breakfast, talked about the cold weather for a moment, and then Nickemeyer began.

"First, let me say for the record that I'm not entirely comfortable with my role here—patient confidentiality and all that. But from what I've been able to learn about events of the past twelve hours, I think it's safe to assume that you, Travis, have been wrongly charged with a murder. I also think it's safe to say that Layla Sommers, wherever she is, is not in a very good place, psychologically. If I can help both of you, then it's worth some level of discomfort."

Nickemeyer smiled a contagious smile at me, so much so that I was compelled to inquire. "What's so funny?"

"Oh, sorry," Nickemeyer said. "It's just that I don't often get to see the object of one of my patient's obsessions."

"Obsession?" I asked.

"Travis," Kathryn interrupted, "Dr. Nickemeyer is offering to help you."

"Are you saying that you would be willing to testify about Layla?" I asked him. His answer was delayed by the arrival of plates heaped with food.

"I think you're missing the point here," Kathryn said. Nickemeyer nodded his agreement. "We're not here to prepare for a trial, we're here to avoid one. A trial could take years, and no matter how good your lawyers are, you could lose. The evidence against you is daunting. A trial is not a risk you can afford to take."

"What's my alternative? To flee the country?"

Kathryn glanced at Dr. Nickemeyer with a conspiratorial look that indicated it was time to bring me in on what they already knew. Nickemeyer moved some blueberries about on his plate with a knife, as if he were an artist preparing his palette. "I think, Dr. Harrison, you could convince—or perhaps I should say, induce—Layla to set the record straight. But you'd have to move quickly. Today."

I looked at Kathryn, who arched her eyebrows in a gesture of hope.

"You've got my attention," I said, suddenly alert again. "But I'm equally curious how Layla could do this to me."

"I think I can help with that as well," Nickemeyer said. "But I'm going to have to talk frankly." He looked at Kathryn and then at me. "You two are engaged, right?"

I guess Kathryn and I both concluded that this was not the time to introduce another problem for the psychologist as we both nodded affirmatively.

Nickemeyer's semipermanent smile disappeared as he leaned over the table toward us. "Some of what I have to say may not be comfortable for you to hear."

"Just say what you have to say, doctor," Kathryn said with a note of irritation.

"All right," Nickemeyer said, leaning back. "Welcome to Psychology 101. Layla Sommers is driven by shame. This shame undoubtedly stems from her childhood. Textbook, really. No one has ever gotten her to confess to a single defining event, but there clearly was one, a severe trauma that I'm certain involved her father. She was likely a preteen at the time. By now, it's like something caught in her throat. If she could ever get it out, there would be a chance for Layla in the future.

"These traumas are often sex-related. They can even occur inadvertently, such as a child walking in on copulating parents." Nickemeyer thought for a moment, running one hand through his unruly hair. "To the child, it might appear that the mother is being hurt, or even tortured. The child might interpret her moans of pleasure as cries of pain or perhaps ascribe anger and abuse to the quite normal throes of passion of the father.

"In more severe cases, these imprints could be the result of violence, such as when a child observes, or hears, her mother or siblings being beaten—again by the father. I'm aware, by the way, that Layla's father killed her mother."

"Did Layla tell you that?" I asked, glancing at Kathryn.

"No. Dr. Bernard told me. I believe a police officer had informed him.

"In the worst-case scenario, sex *and* violence merge into a single event. If a young child observes sexual violence, they may forever confuse the pain they witnessed with the pleasure they themselves experience years later. They may confuse force and submission. They may live their lives being unable to differentiate between those extremes."

Nickemeyer paused and took a bite of blueberry pancake and then put his fork down and wiped his mouth with his sleeve. "Guilt also comes into play," he continued, "for this same child, watching quietly from the shadows, or listening helplessly from her room, is unable to come to the defense of her mother. As the helpless onlooker, she feels equally responsible for her mother's suffering and for her own.

"This unfortunate melding of worthlessness with sexual arousal would lead one to seek, indeed to demand, relationships with abusive partners. Experiencing pain during the act—even life-and-death brinkmanship—would temporarily satisfy her need to replace her mother as the victim and thus ease her unbearable guilt. Though it is short-lived, nothing feels as good to her as those moments of relief. She will go to any lengths to create them.

"The only way out of this vicious cycle," Nickemeyer continued, "or so it seems to the victim, is to find a white knight. She believes that somewhere out there there must be a savior, a protector of mythic proportions who will end all of her guilt and her shame once and for all. A man who will love her for herself and prove to her how wonderful she is. He will dispel all of the evil manifested by her father and keep her safe. And she will have found redemption not just for herself but for her mother as well." A thin smile crept across Nickemeyer's face; he was apparently gratified by the clarity of his analysis.

"Sound like anyone you know?" Kathryn asked me.

"Yes, it does. But I still don't understand why Layla would intentionally hurt me."

"That's exactly the question I asked myself," Nickemeyer said. "The answer has to do with betrayal. Someone Layla thought loved her—her father—ultimately betrayed her trust. Someone whom she thought would protect her ultimately harmed her. She believes, at least subconsciously, that *every* man she ever meets, no matter how shining a knight at the outset, will ultimately betray her. And, as with her father, the pain of that would be unbearable. So, how is she to cope?"

"Betray him first," I said solemnly.

"Give that student an A," Nickemeyer smiled. "But unfortunately, Dr. Harrison, simply betraying this man is not enough. She needs to destroy him. You see, it is the delta—the difference—between her estimation of her savior's goodness and her own that defines the level of her shame. And since she can't seem to lift herself up, the only way she has to lessen her shame is to pull him down."

"She may not be able to help it," Kathryn added, "but she's trying to destroy you in order to save herself."

"Very good, Dr. Orr," Nickemeyer said. "And I'd say she's succeeding. Layla's really quite brilliant. I'm thinking about making her a character in a novel I'm writing."

"Oh, yes, now I remember," I said. "Layla told me that you were an aspiring novelist."

"Yes, in fact I'm quite envious of your success in that field, Dr. Harrison. My latest manuscript has grown to two thousand pages but, like its predecessors, never seems to turn into a book! How do you do it?"

"I had help," I said glancing sideways, but Kathryn seemed in no mood for the compliment.

"So how does all this help Travis?" Kathryn asked, anxious to redirect us.

"Look, we can talk about how clever and manipulative Layla is," Nickemeyer said, "but if I've pegged her right, she is equally subject to manipulation. In fact, if I'm right, you, Travis, can control her like a puppet on a string. Literally.

"You see, she thinks she's brought you down, but if she were to learn that you're just fine and that you forgive her—that you still want to help her—"

"Then the delta, the difference between us, would be greater than ever," I finished for him.

"Exactly," Nickemeyer said. "The depth of her shame would become unbearable to her. She would, as she has many times in the past, see only two remedies to end her suffering."

"She could kill herself," I said, choking slightly on my words.

"Yes," Dr. Nickemeyer said. "Or she can kill you. Metaphorically speaking, one hopes."

"So what does Travis make the puppet do?" Kathryn asked.

Nickemeyer took a sip of coffee and looked at us both. "Here's the uncomfortable part. As you know, Dr. Harrison, Layla frequently tried to seduce you . . ."

"She was sometimes playful," I said defensively, "but I would hardly call it—"

"Travis," Nickemeyer cut me off. "Layla was quite open in our sessions about her efforts. Not to make light of it, but the group became quite intrigued with her 'crusade,' as one of them called it. It was obvious that your rejections both confused and wounded her. But let us not kid ourselves as to *her* intentions when she stood naked before you in a hallway or jumped naked into your lap or pulled you into her bed—"

"You've made your point, Dr. Nickemeyer," I said. "Please move on."

"Travis, may I be blunt?"

"You haven't been?" I said, failing to hide my growing discomfort.

"I simply must know, unequivocally, if you had sexual relations with Layla." He cut his eyes toward Kathryn and then quickly back to me.

"And, as I have told Kathryn repeatedly, the answer is an unequivocal *no!*"

"You did not have intercourse?"

"We did not."

"Oral sex?"

"No sex."

"Anal sex?"

"I'm tiring of this," I said. "Do you have other orifices to check off your list?"

"I'm sorry," Nickemeyer said convincingly. "I really am, but the answer is crucial, and it is your ass on the line."

"Then move on," I said. "You have your answer."

Dr. Nickemeyer allowed for a moment of silence. He formed a triangle with his blueberry mush. "Then the odds are with you," he said.

"The odds of what?" I asked, allowing my frustration to show, or perhaps it was fatigue.

"The odds of getting a certain puppet to do what you want her to do."

"Which is to admit that Travis didn't kill Enos Vasquez," Kathryn said.

"I don't know if she'll even see me, much less if she'll just spit out the truth," I said. "And wouldn't I need a witness?"

"McGowen's law firm employs the top private detectives in the state," Kathryn said. "I think that if you can get Layla to confess, they'll make sure it's all recorded. Then McGowen says that you're home free."

I looked at Nickemeyer, who had suddenly grown quiet. He was observing Kathryn and me as if we were a laboratory study. "What if she won't see me?" I said.

"She might not see you again just to talk," Nickemeyer said. He studied the few remaining blueberries on his plate. "But I'm absolutely certain that she could not resist the prospect of a sexual encounter with you." He looked up at me; I felt Kathryn's stare from the side.

I dropped my chin to my chest and grimaced. "But as I understand it, her desire would be to—"

"Besmirch, humiliate, destroy," Nickemeyer said. "Pick your own word."

"Those are the possibilities?" I asked.

"Actually, there is another possibility, and it's one you should not take lightly." Nickemeyer squinted with intense focus. "There's the Enos Vasquez possibility. Let's not forget that we're talking about a woman who, in all probability, killed a man last night. A man she once said made her feel safe. Smashed his skull with a steel bar. The truth is, Layla may be a very different person today than any of us knows. That uncertainty bothers me, and it should terrify you."

I looked at Kathryn and shook my head in disbelief. "So what do I do?" I asked her.

For the first time during our breakfast, Kathryn found my hand under the table. "Look, Travis, I don't know what this means for us. Let's be honest—we should postpone the wedding for a while and take some time to sort things out. But as of right now, all we know for sure is that you could spend the rest of your life in jail. We're talking about far more than us. We're talking about your career and your life. We have to do—*you* have to do whatever it takes."

"Don't forget we're talking about Layla, too," Nickemeyer added. "She's half the reason I'm here, and she needs help. Admitting what she has done would be an important first step."

* * *

The waitress brought our check and Kathryn quickly grabbed it. Nickemeyer stood to leave. "Thank you for everything," Kathryn said to him. "And good luck with your novel. Sounds like an interesting project." She put down forty dollars and slid out of the booth. "Come on, Travis, I'll take you home. You look like hell."

THIRTY-THREE

"WHAT'S the matter, boy?"

I've often wondered if dogs have the terrific instincts with which they are credited or whether they merely reflect the emotions of their masters. Whatever the case, TJ failed to greet me at the door with his usual tail-wagging effusiveness but instead approached me cautiously, sideways almost, his tail between his legs. I gave him a long scratch, but he never seemed to lose his wariness.

The morning sun was bright, and the early morning rain had left cold, fresh air in its wake. I let TJ out and prevented his reentry when the cold ground under his paws prompted an immediate U-turn. The *Times* had arrived, and though my brain was still spinning from the past twelve hours—and what lay in the next— I determined that a few minutes of normalcy would add the greatest value. I prepared a pot of coffee, shed what was left of my tuxedo, and put on jeans and a sweater.

Coffee in hand and the *Times* under my arm, I was en route to my study when I glanced at the caller ID. Reluctantly, I checked it and was relieved to find only one message. It was from a man I'd never heard of: Joe Shoppe. I retrieved the message and learned that he was the private investigator who would be working with

me. He said that he wanted me to know that Layla had not returned to her apartment, where police lines still encircled the
grounds. Rather, she had checked into the Flamingo Motel on
South Congress under her own name. He gave me the phone number and her room number—127—both of which I wrote down.

I had been urged by Nickemeyer to contact Layla as soon as
possible. The implication was obvious, so I dialed the number that
Shoppe had provided.

"Flamingo Hotel," a husky, smoker's voice said.

I hung up. I couldn't bring myself to make the call. Not yet.

I decided to shower first and let the heavy stream of hot water
soothe my body and my mind. I turned the shower off and
snapped the drain closed with my big toe, allowing the tub to fill.
I lay down and let the water consume me.

I've never liked baths, especially in small tubs like mine, where
I had to choose which half of my body to soak. I also don't like the
sight of my flesh jutting out above the water line like a chain of
unrelated islands. But the heat relaxed me, and shutting my eyes,
I came upon a brief, meditative relief. Temporarily gone from my
mind were my arrest and my night in jail. Gone was Gail's warning that, at this point, there were no good outcomes for me. Momentarily silent was Nickemeyer's chilling conclusion that Layla
sought to destroy me. Marriage did not cross my mind.

As the water cooled, however, reality leeched back in. And
though philosophy had never been my favorite subject, I'd read
my share and suddenly felt deeply philosophical. From some distant class, I recalled, perhaps imperfectly, the words of Friedrich
Nietzsche. Would I live my life—without the slightest change—
over and over again?

I saw Layla's razor in the corner of the tub. I took it in my hand
and turned the base of the handle, opening the top. I took out the
sharp, double-edged blade inside, carefully holding it between my
thumb and forefinger. How much did it hurt, I wondered. I placed
the blade on my wrist—just rested it there. The razor was so sharp

that I thought for an instant it might not hurt. Of course, Layla had also had wine and pills. I pressed down on the blade. Just how deep did the cut have to be to succeed? *Succeed?* It was an odd choice of words, I realized. And how long would it take? I slid the blade gently across my wrist and drew just the tiniest edge of blood. And how long afterward could a tourniquet save it all for another day?

Of course, I wasn't planning to cut my wrists. Not only would I never subject Kathryn or Ben—or whoever might find me—to such a scene, but men don't cut their wrists and they don't take pills. The statistics prove overwhelmingly that men do what they've always done; they put the barrel of a gun to their head and they pull the trigger.

For the first time in almost a decade, I thought about the revolver in my bedside table.

The next time I pulled the trigger, it would fire.

THIRTY-FOUR

"HELLO?" Her voice was weak.

"Layla, it's me, Travis," I said. There was a nasal wisp of air on the other end of the line and nothing more. An eternity passed. "We need to talk."

"I thought you were, like, in jail or something." She groaned as if the words caused physical pain.

"No, no, I'm fine. But I'm worried about you. I want to see you."

"Why would you ever want to see me again?" she asked. I could sense the slight but encouraging rise in the pitch of her voice.

I swallowed hard, balancing my instincts against Nickemeyer's advice. "Because I . . . I care about you."

"You *care* about me? How could you possibly—?" She stopped suddenly.

"There have been some misunderstandings," I said. "Things were said and done in the heat of the moment. We can't let this . . . we've been through too much together, you and me."

"You and *me?*" she said wistfully.

"Come over this evening and we'll clear the air." The long silence that followed made me anxious. "I really want to see you," I added.

"You do?" she sang, her voice up an octave and syrupy. "You want to see me? Just you and me?"

"And TJ. He misses your nails. He'll barely let me scratch him anymore."

She laughed.

"What about Kathryn?" she asked.

"You know, Layla, I'm not sure it's going to work out between Kathryn and me."

"I knew it!" Layla burst out. "I knew she wasn't right for you. This could be the best thing to happen to you."

"So you'll come tonight?" I asked.

Her hesitation bothered me. "No, Travis. I think we should wait," she said. "Let's wait a week or two, until things clear up a little for both of us."

"They're clear for me, Layla," I said, more urgently than I had intended.

"I'm in kind of a weird place, Travis. Mentally. I'd better let you go."

"No, wait!" I feared that time for diplomacy was running out and had to defer to Nickemeyer's cunning tactics. "I want you Layla," I said. "I can't wait a week or two. I want you tonight."

"You *want* me?" she said. "What does *that* mean?"

I swallowed hard. "You know what it means. I've wanted you all along, and tonight, I'm going to have you."

*   *   *

As I've said, Sundays have always been special to me, but as word of my arrest became public, a better word for that particular Sunday would have been chaotic. Within minutes of Layla's agreeing to come over that evening, my phone started ringing and never stopped. It was as if the foundations of my life were being loosened, plank by plank, with each call.

First, Dean Schramm called on behalf, he said, of both himself and president Nevitt. He insisted that they both wanted me to know how very, very sorry they were that I had gotten caught up in this mess, and having been updated by Dr. Orr, they were both confident that I would be exonerated when the facts came to light. *However,* until that time came, they *assumed* that I would want to take a leave of absence while working through it all. Schramm had generously assured me that I could have my office back at some point, but since "things" were likely to take a while, it would be best to let someone else use it in the interim. When I told him that I expected to *teach* in the interim, he had scarcely been able to contain his laughter. *Oh, my . . . uh . . . no, no. Nevitt and I, well, I don't think, you know, the sensitivity on these matters today . . . it would just be best for all concerned . . . I'm sure you would agree, and . . . well, we'll just store your boxes in the basement . . . you know, until things . . . and if we can be of . . . well, we're pulling for you . . .*

*   *   *

The next plank came loose a little after noon when I received a call from Cindy O'Connell, my editor at Knopf. I had only met the woman once and had only spoken to her a few times on the phone; she preferred to deal with my agent, Saul Westberg, who actually did the bulk of my editing.

"We were so thrilled to see your book in the one position," she said. Her voice was deep and masculine. The paper happened to be lying next to me, and I picked up the *Book Review* with an ironic smile. I decided not to even mention the crises in my life, when Cindy's deep voice suddenly turned shrill.

"We are, however, naturally distraught over your legal situation, but want you to know that you have our . . . well, we certainly hope that things work out for you."

Had Kathryn called her, too, I wondered? Or was it possible this story—*my* story—was already on the wires?

"I'm sure you can appreciate that we feel it is best to, uh, postpone the book-signing tour. We're afraid the publicity would not be about the book and, thus, not a very good investment for Knopf."

215

"Sure," I said. "Maybe in a month or two."

"Well, we'll have to watch sales patterns very closely over the next few weeks."

"I see. Well, maybe some time away from teaching will speed up the progress of my next book."

"Uh, yes. About your next book . . . I hate doing this, but our lawyers insisted that I remind you that our contract includes an escape clause subject to acts of 'moral turpitude' by the author—"

I hung up.

Joe Shoppe called again at least five times, as if his job depended on updating me with every technical detail. Three of his calls came while several of his technicians were already in my house wiring rooms for sound. One of them, a massive bald man dressed in white, whom the others called Ears, kept asking me as he walked from room to room, "Think ya'll might do it in here?"

I finally asked him, "Do *what*, Ears?"

He smiled, and winked, and said, "You know—*talk*."

Ben called twice, one call lasting almost an hour. It was the best hour of the day as it passed the most quickly. "Five thousand bucks to be there," he said jokingly, and then, "Whatever happens, I'm here for you, my friend."

"I know that, Ben."

* * *

Between the constant stream of calls I had gone to my bedroom several times with the idea of napping, but every time the phone rang I knew there was a chance that it was Layla. It would only be bad news if she did call, which heightened my anxiety with every ring.

Perhaps the most telling moment of that afternoon came when my real estate agent, Flo Landers, came by. Flo, who always dressed in a pink pantsuit, knocked on the frame of my open front door until she captured my attention. When at last I noticed her, my heart sank. I assumed she needed my signature on the revised contract. Having apparently lost my spot at Kathryn's, that was the first moment I realized I had only two weeks left at Preston Street and nowhere else to go.

"Hello, Dr. Harrison," Flo said. There was an edge of bitterness to her voice. "I hate to be the bearer of bad news, but the buyers have changed their minds."

"About the move-in date?" I asked.

"About the house," she said. "They found another one, and since you breached the contract, there's really nothing you can do. You'll have to return the earnest money. I came by to take the CONTRACT PENDING notice off the sign. We'll just have to start over."

"No!" I almost shouted. "Listen . . . Flo . . . a lot has happened in the last few days, and I'm going to take the house off the market for a while." I had not felt such a surge of hope rush through my body in years. I found myself literally propelled down the porch steps where, for the third time in my life, I yanked the FOR SALE sign from the dirt. After Helen, after Randi, and now, after Layla.

"But Dr. Harrison, our listing agreement—"

"Sorry, Flo, but the house is not for sale." I carried the sign to the street and laid it in the grass next to her SUV.

"Do you want me to try and lease it for you when you move in with Dr. Orr?"

"I'm not moving in with Dr. Orr," I said.

"But I thought—"

"I thought so too, Flo," I said. I didn't mean to be flippant or rude, but I used the ringing phone as an excuse to avoid further explanations. "I've got to get back inside now."

She left with a perplexed look on her face.

*   *   *

Eventually, the activity around the house wound down. The only person who had not called during the day was Kathryn. At about five o'clock, I walked into Randi's room and in less than an hour had returned every hint of Randi's existence back to the cardboard boxes. This time, however, I had done so because I finally under-stood what her death had done to me, not because I was avoiding it. This time, I took the boxes to the garage.

By six o'clock, I was preparing to shower and change. I was still euphoric that I was not going to have to move out of my house and that my dogs would not have to meet their new owners—the ones I had yet to find. And for reasons that were hard to under-stand and impossible to articulate, I was also growing excited over the prospect of seeing Layla. She was due in an hour.

A knock on the front door jarred me from my solitude; Layla had come early.

THIRTY-FIVE

BEFORE I opened my door that Sunday evening, I had never seen Layla in a dress. I had seen her in jeans, clingy Lycra running shorts, her silk robe, soap bubbles, and wearing nothing at all. But I had never seen her in a dress.

Though it was cold outside, her dress was short and sleeveless—a simple ecru canvas dress that caused a certain stiffness to her movements. Her legs, arms, and neck shone as if buffed. Her hair, slightly unkempt, fell long and soft over her shoulders. Ironically, nothing was ever quite perfect about Layla's appearance, yet the result seemed to always approach perfection.

My attention was immediately drawn to her eye, which had a black circle beneath it. I then noticed other marks on her face.

"Did Enos do that?" I asked.

"I'd rather not talk about it," she said. "Not yet."

I opened my arms and she slowly walked into them. "You look beautiful," I said. As I held her, I stroked her silky copper hair, and the cool breeze from the open door enveloped us. "Let's move inside."

We sat on the sofa in front of the fireplace, where three small logs burned. Classical music played from the study, and neither of us said much. The short canvas dress forced Layla to position her legs slightly sideways; she adjusted them into Picasso-like geometries.

TJ appeared at her side and copped a long-nailed scratch as I retrieved two glasses of wine from the kitchen. *Red wine.* Layla's nails were carefully painted in her favorite color—purple—which matched the hue of her lipstick. Her lips, naturally full to begin with, appeared engorged against the offsetting ruddiness of her skin and her luminescent copper hair. The bruise beneath her eye made her the single most pitiable person I had ever seen, despite what she had done to me.

We offered up a wordless toast, tapping our glasses lightly, and began sipping on the warm redness. She held the wine glass in her left hand while keeping her right delicately poised along a fleshy expanse of her thigh. Neither of us seemed to know where to start.

"My book hit number one on the *Times* list today," I said at last.

"Oh, that's terrific, Travis," she said, giving me a friendly pat on my arm. It was a gesture of underwhelming enthusiasm and worried me.

The first bottle of wine went quickly and I opened a second. She seemed hypnotized by the flickering flames of the fire and kicked off her platform shoes. She let her body sink down a few inches into the sofa and, as if succumbing to the wine, finally leaned against me. She shut her eyes and kept them shut for quite a long while; she, too, had probably had a sleepless night, but I couldn't let sleep come to her too soon.

"I guess we should talk about what happened," I whispered.

She shook her head vigorously. "Anything but that. I just want to put that behind us."

"And we can," I said, "but not until we've talked about it." I knew the effect of words on Layla, but I was too tired to be subtle. "Layla, you're going to have to tell the police what really happened."

She did not move from my arms, a good sign, I thought.

"What do you want me to say?" she asked. "What if I tell them everything," she said. "Then what?"

"Then we'll both be okay. They'll drop the charges against me, and as for you, well, judging from the bruise on your face—" I turned her head toward me and touched the bruise lightly with the back of my hand. "They'll almost certainly rule self-defense. I know you've been through something horrible—"

She turned her head away and stared into her crimson glass. "What I meant was, what happens to *us*?"

"We need to find a way to play a role in each other's lives. Each of us offers something to the other. We need to match those needs up in ways that are healthy and positive."

She turned her head sharply toward me. Her eyes were hazy with tears, her full purple lips quivering. I could feel the tension vibrating in every cell of her body. It made my throat dry. I didn't know what I had said, but like waking a slumbering beast, I knew I would soon find out.

"I don't understand you," she started and then stopped. She reached for the paper napkin under her wine glass and pressed it hard against her eyes. She sniffed and leaned her head back to take a broad gulp of air. "You talk about *us* as if we came with a user manual and you could pick the features you want—healthy, positive, rational. Don't you ever let go, Travis? Don't you ever *feel*?"

"You know I do. I cried all night in your arms—"

"*No!* Tonight is not about Randi. I ache for you and your losses. They are incomprehensible to me. But tonight is about you and me. Two adults trying to figure things out. Like why you are not attracted to me."

"Not attracted to you?" I protested.

"Sexually, Travis! Sexually."

I started to respond, but she abruptly stood and walked to the fireplace, then turned to face me. Standing before me, her sinewy limbs trembling, her hair reflecting the chaotic dance of the flames as if it, too, was on fire . . . the short dress, her purple nails, and purple lips . . . tears streaming from her brilliant brown eyes . . .

She stared me down, raised both arms in priest-like fashion, and asked in a plaintive wail the most gut-wrenching question I had ever heard posed:

"What is *wrong* with me?"

Her thick, plum lips continued to tremble, and she wiped her eyes with the backs of her hands. Her stomach filled and contracted with her effort to squelch her sobs.

I went to her and gently wrapped my arms around her again. I let my right hand slide down the outside of her skin-tight dress to the small of her back and, with my knuckles, firmly rubbed the distinct muscles on either side of the base of her spine. With my left hand, I raked my fingers through her flaming copper hair. I could see the reflection of the flames in it, yet it was cool to the touch.

"The only thing wrong with you, Layla, is that you are so extraordinarily beautiful that you terrify me." She took a deep breath and looked at me through misty eyes. "It is because I was so attracted to you, right from the first, that I had to build such impenetrable walls between us. I had just met you, and I was not ready to risk a relationship—an impending marriage—that I had invested years in. I barely knew you, and for God's sake, you reminded me of my *daughter!*"

"But I'm not your daughter, Travis. I'm a grown woman."

"I know that now. You're a woman who knows more about me than anyone on Earth. You know more about me than Ben, more than Kathryn. Sometimes, I think, more than myself."

She checked a laugh, nodded, and uttered some slurry, hopeful sounds of concurrence. Then, as if standing on a slow-moving conveyer belt, her body inched closer to mine; she buried her tear-stained face in my chest. I contracted my arms so tightly around her that I could feel her ribs with my forearms; she pressed her hips forward firmly, giving me a hint of the unthinkable. The irreversible.

She wiped more tears on my shirt and held me as tightly as I held her; I could still feel her body trembling. She sniffled and shook her head sharply at last, as if trying to regain her wits. She tilted her head back and looked at me.

"I'll tell the police whatever you want me to tell them," she said softly. "Just don't let me go again."

"I won't."

"Things with Enos got out of control. It was probably my fault, but he started hitting me too hard. I couldn't get him to stop. He shoved me to the floor and took off his belt. I looked around me and saw that steel bar you brought that night. He leaned over to try to get me back on my feet and—"

I put two fingers over her mouth. Seconds away from my exoneration, I suddenly remembered "Ears" and all the newly installed wires running throughout my house.

"We need to get out of here," I whispered, evoking an understandably confused look from Layla.

"Why?" she asked.

"Just trust me," I said.

She hugged me tightly and kissed me on the cheek. "I do," she said. "You know I do."

*   *   *

We drove in silence to the Flamingo Hotel on South Congress and pulled into the circular drive that leads to all thirty rooms. I parked in front of her room, number 127.

Without a word, we got out of the Wagoneer and walked to her door. She fished through her purse for the key.

The room reeked of mildew, cleaning fluids, and decades of cigarette smoke; it was dank and small with brown carpet worn to the slab in spots. The bed was covered with a paper-thin blanket that had sported quilted gold patterns a thousand washes ago. Televisions could be heard from the rooms on either side.

Layla sat on the edge of the bed, staring at her feet as I shut the door. As she sat there, head bowed, I had never seen her look so tired, so alone. She simply stared at her feet and her platform shoes, seemingly unaware of my presence. Her knees were pressed together and her long legs angled to one side.

I sat down next to her and put my hand in the center of her back. Beneath my fingers, I felt the ridge of her spine and worked my fingers around it in soft circles. "What is it?" I asked.

She shook her head, *no.*

"Layla, talk to me."

My back rub seemed to be having a soothing effect as she adjusted her body slightly to give me a better angle and a greater surface to rub. As I did, she began to sniffle and then coughed twice as if something was literally bubbling up from inside of her.

"You're going to think I'm so fucking pathetic," she managed, wiping her eyes.

"I'm going to think nothing of the sort," I said.

"God, you poor man, having to deal with me."

"I've never felt more worthwhile," I said.

"That's why I feel so stupid," she said. "I keep allowing myself to think that you really like me."

"I *do* like you," I protested.

She patted me on the knee and forced a sympathetic smile. "I don't mean it that way," she said. "You've been wonderful to me. What I mean is that I allowed myself to think that you were, like, falling for me."

"The problem, Layla, is that I can't imagine why you would want me to fall—"

"I mean, we talked about Helen and Randi," she interrupted. "We cried about Randi. We got into such a nice routine with our meals and everything. I've never felt so comfortable, so safe—so loved. And it felt good, Travis. For the first time in my life, I thought maybe I deserved something like that. I thought maybe it was my turn. You even bought me those sheets . . . "

"Go on," I said, massaging the thin muscles in her neck.

"I thought if I fixed dinner for you and dressed up a little, looked a little more mature, you know, like Kathryn . . . then I wore that ridiculous fox-hunting outfit . . . tally-ho, or whatever the fuck they say."

"You were spectacularly beautiful," I said.

"Whatever I was, whatever I am, it doesn't seem to work on you. What other men have always wanted, you're not interested in." She shrugged her shoulders in a playful "I don't get it" gesture. "What do I have to do?"

"You have to build a life for yourself, and you have to stop trying to hurt yourself."

"You want me to not kill myself."

"That, above all," I said.

"You know, maybe I'm young and stupid, but I don't understand why everyone thinks death is such a big fucking deal. Seems to me that life is the hard part. The only thing that's kept me going this long is the knowledge that life is always optional. I can follow the light, or I can put it out. I think you have that confidence too, Travis."

"I said you knew me better than I know myself, but it doesn't change the point. Even if I'm willing to face my own death, I would still find yours unbearable."

Layla shook her head and pointed at me. "You see, when you say things like that, I concoct these great fantasies of how much you love me!" She let out an enormous, high-pitched groan.

"When you're wanting children, I'll be wanting grandchildren—the kind you spoil for two hours and then send home."

"But when you're ninety, you'd have a hot young wife to change your diapers!" she laughed. "Look, I know now that there was never a chance for us, that I was just another stray that wandered into your life."

"That's not true."

"It is true. I'm like one of your dogs that you take in until you can find them another home."

"At first, perhaps, but the fact is, they're all still with me."

"Yeah, but they sleep outside and eat out of bowls," Layla laughed through her tears. "I'm quite sure that was my fate as well."

"Layla, you have your whole life in front of you. You need to finish college, find a career, marry, and have children if you want. I've had my chance at life, and I admit that it didn't work out exactly the way I'd hoped. But I'm not so naïve as to think that life gives us a second chance. It's your turn now.

"What you've experienced while living with me is my daily routine. It's a routine because I've stopped searching for anything more. Because I've settled for the life I have. It's what I'll be doing three, ten, and maybe thirty years from now. It felt safe to you since you had been in a dangerous place, but when you get back on your feet, life with me would bore you to tears. My routine would quickly become your insanity."

"And we all know I've got plenty of that already," she smiled. "But I don't care about college or family."

"Which is absolute proof that a relationship with me does not benefit you. Where would you be when I died? You'd have no degree, no career, no husband, no children. I'm not worth it. No one is."

I stood from the bed and paced the small, dank room. Standing some few feet away from her, I could think of only one thing to say. There was nothing left for us but the truth.

"Why do you try to kill yourself?" I asked.

"Trying to determine whether you might have to pluck me out of a bathtub again?" she asked.

"Yes," I said. "Don't you think that's reasonable?"

She folded her arms across her chest. "Are you saying there is a chance you might want me in your life? Or am I setting myself up for another kick in the gut?"

"I'm so tired that I don't know exactly what I'm saying," I said. "But I do know that I love you."

Her mouth fell open. She put her hands over her face for a moment, and then let them fall to her thighs. "That's the first time you've ever said that."

I shrugged my shoulders. "I should have said it sooner." I sat down next to her on the bed again. She took my hand in hers.

"Everyone would like to get rid of the thing they hate most in life," she said. "In my life, that's often me. I sometimes feel guilty and worthless, and I just can't make the argument that life is worthwhile."

"Was there something in your past?"

"Been talking to Dr. Nickemeyer, have we?" she said without malice. "I've been to half a dozen shrinks, and they all dig like dogs after a bone for my so-called primal scene. When they can't find it, they get so flustered that they either try to commit me or screw me! Usually the latter."

She smiled, reclaimed her hand, and folded her arms tightly; she crossed her legs at the knees. She sighed deeply.

"I was nine years old," she began. "We lived in Deridder, Louisiana. My dad—even the kids called him Darryl—ran a garage shop, and he drank too much. He's a big man with a big handlebar mustache who never really grew up. He'd get into fights all the time, often starting them for no good reason. You know, someone would make an innocent comment, and he'd say, 'What in the hell do you mean by that?' He was always looking for trouble.

"Mom was the best. She was a good old hippie who loved nothing more than her children. Which is a good thing considering she had five of them. Hers was not a job I would want—cooking, cleaning, getting the kids to school and a hundred other places. But she loved it. She painted little flowers all over the windows, painted the doors purple. She thought that the dust on butterflies' wings was angel dust and that grass cried when you cut it. Stuff like that.

"Our house was small—sort of like yours. Only one bathroom, yet we had seven people vying for it. As I told you before, modesty was not an option for us. We'd use the bushes outside if we really had to go, and we all ran around naked or in our underwear. There was never enough hot water, and what there was, we all knew to save for Darryl. My parents had a small bedroom; I shared the other one with my four brothers.

"Darryl hit all of us a few times, but he wasn't what I would call violent, except when it came to Mom, and man, he would just whale on her." Big tears fell from Layla's eyes. "My brothers and I would sit in our room, listening, silently crying. It's odd, but the sound wasn't as dramatic as you would think. It was sometimes just one dull thud followed by another. I think it would have been easier to deal with if there had been screaming and furniture crashing or dishes being thrown. But it was just dull thuds and muffled groans.

"The boys would always talk about doing something. They'd talk tough, but even Eric, who was six feet tall and two hundred pounds at the time, wasn't about to take on Darryl.

"One night, Darryl came home late from work, shouting and knocking things over. I don't know what had set him off; I just heard him yelling at Mom. I peeked out my door and saw that his face was covered with blood. He had a half-empty bottle of whiskey in his hand."

Layla crossed and uncrossed her arms and then crossed them again. She inhaled deeply and her eyes looked off into the distance.

"He grabbed Mom by the hair and pulled her into their bedroom. I could tell from her voice that she was really scared. She had always taken the beatings with the silence of a martyr and the sex, too, I guess, but this time was different. She sensed it and so did we.

"My two oldest brothers, Eric and Jimmy, were gone at the time, but Billy and Dwayne and I huddled together and listened to sounds that were barely human." Layla's shoulders began to tremble; her eyes became glazed, distant. I knew she was hearing those sounds again; I put my arm around her shoulders.

"As Mom's screams worsened, I picked up a baseball bat and told my brothers that we had to save her. Scrawny little Billy grabbed an old tennis racket, and Dwayne picked up a BB gun. We headed down the hall.

"But as I approached my parents' door and looked back, I was alone. My brothers' faces stared out of our doorway with eyes as big as an owl's, their feet frozen to the floor.

"My parents' bedroom door was cracked open and I could see a silhouette on top of the bed that was, at the time, incomprehensible to me. I realize now that my mother was on her knees and Darryl was behind her. He had wrapped his belt around her throat and was pulling on it like the reins of a runaway horse.

"I eased around to the side of the bed, the bat cocked. Mom saw me out of the corner of her eye and shook her head, *no,* pleading with me in the only way she could, not to hit him. I could see veins as thick as ropes bulging from her neck. Her eyes were huge.

"But I did hit him. I hit him with the bat as hard as a sixty-pound girl could, right at the base of his spine.

"He screamed out, his head flew up, and his back arched from the pain. He fell clumsily off my mother and then tore the bat from my hand. He grabbed me by my hair and pulled me up onto the bed. He kneeled over me, his huge penis in my face."

I felt Layla pull away from me slightly, and I removed my arm from her shoulder.

"My mother screamed at him as she reached up and sunk her nails into his back. He grimaced from the pain, wheeled around sharply, and in one swift motion, almost like a reflexive jerk, hit her in the head with the bat. It was the most sickening thud I have ever heard, like a watermelon bursting. It happened so fast—just like *that!*

"From what I could tell she didn't take another breath, and Darryl and I just stared at her for what seemed like an eternity. Finally, he turned to me and said, 'Look what you've done.'"

Layla looked at the dingy motel floor. Her shoulders drooped and she crossed her legs tightly. "He wrapped one of his huge hands completely around my throat, and just as I thought I was going to suffocate, he let go. Then he raped me. Afterward, he left me in the bed with Mom, both of us in a pool of our own blood . . .

"I haven't seen Darryl since he went to jail, but Eric wrote me about a year ago to say that he'd gotten out. Served less than ten years of a twenty-five year sentence for manslaughter. I never told anyone about the rape, though I could tell from the way that my brothers looked at me that they knew. I never wanted to see any of them again, either.

"What I think about—and I think about it every day—is that Darryl wasn't going to kill her until I walked in, until I delivered the bat to him. Not a day goes by that I don't wish it had been me instead of Mom.

"There! I finally told someone." She held her stomach and moaned. "Aren't I supposed to turn into Mary Fucking Poppins now, or start singing something from *The Sound of Music?*

"I want to forget all that, Travis. I'm tired of seeing it every day. When will it go away?"

*   *   *

After that, I would guess half an hour passed in silence. Eventually, her body softened and we held each other again, still sitting on the edge of that board-hard bed. If I had one regret at that instant, it was that I felt I had taken more from Layla than I had given. Despite what others would think, in so many ways, she had proved to be what I needed most in my life, exactly when I had needed it. She had pulled the memory of Randi from me and helped to excise a painful tumor on my soul.

She leaned closer to me and placed her hand on my leg. "I feel so safe when I'm with you," she said.

As I sat on the edge of that bed next to her, as I held her, I didn't care about anything else—not Kathryn, not Dr. Nickemeyer, not even the murder charge. At that moment, all I wanted to be was whatever Layla Sommers needed me to be, exactly when she needed it.

As I pulled her tightly into my arms, all I wanted was for her to have a second chance.

THIRTY-SIX

NOW, AS I sit alongside this cold and desolate highway, I haven't seen Layla in over a year.

The Cadillac that roared past me is long out of sight; I study the rearview mirror for the next approaching vehicle. My Buick— Puddy's Buick—sputters a bit. I'm not sure what I will do if it dies. I miss my old Wagoneer but find consolation in the certainty that Mr. Newby will take good care of it; he paid more for it than I had paid him. And, together with my book advance and the sale of some stocks I had owned, I had managed to repay the legal expenses incurred by Kathryn. I had also pledged my future book royalties against a small loan, but the book tour had been cancelled, and without any help from Knopf sales had quickly plummeted. My first novel would apparently be my last.

I had all but begged Dean Schramm to let me keep my office in Garrison Hall. Somehow I knew that if I left there, if I buried twenty-five years of materials in some storage shed, the metaphor would take on a life of its own. He gave me a week, and it had taken all of that just to pack up. Without complaint, Ling bore the brunt of the heavy lifting, while Ben took whatever he could hold on his lap, via countless elevator trips.

Not surprisingly, Layla, and her bruised face, had been convincing before the grand jury. Prior to that, she had explained to a skeptical D.A. that I had nothing to do with Enos's death. Yes, I had broken in through her kitchen window but not on the night Enos had died. Yes, I had introduced the steel bar into her apartment, but I had never hit Enos with it. The evening of Enos's death, she told the grand jury, had been no different than dozens of others the two of them had planned and executed before. Until, that is, Enos apparently took some tainted drugs that had made him violent, prompting her to hit him in self-defense. Three times, as she recalled.

The charges against me had been dropped, and Layla won a ruling of justifiable homicide. The D.A., Dr. Bernard, Dr. Nickemeyer, and Judge Patton, a kindly old man, conspired to impose a year of psychological treatment for Layla in return for the favorable rulings in her behalf and in mine.

Dr. Nickemeyer considered half a dozen places nationwide that specialized in the shame-based disorders of young women and had ultimately selected the Harbinger Institute outside of Odessa, Texas, for its small size and stellar reputation. I hoped it was as good as he said because the program cost a fortune. Layla thought the state was paying for it, but it wasn't. I was. And, having liquidated my other assets to repay Kathryn's legal expenses, I was left with only one option to fund Layla's care; I sold my house on Preston Street.

I moved into a small efficiency apartment that did not allow pets. I had worked for weeks to find good homes for my dogs, interviewing each prospective owner at length. I had especially made sure that Madison's new owner loved to throw the ball, even though I had never been so sure about Madison. Ben had agreed to keep TJ until I had more space.

I think about those damn dogs constantly.

No longer on campus each day, I had scarcely seen Kathryn over the past year. She had written me one long letter—her attempt to close the chapters of our time together on a positive, if irreversible, note. She could have saved the four pages in favor of the last paragraph where she mentioned that she was going to help Dr. Nickemeyer shape up his novel. In other words, Kathryn had found her next project. Since he was decades younger than she, I had to smile at the irony.

If I had never met Layla Sommers, I suppose I would now be in front of a fireplace in Kathryn's big house, nestled into a leather recliner with a good book in my lap and TJ at my side. I would be teaching and molding young minds while working on my second novel and listening to Ben's stories.

I would also believe that Randi had died instantly.

I would believe that I had never told her goodbye.

*   *   *

The vicious north wind continues to buffet my car; it seeps through cracks, chilling me to the bone despite my heavy canvas jacket and once-hot coffee.

I jerk my head to the left as an old Ford pickup truck passes by. I haven't even noticed the truck in my rearview mirror, but as it passes, I turn quickly enough to make out Louisiana plates. The black truck pulls into the circle drive in front of the brick building, the Harbinger Institute. It comes to a stop, but no one gets out.

I set my coffee down carefully on the console and raise the binoculars. I see exhaust coming from the twin tailpipes of the truck, but due to the angle at which it is parked and the dark tint of the windows, I cannot see inside.

Then the front door of the building opens. My throat constricts, my mouth is suddenly cotton. *What in the hell am I doing here?* I slump a bit lower in my seat.

At the insistence of the Harbinger, Layla and I have not spoken in a year, nor have we corresponded. Though I have written her at least two dozen letters, they remain in a box in my small apartment.

Why am I here? Ben kept using the word *closure* as he had urged me to make the trip. Funny, but that's the same word Layla had used regarding Randi. "Don't approach her," Ben had said. "There's time for that, and you should give her a chance to make the first move. But you've been wondering about her for a year now, so go and look at her and study your feelings as you do. You'll know that she is either a part of your past or that the final chapter between the two of you has yet to be written."

I focus my binoculars and slide the zoom lever to the highest magnification. Just outside the front door of the building, two women appear and hug each other. One wears a navy blazer and has shoulder-length gray hair. The other wears a heavy black wool coat and a hat—a wide-brimmed leather hat with a braided leather band. She carries a blue backpack over one shoulder. After several attempts to separate, only to be overcome by the need for an additional hug, the two women part.

The woman in the black wool coat—Layla Sommers—leans into the wind, one hand on her hat, and makes her way toward the pickup where the passenger door is flung open from the inside; the wind nearly tears it off.

As she reaches the truck, Layla tosses her blue backpack in and then turns and looks at the building once more. At that moment, the stiff north wind blows her hat off like a shot. It sails through the air before landing in the snow some ten yards away. She chases it. She is laughing. The fresh, powdered snow comes up to the middle of her shins. The hat blows farther, and Layla steps over the low-lying barbed wire fence and continues her chase.

Her pursuit of the hat brings her directly toward me, her face and head uncovered. She moves slowly through the snow, which allows me to study her closely. Her long copper hair has been cut to chin length, which makes her face look longer, in turn making her look older. Much older. While there had always been a frustrating and intoxicating duality of woman and child in Layla, she now shows no trace of the latter.

RESURRECTING RANDI

She bends over to retrieve the hat just as a gale-force wind sends it jetting and rolling some thirty yards closer to me. She shakes her head and looks back at the pickup. The driver's door swings open and a big man gets out. He wears jeans and a heavy denim jacket along with black leather work gloves. He has a long handlebar mustache.

He signals Layla to return to the truck.

Layla takes several more steps in the direction of her hat but the wind picks it up yet again and sends it spinning up the road like a tumbleweed. She stops and looks in the direction of the hat. Then, she looks at me.

I'm confident she can't see me inside my car at that distance, and I doubt that she would recognize the Buick. Still, is she wondering what that car is doing parked on the side of the road?

Through the binoculars, Layla's face fills my view. She looks right at me; her brown eyes cut into my soul. It is as if she is saying, thanks for coming. Or is it as if she is saying goodbye?

Closure?

She throws up her hands in exasperation at the continuing trek of her hat; she turns toward the truck. When she gets there, the driver, who is waiting for her, gets in on his side, she on hers. They do not speak.

They sit for a while, trails of smoke curling out of the dual exhausts, but my attention drifts. As if on a string, Layla's hat continues to bounce and dart directly toward me. I get out of the Buick, straining to open the door against the wind, and sift through the snow on the side of the road. I approach the barbed wire fence and carefully separate two strands of wire with my gloved hands and ease through the fence. The wind sends the hat tumbling to within two feet of me. I lunge forward and grab it. My shoes and pant legs are soaked. My toes are numb.

I hurry back to the Buick. The Ford begins to move. My stomach turns to knots at the thought it will turn away from me. My heart races at the thought that it will turn my way.

236

It turns my way.

I slip as I hustle back through the fence and stumble toward the highway. My entire body is covered with snow. The black truck grinds slowly in my direction; I hold the hat up in the air but the Ford sails right by, picking up speed.

As I turn to watch, the Ford pulls to the right side of the road and sits there for what seems like an eternity. Then, it slowly makes a U-turn and eases up directly behind my Buick.

There it lingers. I look into the windshield where Layla and the driver are talking. They are highly animated. The cold is starting to bite through my pants when the passenger door of the truck opens. Layla steps out and approaches me.

Her arms are folded tightly across her chest, holding her wool coat secure. Her short hair whips under the wind. Her cheeks are painfully red from the cold; I have never seen anything more beautiful in my life. Like the first time I saw her, there is a gnawing hunger in my gut.

"So, here you are to save me again," she says calmly, taking the hat from me, staring at it. "How have you been, Travis?"

"Fine, just fine," I lie. "And you?"

She laughs sharply and turns toward the Harbinger. "Oh, it was a barrel of laughs," she says. We both kick aimlessly at the ground. "How're TJ and the gang?"

"Well, it's just TJ now," I say. "And, actually, Ben's keeping him for a while—I'm living in an apartment. You know, just until—"

"You're still teaching, aren't you?" she asks.

"I'm taking some time off."

"Kathryn?"

"You wouldn't believe me if I told you," I laugh, but my voice cracks.

The horn of the truck honks. Layla looks behind her nervously. "I really better go," she says.

"I've missed you, Layla," I say, suddenly panicked.

"You wouldn't even know me now, Travis," she says. "I have to admit, that place was good for me; I'm a different woman. Maybe you were wrong about second chances—"

"We should spend some time together," I say a bit too urgently.

She smiles and looks away. "Our ages, Travis. Our interests. You were right all along. I can finally see that."

"I don't mean as a couple," I say. "You'll want to get married and have children some day, but Layla—"

"I've decided I want to travel," she says.

"I'm free to travel," I say quickly. "We were good for each other, weren't we?"

She laughs and her face is radiant. "Oh, yeah, you no longer have your job, or your house, or your fiancée, or your dogs—and I killed a man and spent a year in a psych ward! We were *great* for each other!

"I'm so sorry, Travis . . ."

"No, please . . . don't."

The horn honks again and the large man gets out and walks toward us.

"Darryl," Layla says to me, grimly.

"Is there a problem?" Darryl says as he approaches; he grabs Layla by the arm. There are deep, old scars on his face, and even through the wind I catch the sickly sweet smell of alcohol on his breath. I swear to myself that if he tries to force her to leave, I will get the revolver from the car and use it without hesitation.

"No problem," Layla says, pulling her arm free. "This is Dr. Harrison, the man I told you about. He just came to make sure there was someone here to pick me up. I told you he was sweet." Layla reaches out and places her hand on my shoulder. I want to hold her. I want to protect her from this man, her father.

"Darryl Sommers," the big man says as he offers his huge gloved hand for me to shake. My hand disappears in his enormous grip. I imagine that hand around Layla's nine-year-old neck as he rapes her. "It's goddamned cold out here, Layla," he says, "and we've got a hell of a long drive. Keep it short, will you?" He walks toward the truck.

"You told him about me?" I ask.

"Yeah. He's been coming all the way from Deridder once a month for joint counseling. I guess we're trying to put things back together."

"Do you feel safe with him?"

She pauses for a moment. "Not really. I can't until he's off the booze and that hasn't happened yet. In fact, I'm scared shitless about moving in with him. It's the same old house, you know."

"Then move in with me!" I say urgently.

The horn honks again and we both jump. She hugs me quickly but does not kiss me, not even on the cheek. "I gotta go," she says. "You don't want to make Darryl mad."

There are so many things I want to say to her. I want to thank her for healing a wound within me. I want to tell her that I understand her actions, even those that hurt me most. I want to be a part of her life. I want to grab her and *force* her to come with me. Instead, I nod and look past her, somewhere out over the white horizon. She gives me another moment as if she, too, is hoping that I will find the right thing to say. "Be safe," I say at last. As she smiles and turns to leave, I am left with the toxic residue of my pathetic final words.

I lean against the Buick as Layla gets into Darryl's truck. It makes another U-turn and builds speed rapidly as it straightens out on the empty highway. On the flat road, I am able to watch the truck turn into a black dot on the horizon.

For a moment, the dot seems to hang on the horizon. I think maybe it has stopped.

*   *   *

The heat inside the Buick feels good, though my feet are still throbbing from the cold. The wind whistles through the cracks in the old car; I reach for the revolver and cock it. Unlike the last time, a bullet advances into the chamber.

I look also at the cell phone in the passenger's seat and know that I have one last promise to keep. Ben is expecting my call.

"Did you see her?" he asks, anxiously.

"Yes, I talked to her."

"And?"

"She looks different. Older. She's cut off most of her hair. I think she's going to be okay."

"And you? Are you going to be okay?" Ben asks.

I look at the gun I have set in my lap. "I think she was worth it, Ben," I say. "Even if I never see her again, I think she was worth it."

"I want to hear all about it when you get back," Ben says. "I'm going to force a couple of martinis down you."

"How's TJ?" I ask.

"Spoiled rotten. That dog sure likes bacon!"

There is a long silence, and then Ben says, "By the way, I saw a friend of yours today."

"How is that possible, Ben," I say, "when I'm talking to my only friend in the world?"

"It's Shawn," Ben says. "He's back. Spent a year in Mississippi taking care of his mother before she passed on. Said to tell you that he wrote a book. You won't believe this, but he's actually got an agent who says it's pretty good!"

"Tell him I'm happy for him," I say.

"You tell him," Ben says. I sense the urgency in his voice. "When are you coming back to Austin?"

"I've got to go, Ben . . . it's cold up here . . ."

"Travis! Do not hang up that phone. Listen to me . . . you *are* coming back . . . *Travis!*"

I pick up the gun again and hear the curious words of my father. *Always leave the first chamber empty. That way, you'll have to pull the trigger twice if you really want to kill something.*

Tears begin welling, and I don't know if they are for Helen, Randi, Layla, or perhaps even for myself. I think of all the women I have loved—and lost—and wonder whether I was good to them. I believe that I was, and with that thought, I feel an amazing tranquility, an unbelievable peace.

I look in the rearview mirror one last time. I'm looking for a black dot on the horizon, but this time the horizon is clear.